Peach AND Plum

Here We Come!

For Trudi

About This Book

This book was edited by Rachel Poloski and Esther Cajahuaringa,
and designed by Carolyn Bull. The production was supervised by Bernadette Flinn,
and the production editor was Marisa Finkelstein.

Little, Brown and Company
Hachette Book Group
1290 Avenue of the Americas, New York, NY 10104
Visit us at LBYR.com

First Edition: August 2022

Little, Brown and Company is a division of Hachette Book Group, Inc.
The Little, Brown name and logo are trademarks of Hachette Book Group, Inc.

The publisher is not responsible for websites (or their content) that are not owned by the publisher.

Library of Congress Cataloging-in-Publication Data
Names: McCanna, Tim, author, illustrator.
Title: Peach and Plum, here we come!: a graphic novel in rhyme / by Tim McCanna.
Description: First edition. | New York : Little, Brown and Company, 2022.
Series: Peach and Plum; 1 | Audience: Ages 6–9.
Summary: In Fruitdale, best friends Peach and Plum enjoy many fun summer activities,
such as playing ball, going to the beach, and riding a bike—although Plum often seems
to find the downside of fun. Told in rhyming text.
Identifiers: LCCN 2021038961 | ISBN 9780316306102 (hardcover) | ISBN 9780316306201 (paperback)
ISBN 9780316344180 (ebook) | ISBN 9780316347242 (ebook other)
Subjects: LCSH: Friendship—Comic books, strips, etc. | Friendship—Juvenile fiction.
Play—Comic books, strips, etc. | Play—Juvenile fiction. | Stories in rhyme. | Graphic novels.
CYAC: Graphic novels. | Stories in rhyme. | Summer—Fiction. | Friendship—Fiction. | Peach—Fiction.
Plum—Fiction. | Fruit—Fiction. | LCGFT: Graphic novels. | Stories in rhyme.
Classification: LCC PZ7.7.M41264 Pe 2022 | DDC 741.5/973—dc23
LC record available at https://lccn.loc.gov/2021038961
ISBNs: 978-0-316-30610-2 (hardcover), 978-0-316-30620-1 (paperback), 978-0-316-34418-0 (ebook),
978-0-316-34691-7 (ebook), 978-0-316-34713-6 (ebook)

PRINTED IN CHINA

Hardcover: 10 9 8 7 6 5 4 3 2 1
Paperback: 10 9 8 7 6 5 4 3 2 1

Peach AND Plum

Here We Come!

Tim McCanna

LB

LITTLE, BROWN AND COMPANY

New York Boston

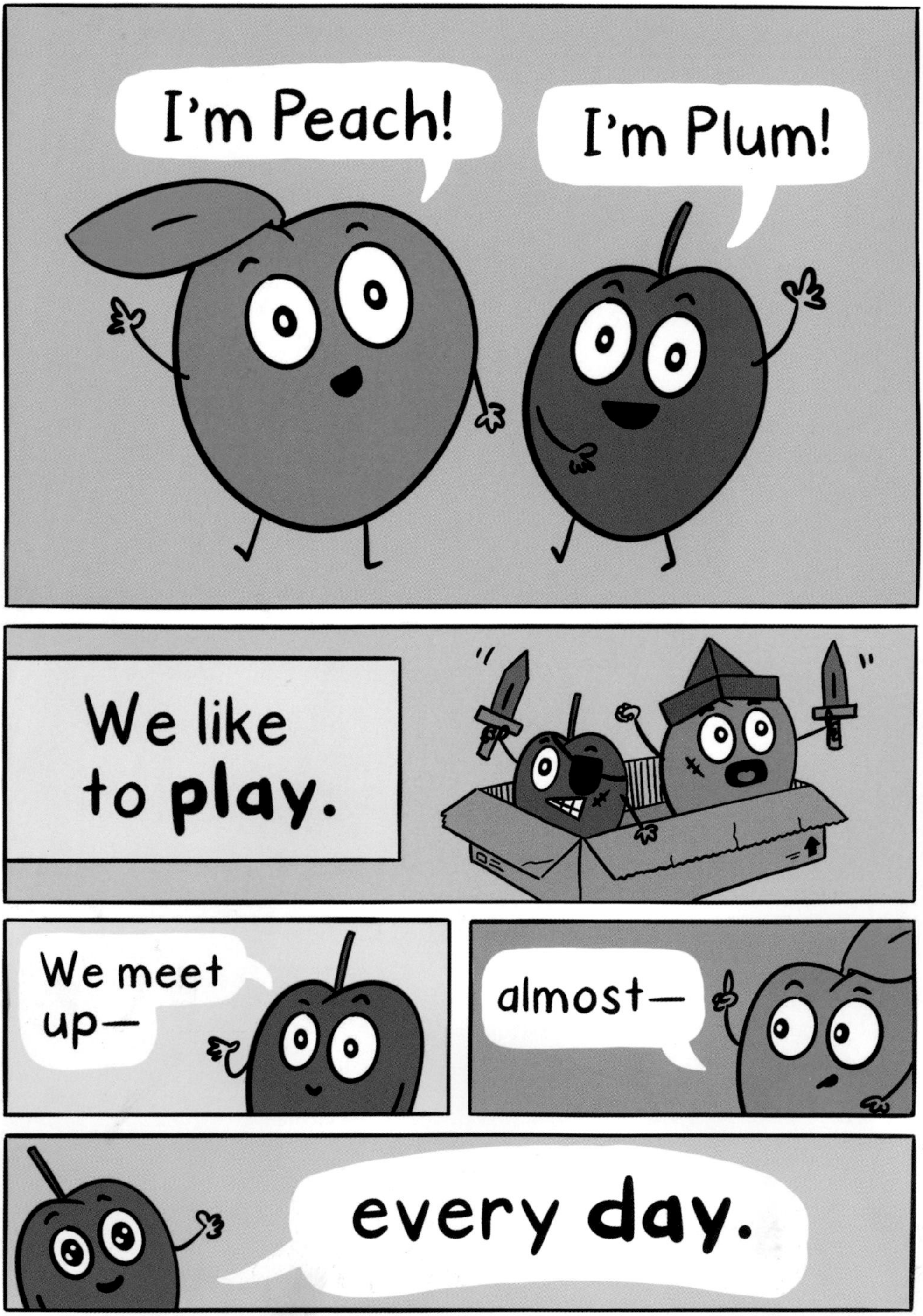
I'm Peach!
I'm Plum!
We like to play.
We meet up—
almost—
every day.

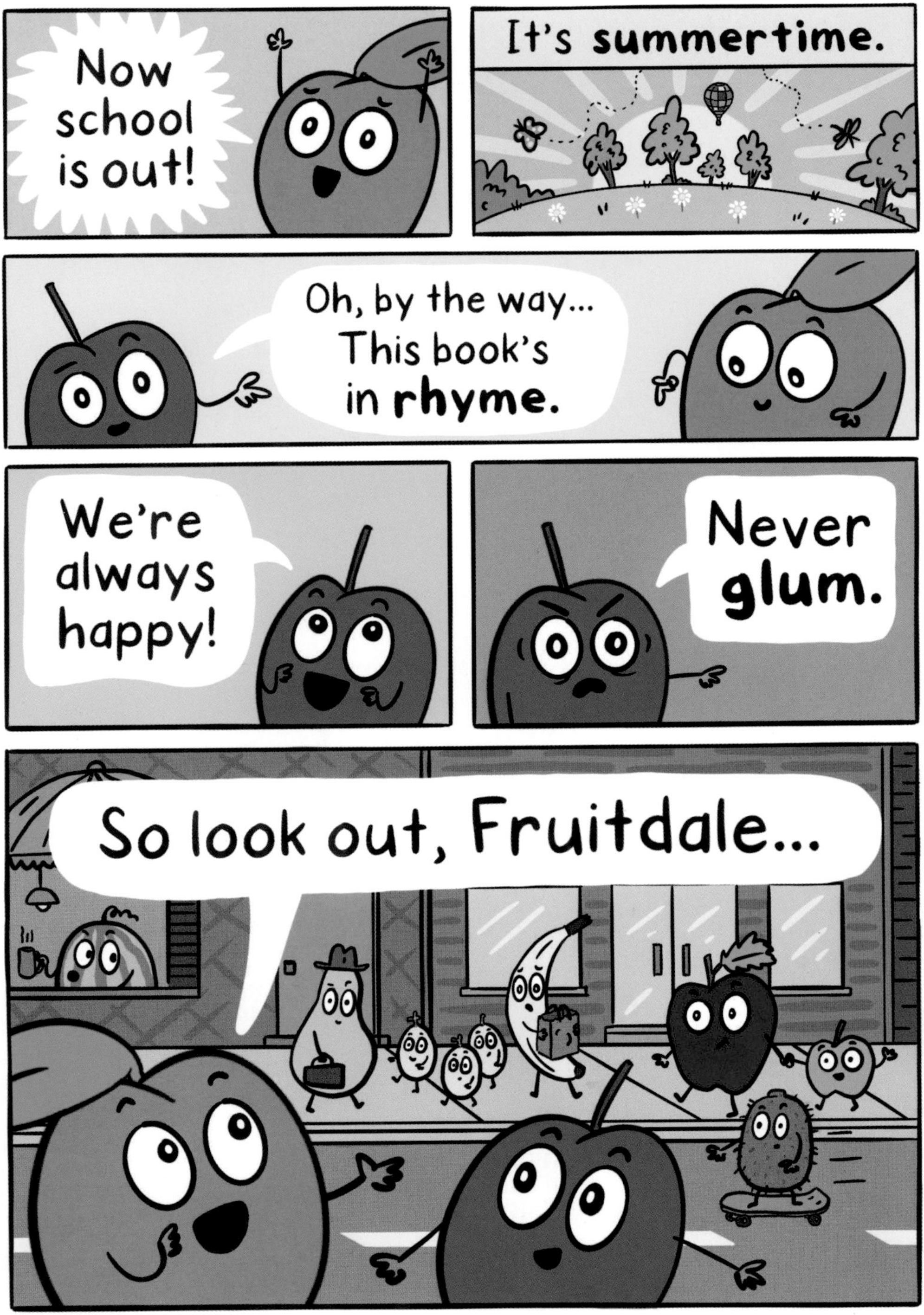

Now school is out!
It's summertime.
Oh, by the way... This book's in rhyme.
We're always happy!
Never glum.
So look out, Fruitdale...

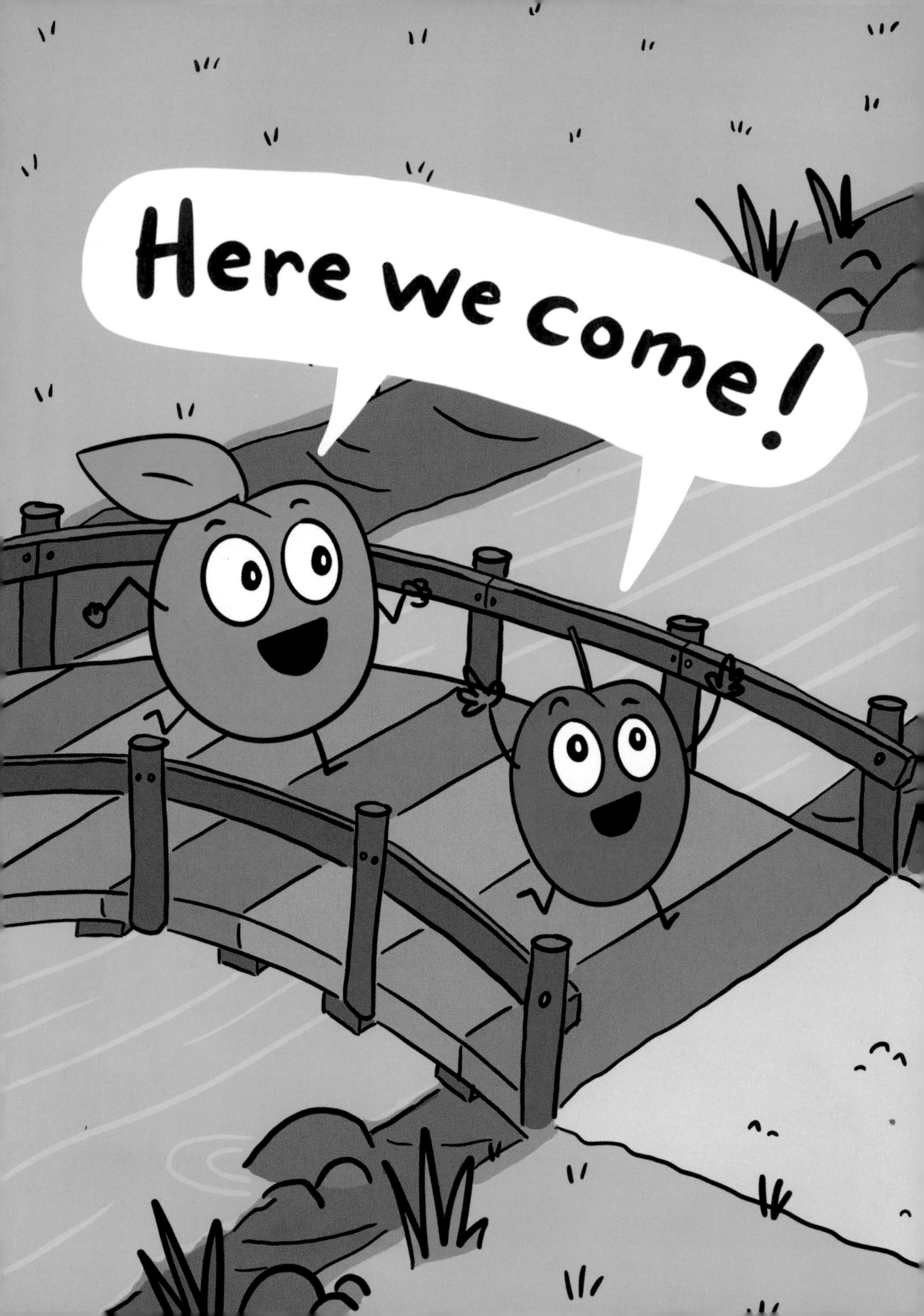
Here we come!

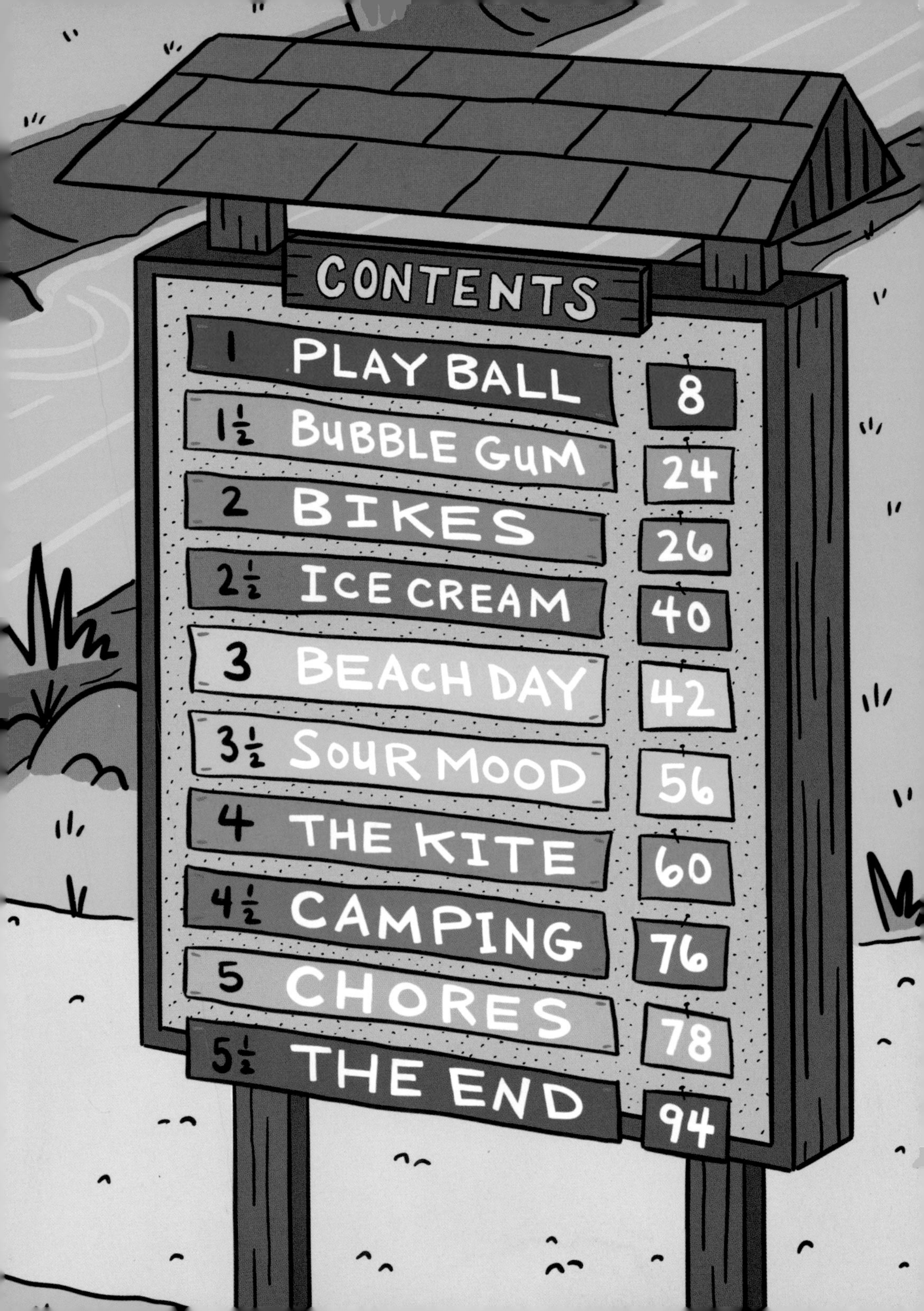
CONTENTS
1 PLAY BALL 8
1½ BUBBLE GUM 24
2 BIKES 26
2½ ICE CREAM 40
3 BEACH DAY 42
3½ SOUR MOOD 56
4 THE KITE 60
4½ CAMPING 76
5 CHORES 78
5½ THE END 94

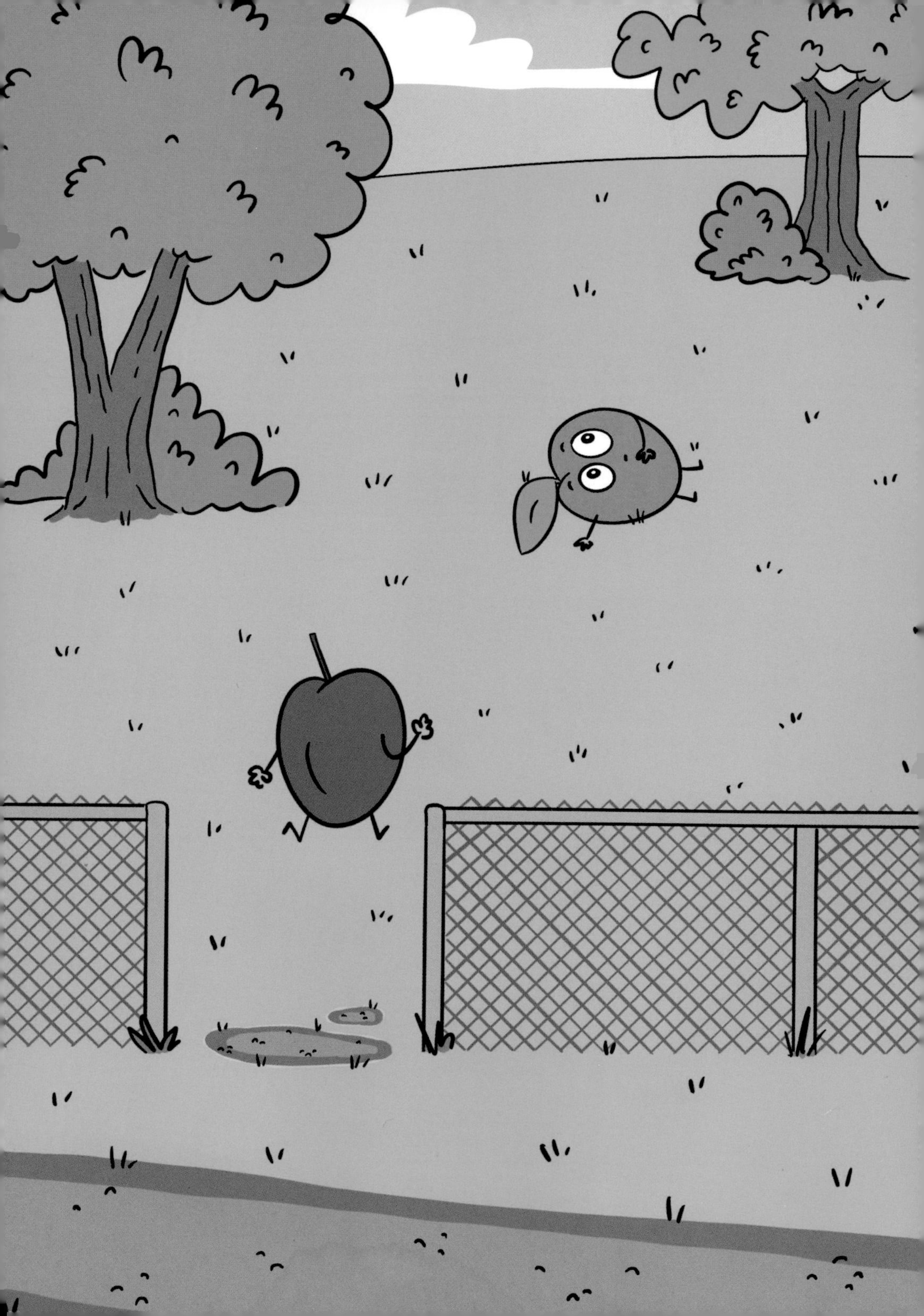

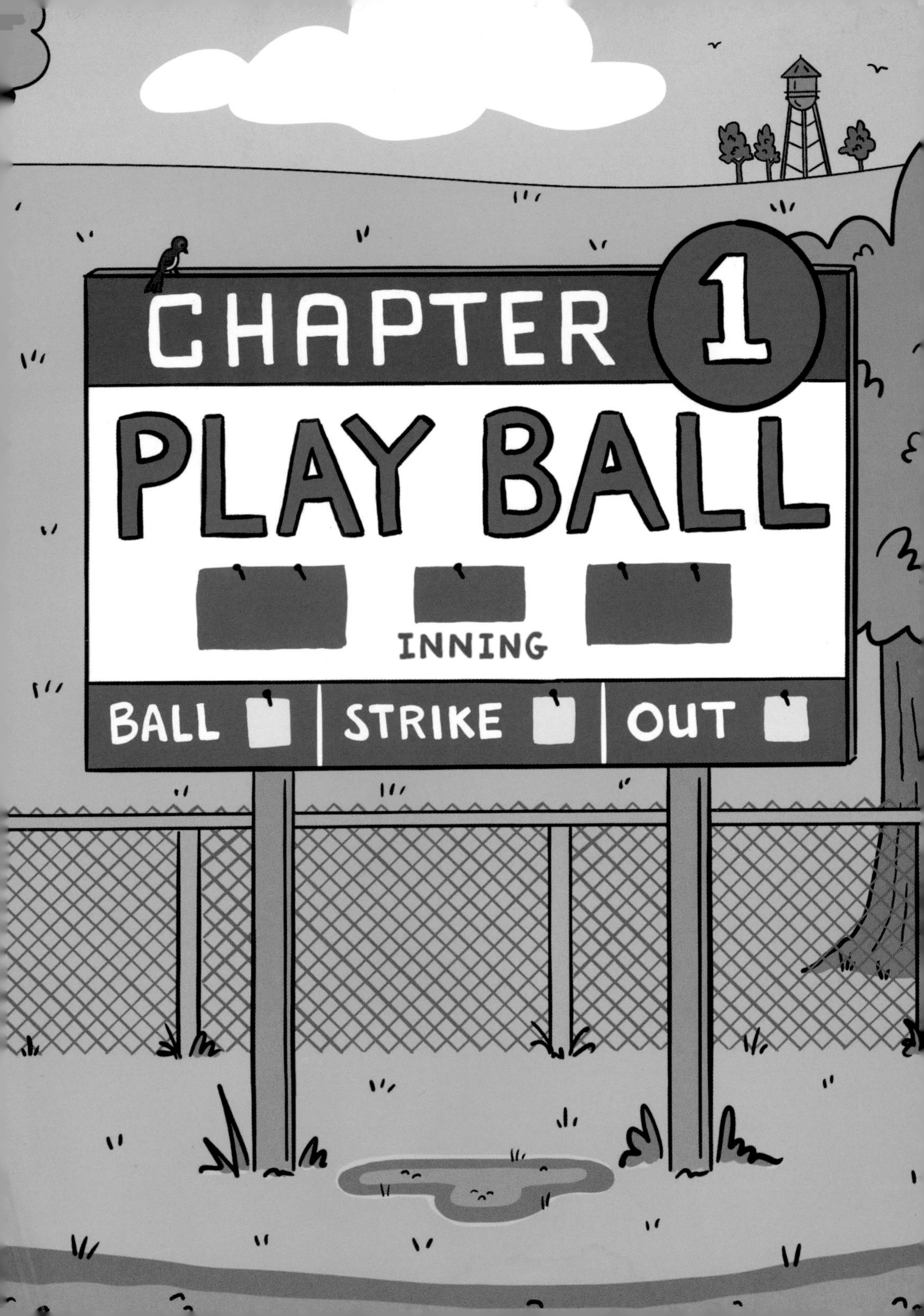
CHAPTER 1
PLAY BALL
INNING
BALL
STRIKE
OUT

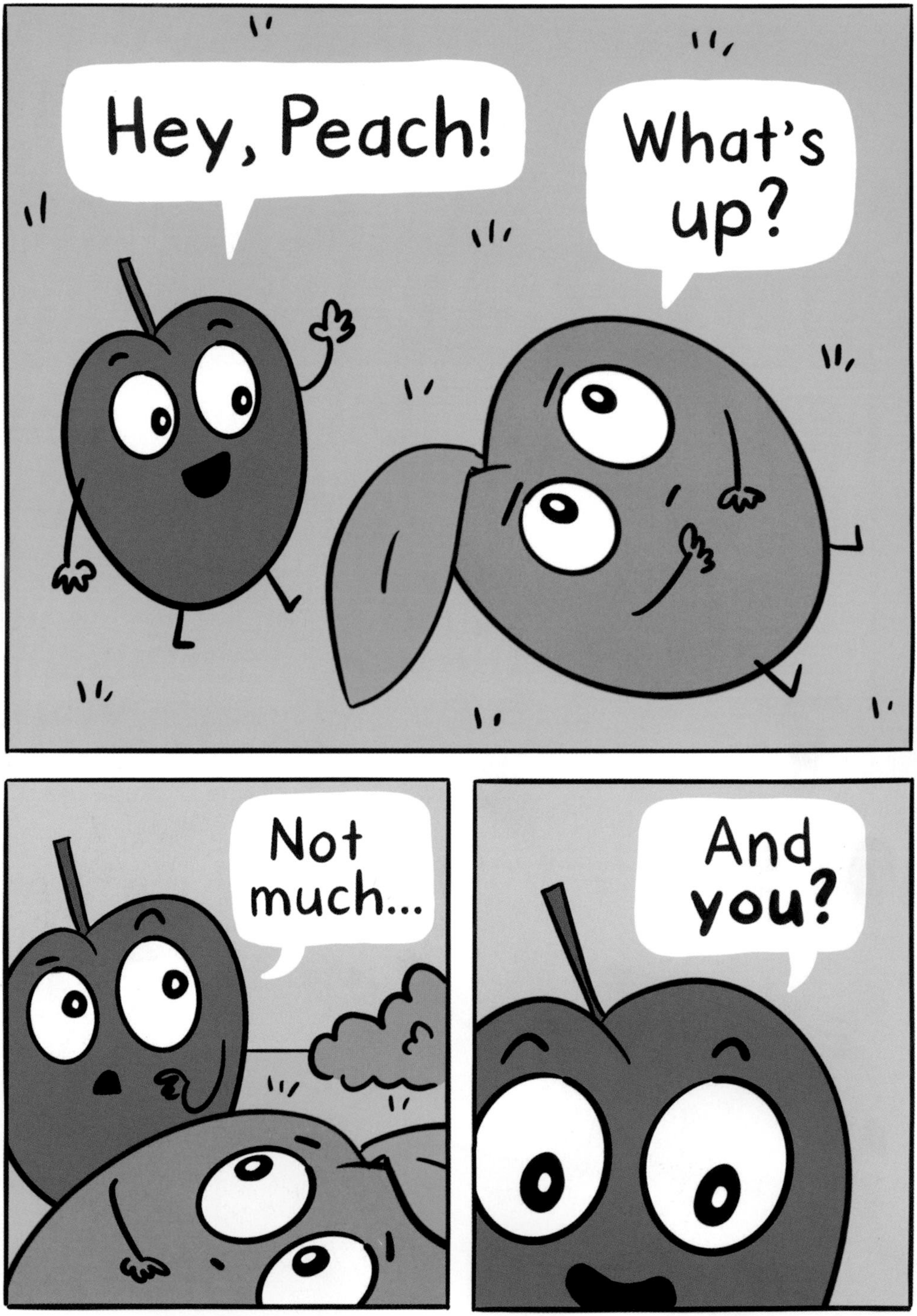

Hey, Peach!
What's up?
Not much...
And **you?**

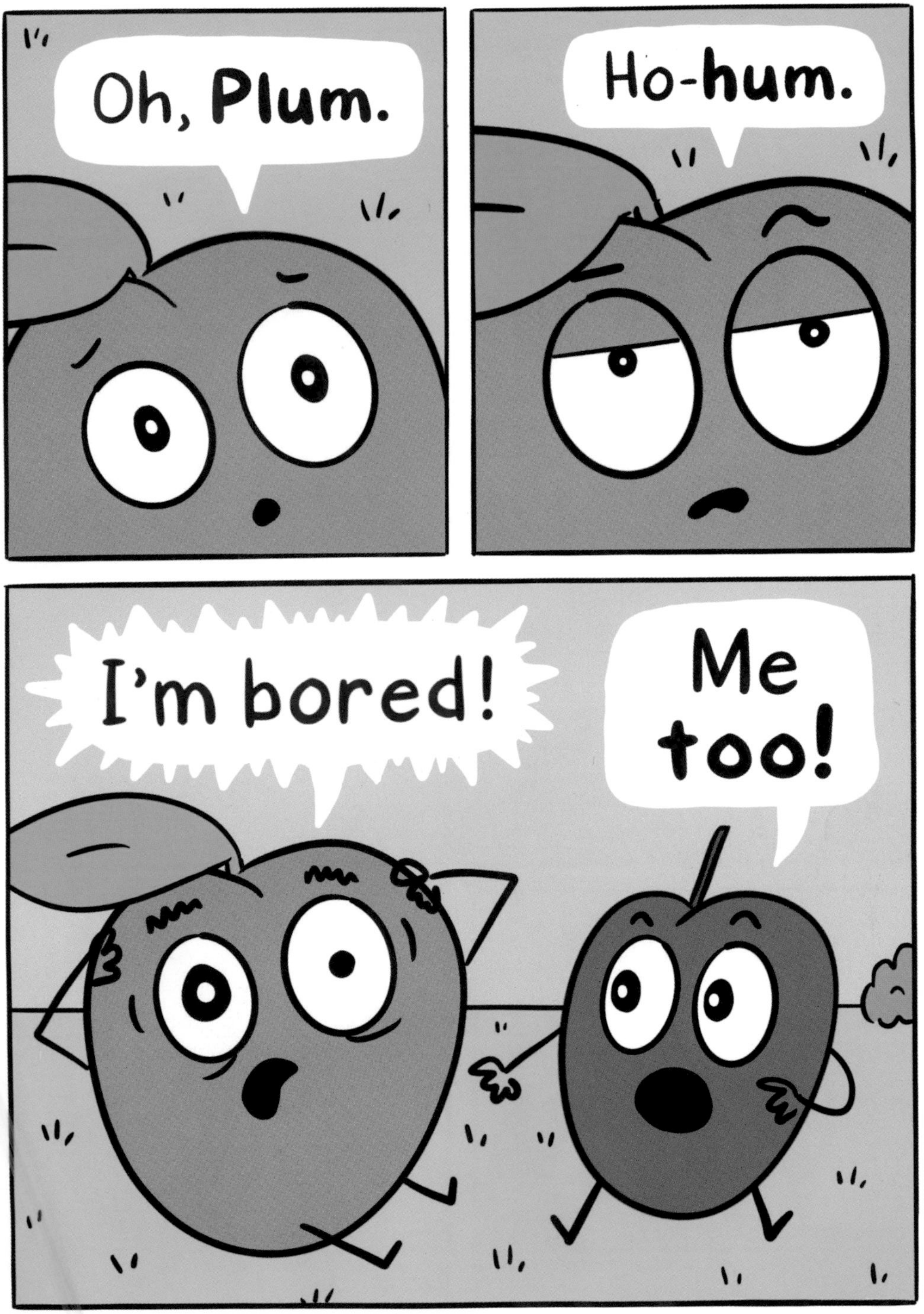
Oh, Plum.
Ho-hum.
I'm bored!
Me too!

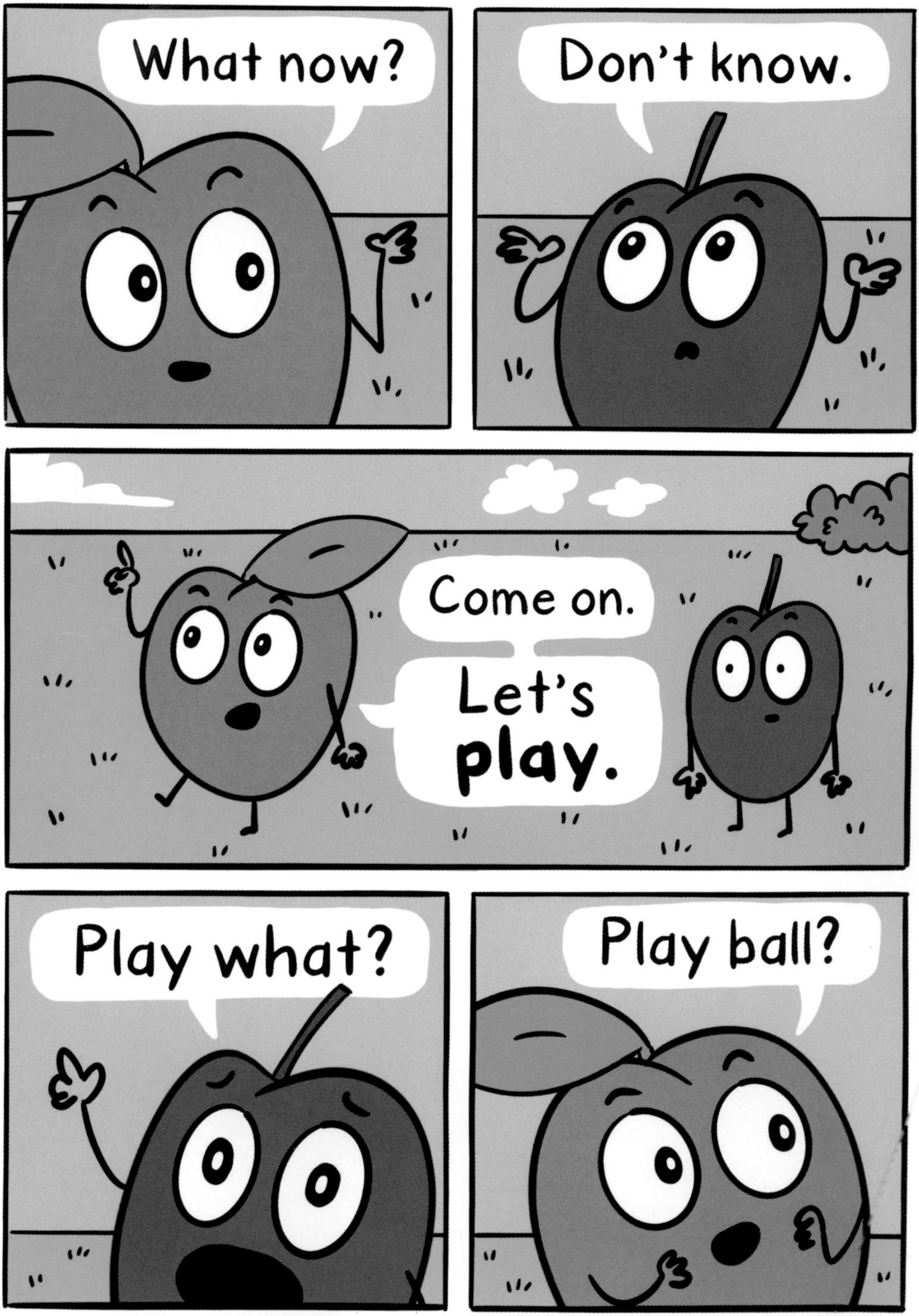
What now?
Don't know.
Come on.
Let's **play.**
Play what?
Play ball?

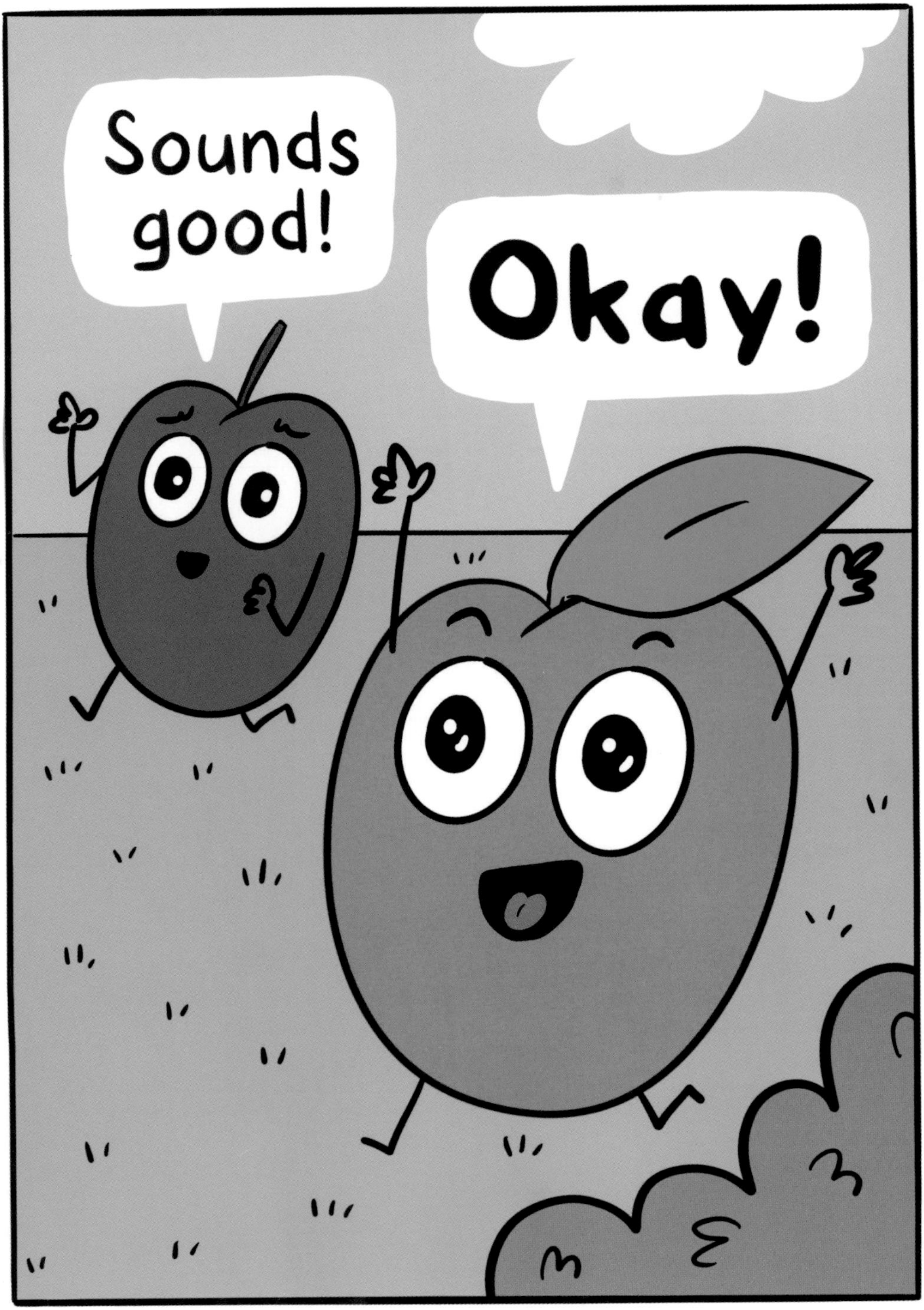
Sounds good!
Okay!

One glove.

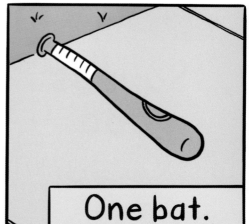

One bat.

I'll pitch. You **hit**.

Too high.

Too low.

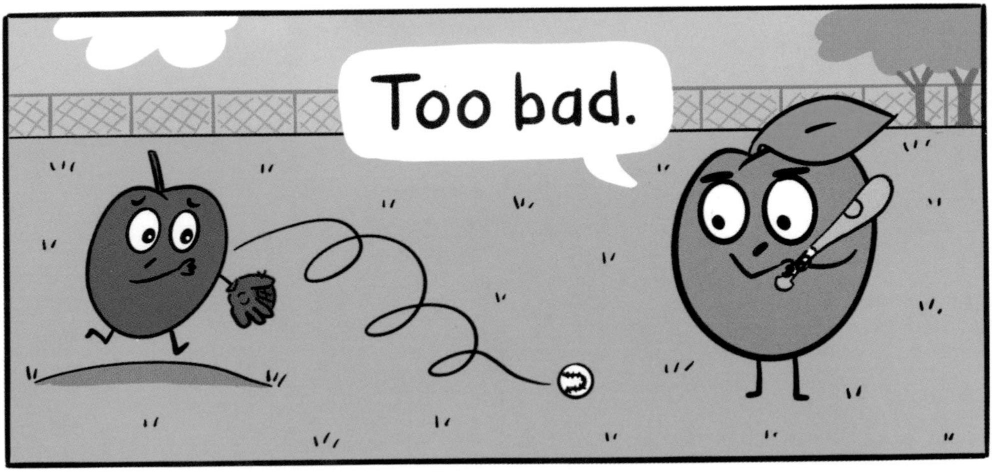
Too bad.

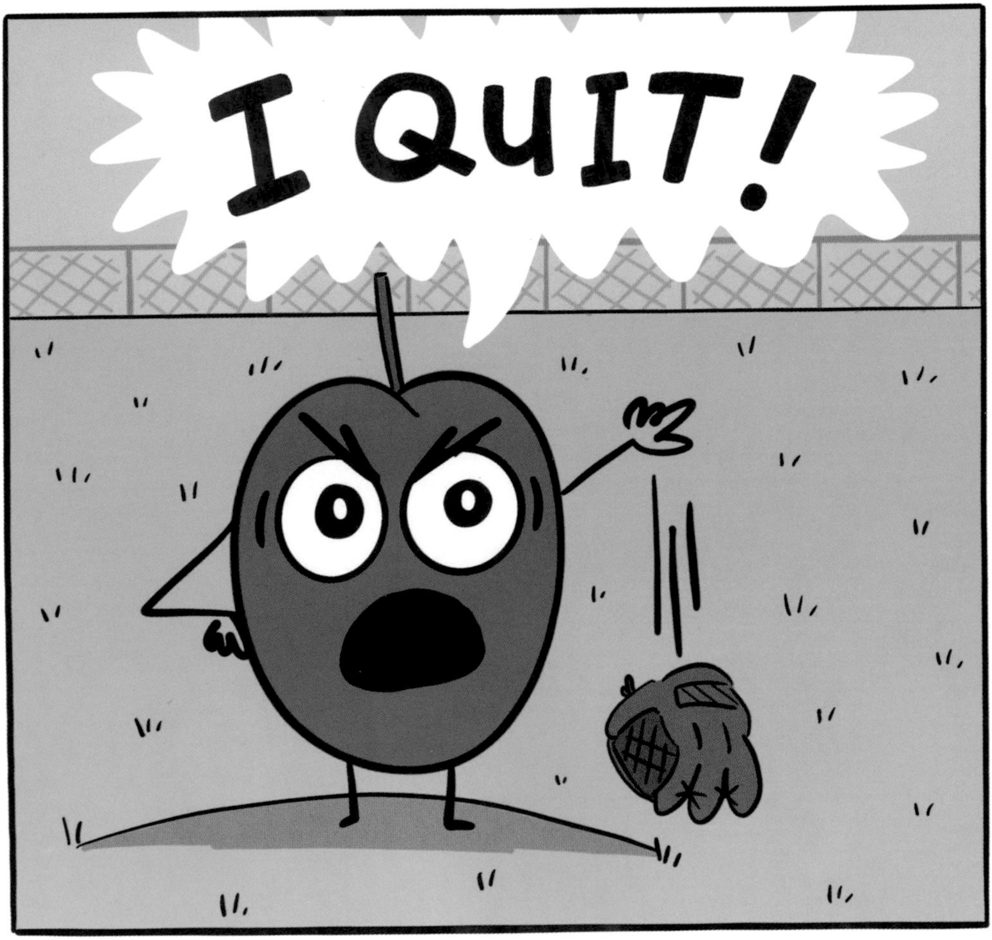
I QUIT!

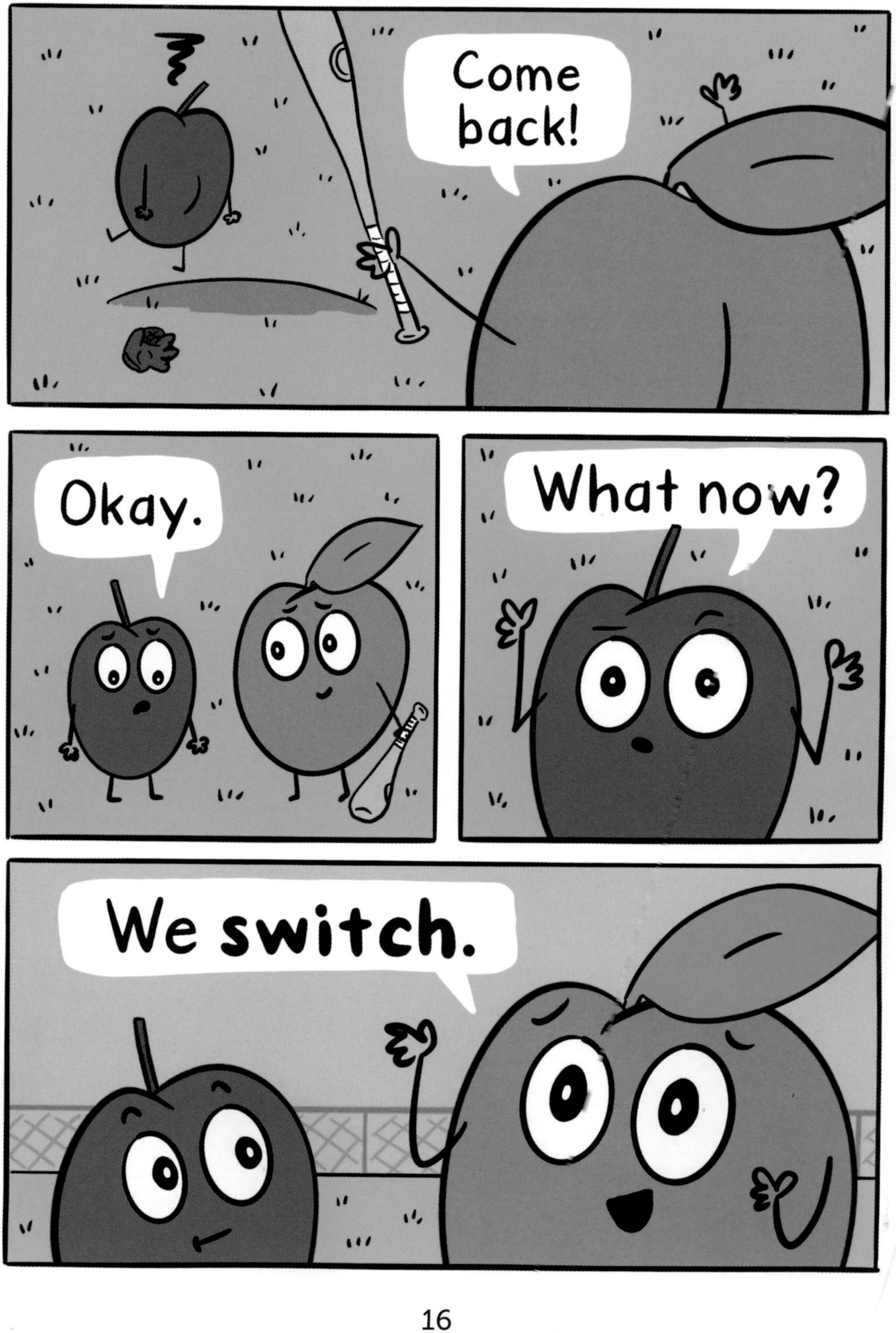
Come back!
Okay.
What now?
We switch.

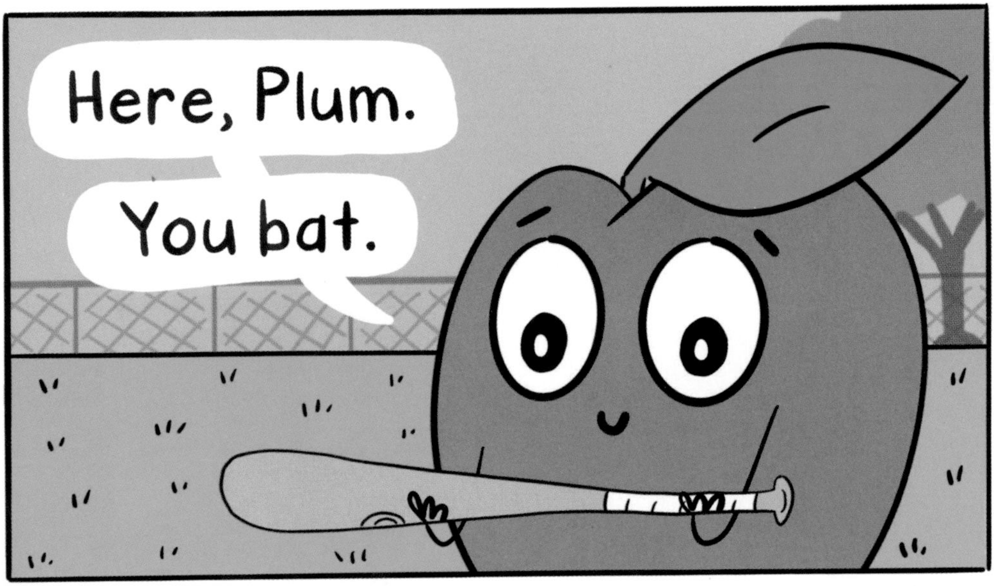
Here, Plum.
You bat.

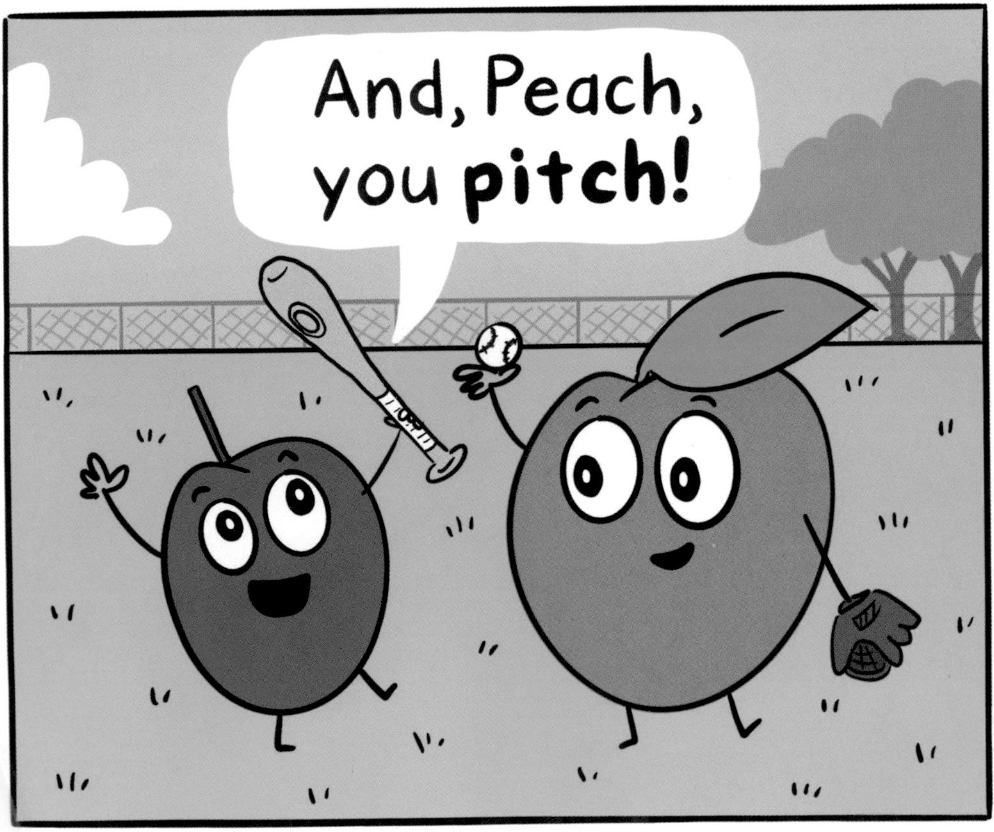
And, Peach, you **pitch**!

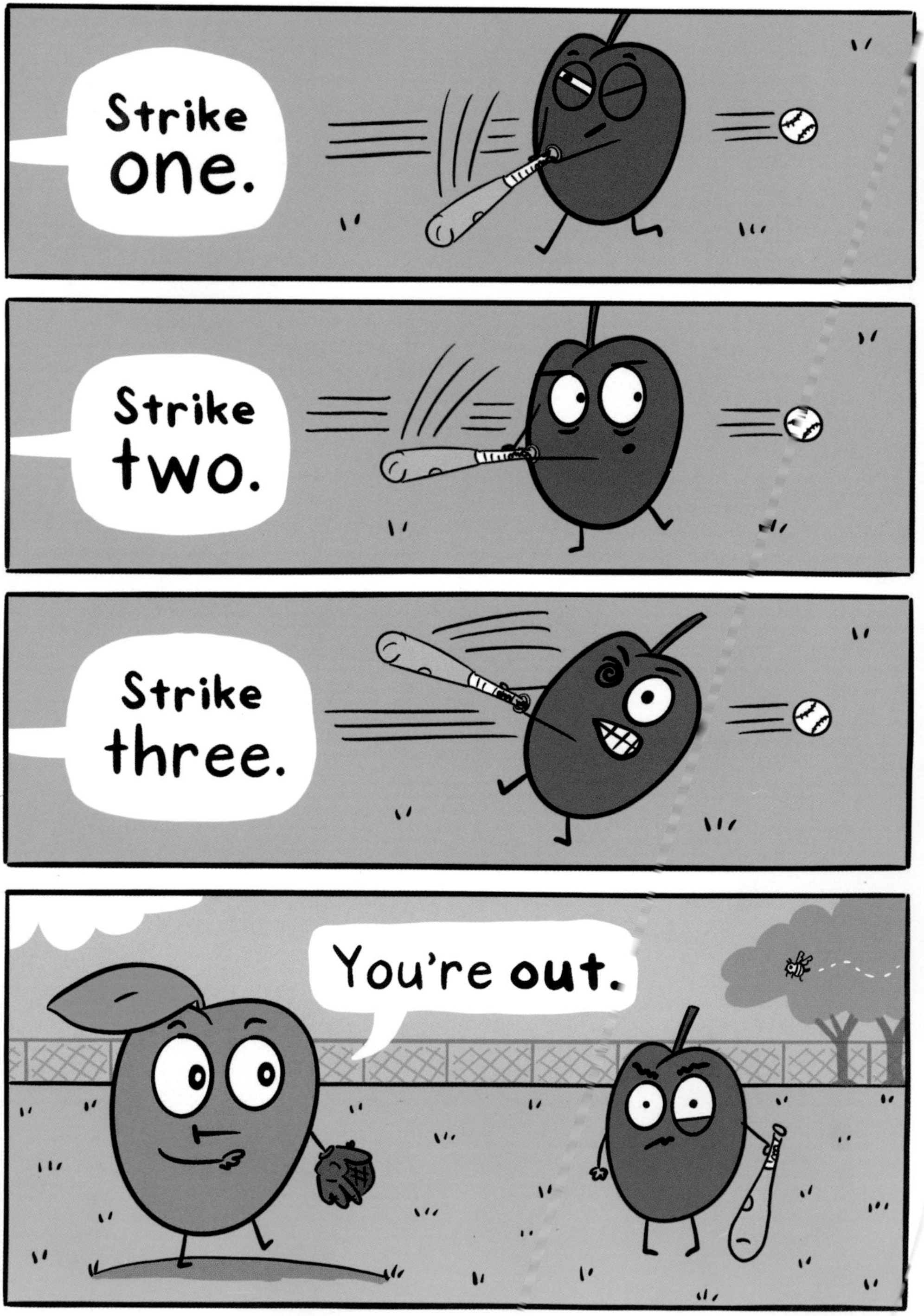
Strike one.
Strike two.
Strike three.
You're out.

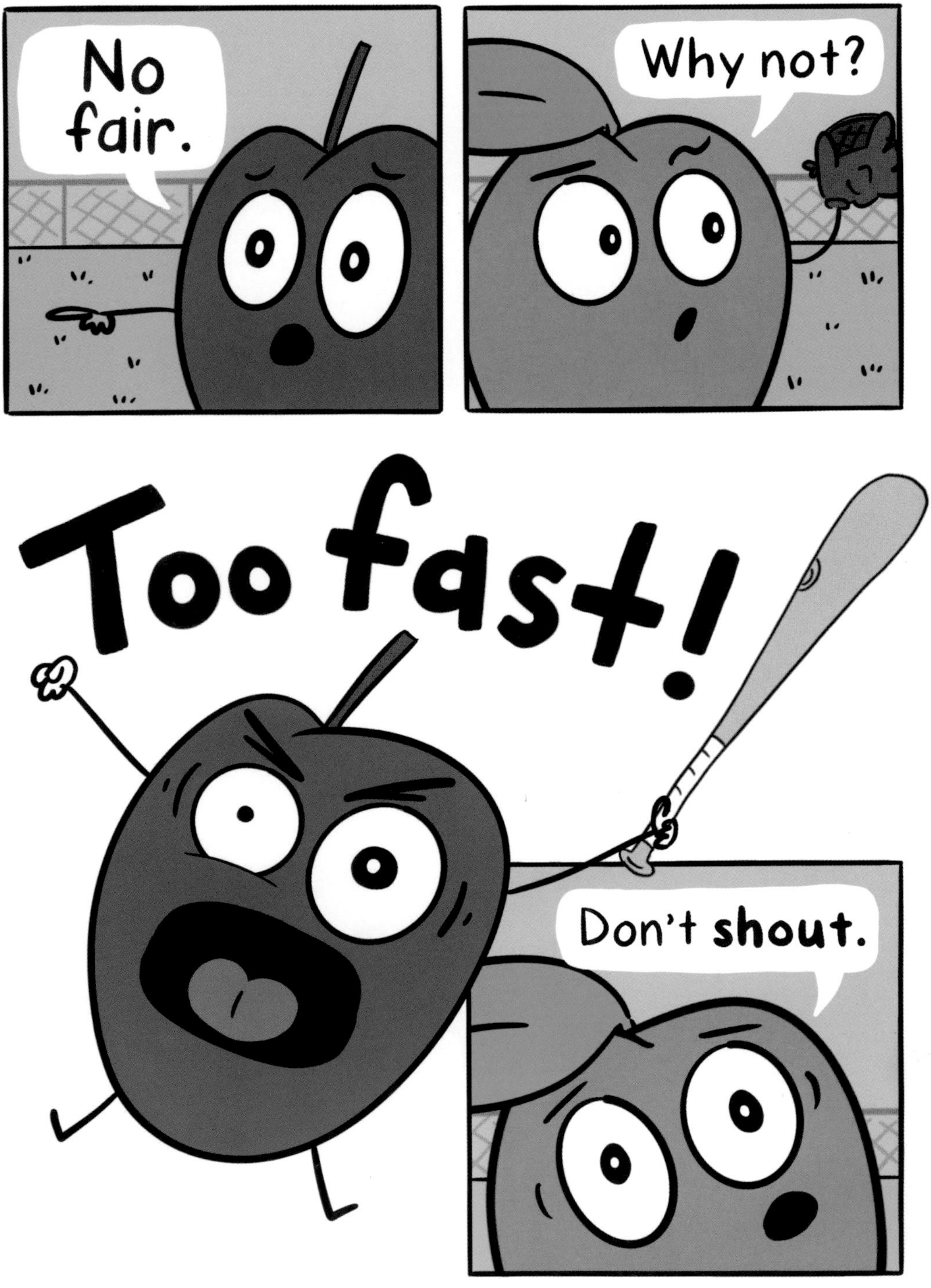
No fair.
Why not?
Too fast!
Don't **shout**.

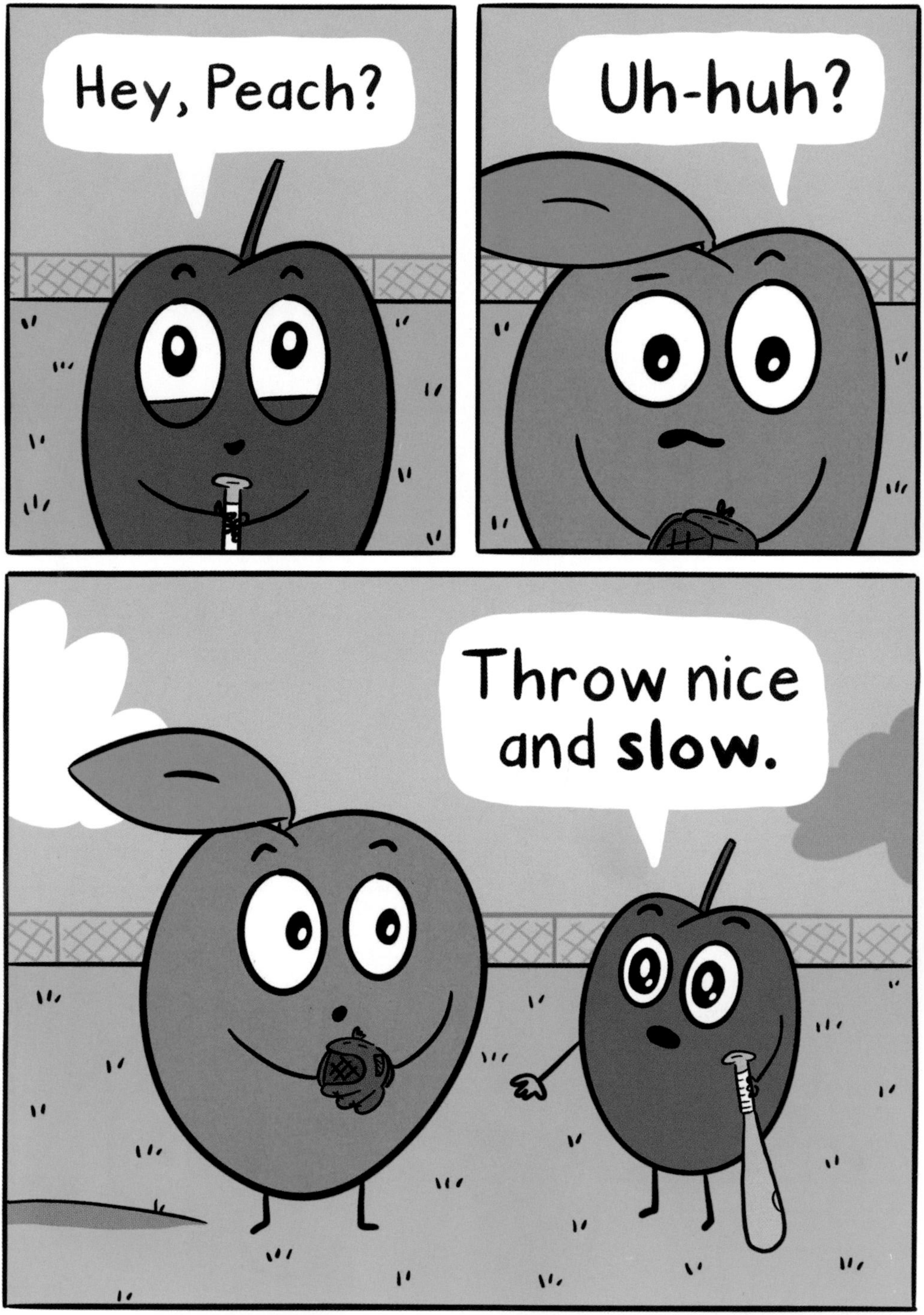
Hey, Peach?
Uh-huh?
Throw nice and **slow.**

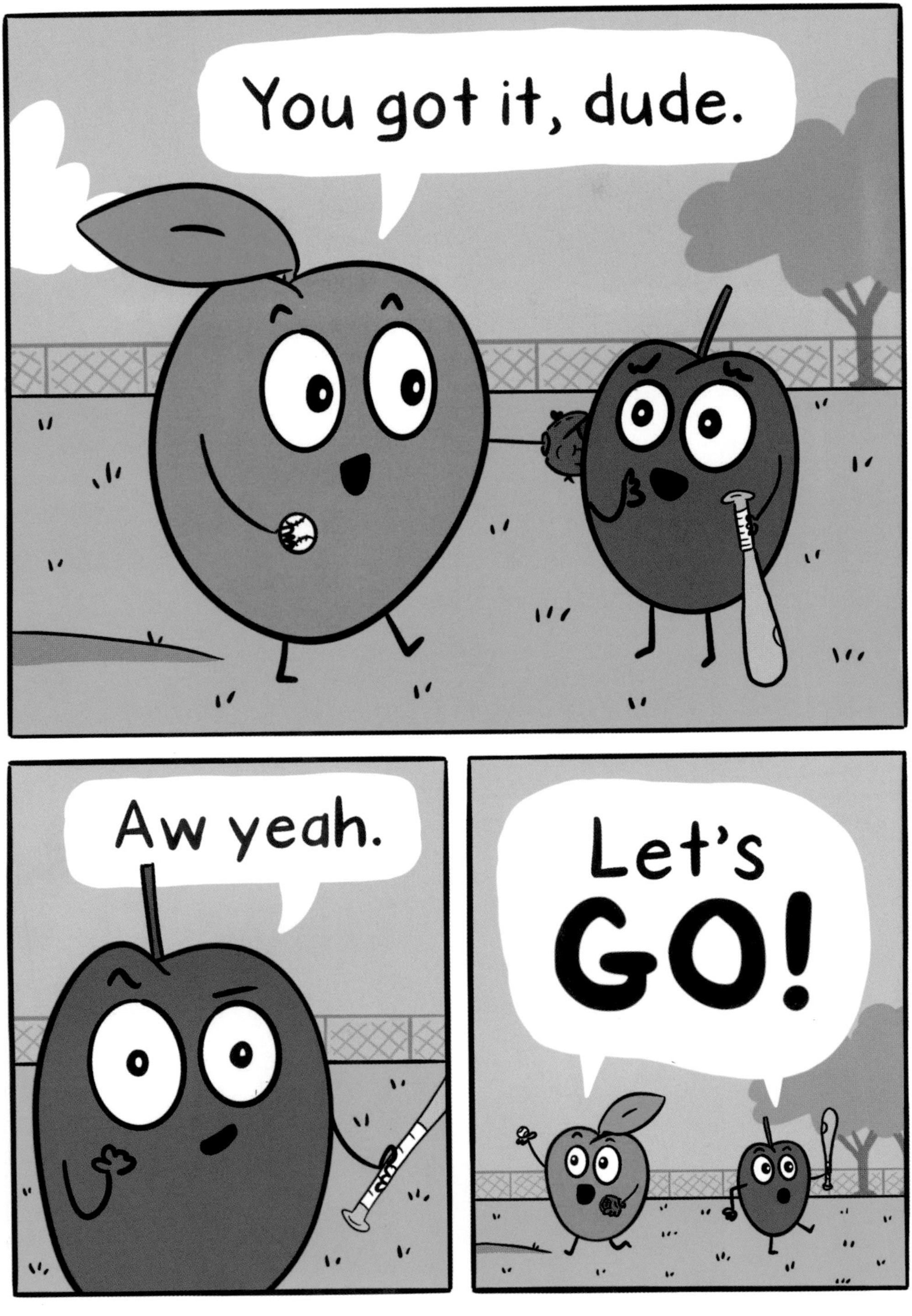
You got it, dude.
Aw yeah.
Let's GO!

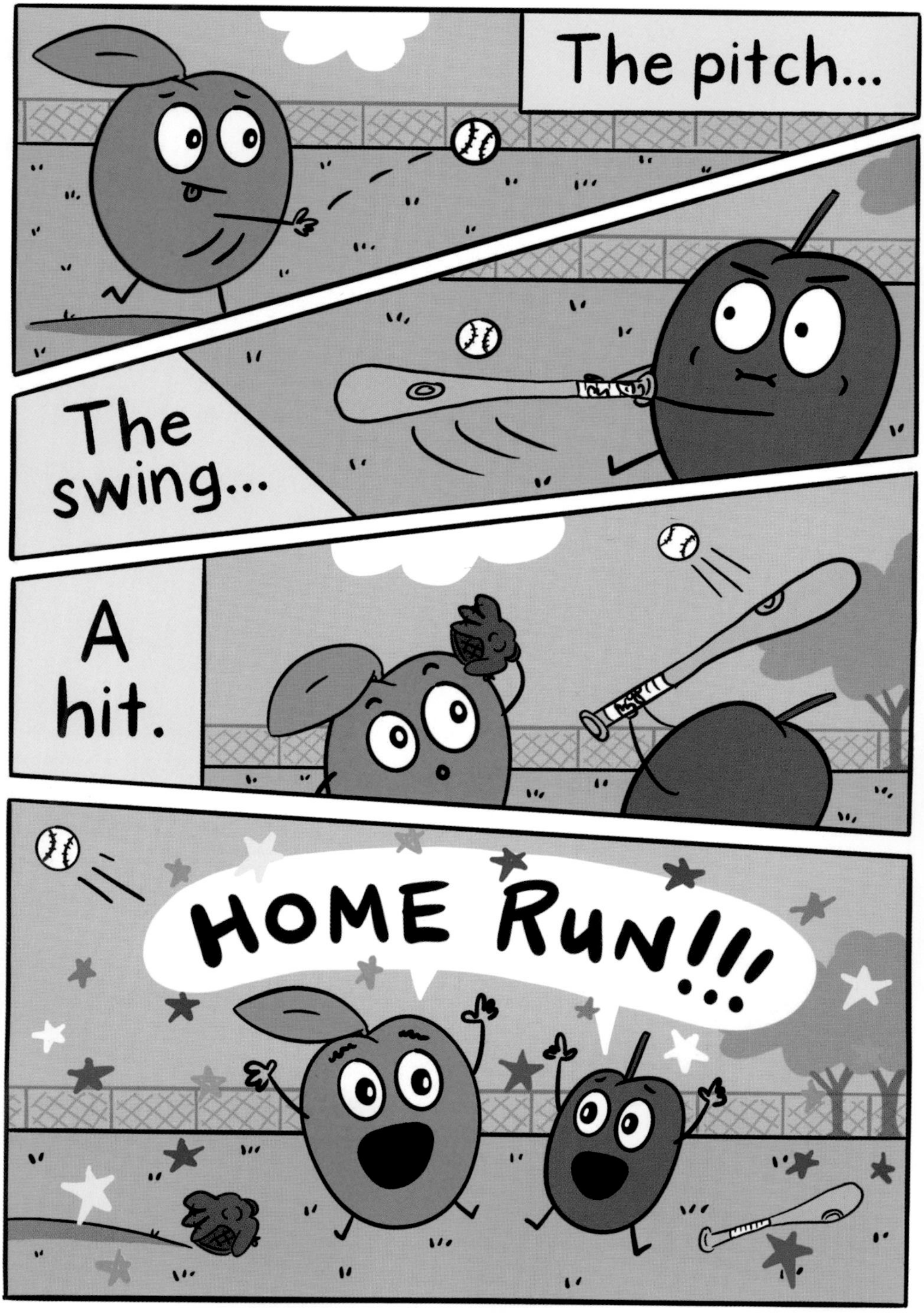
The pitch...
The swing...
A hit.
HOME RUN!!!

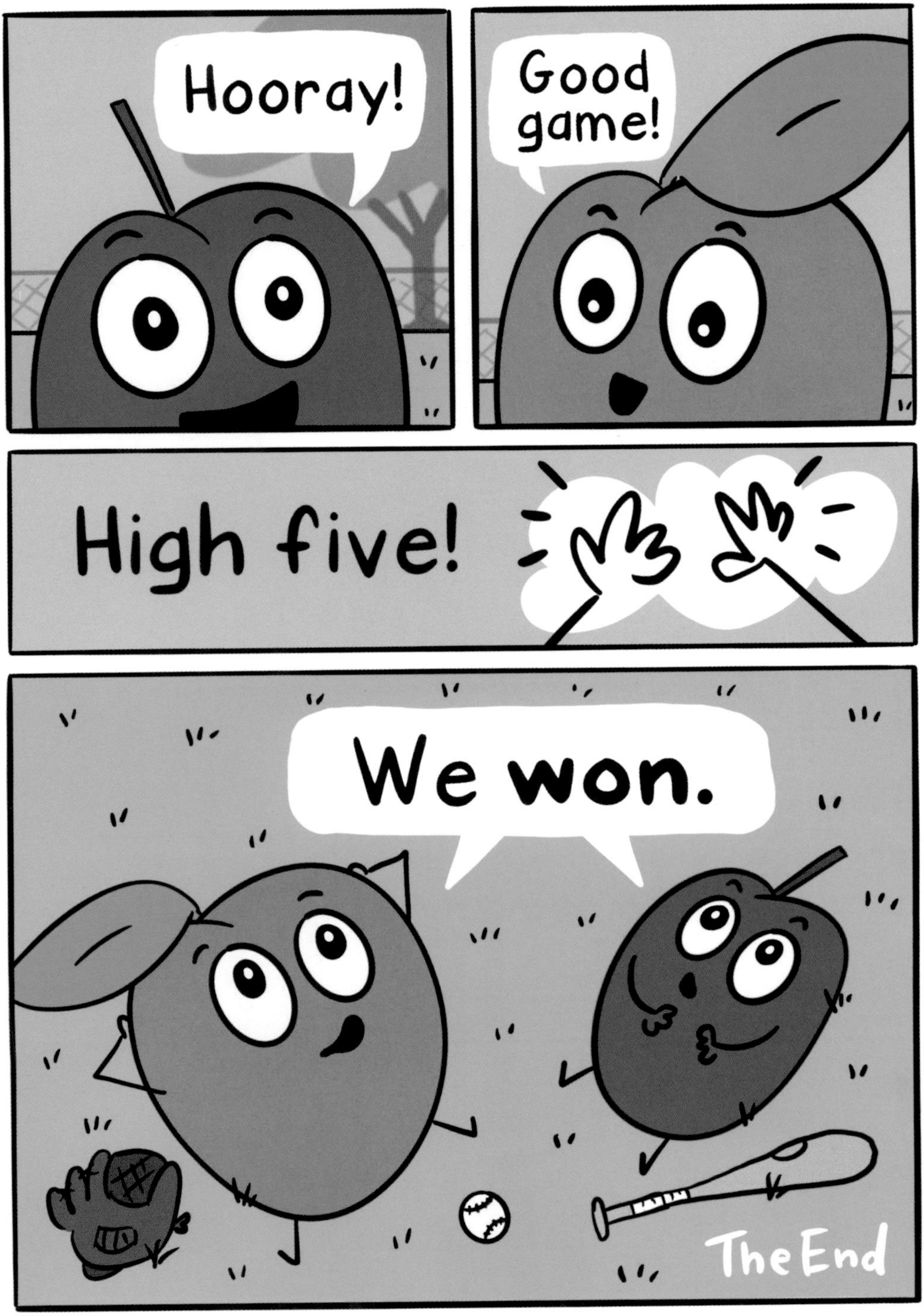
Hooray!
Good game!
High five!
We won.
The End

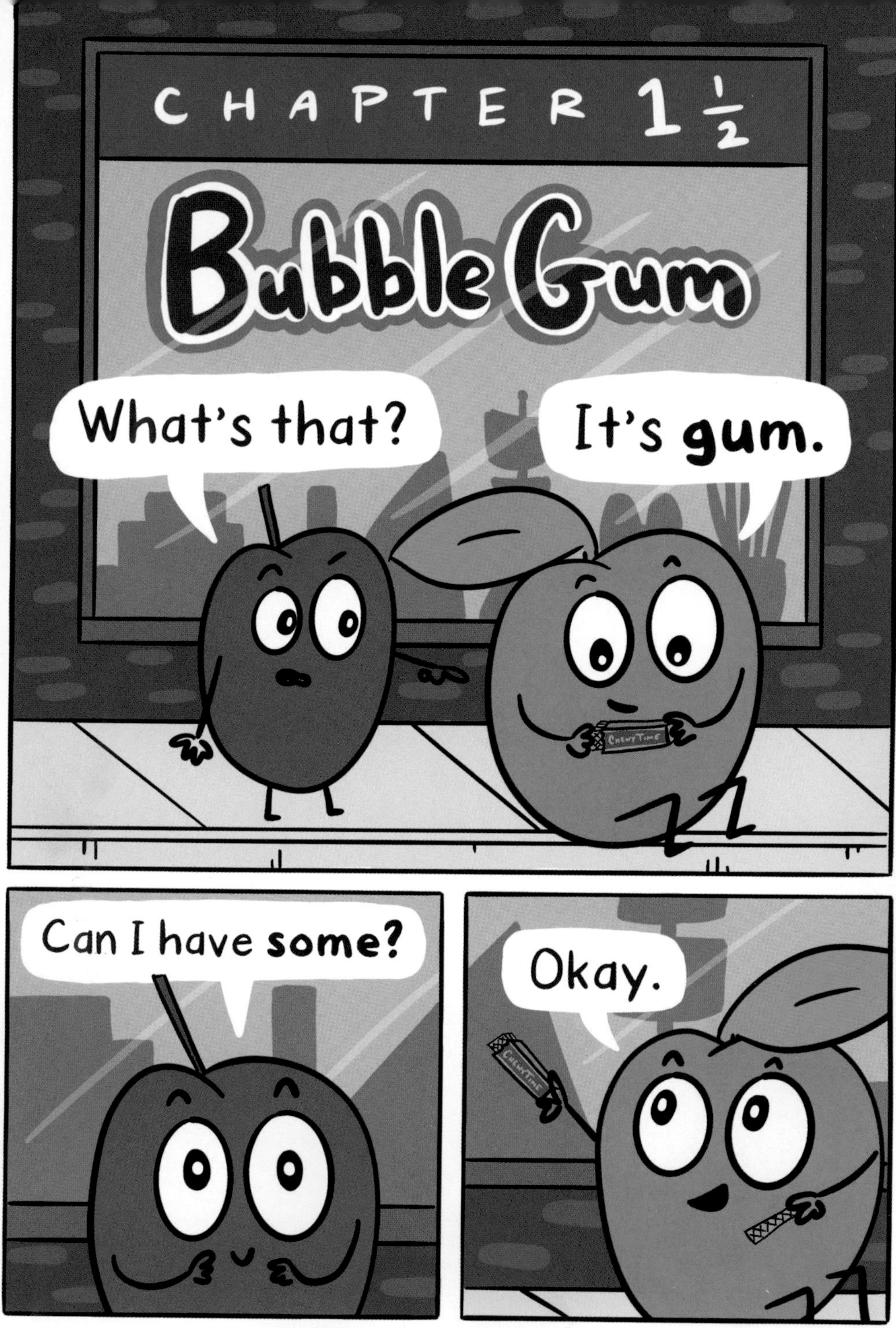
CHAPTER 1 1/2
Bubble Gum
What's that?
It's **gum.**
Can I have **some?**
Okay.

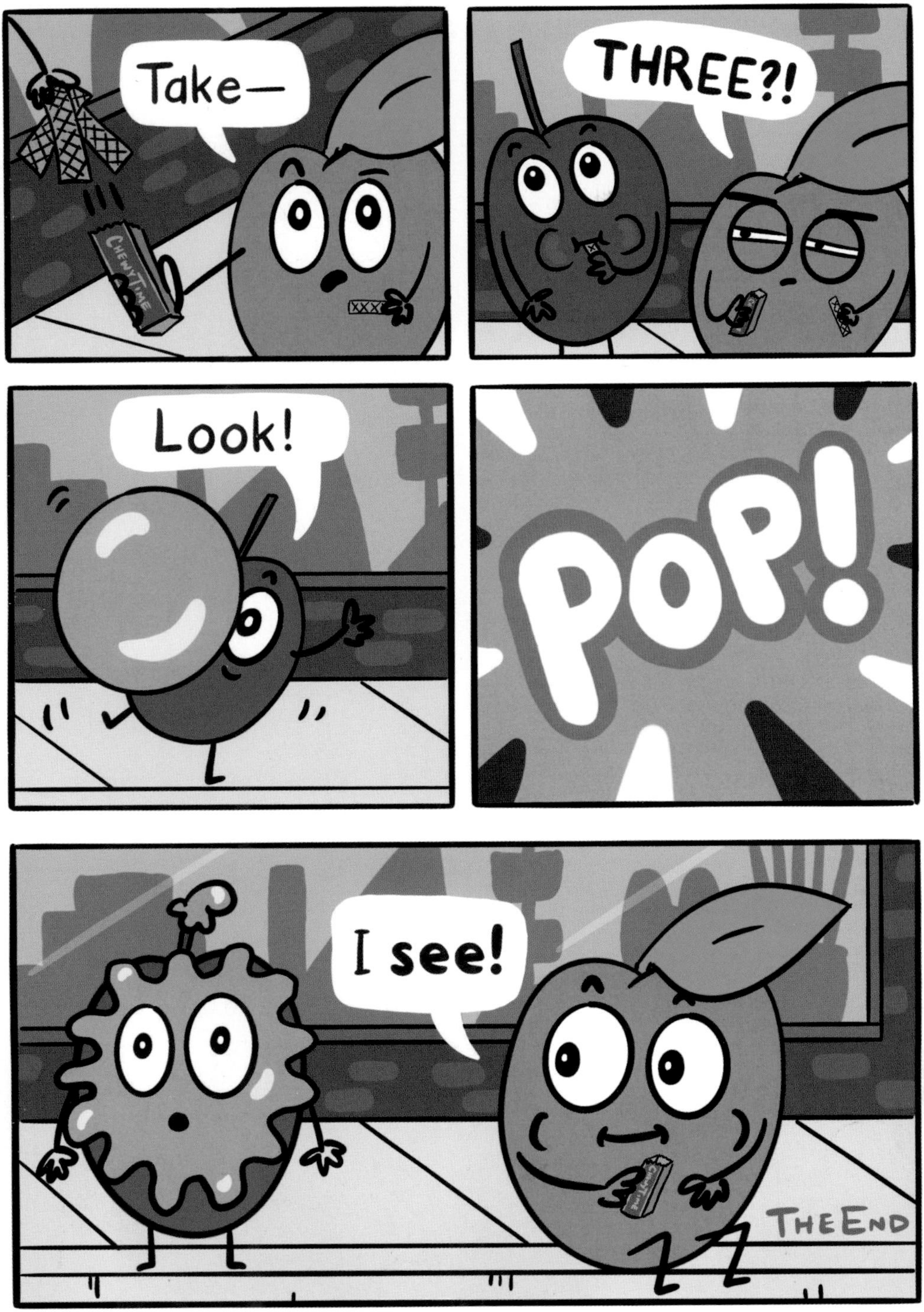
Take—
CHEWY TIME
THREE?!
Look!
POP!
I see!
CHEWY TIME
THE END

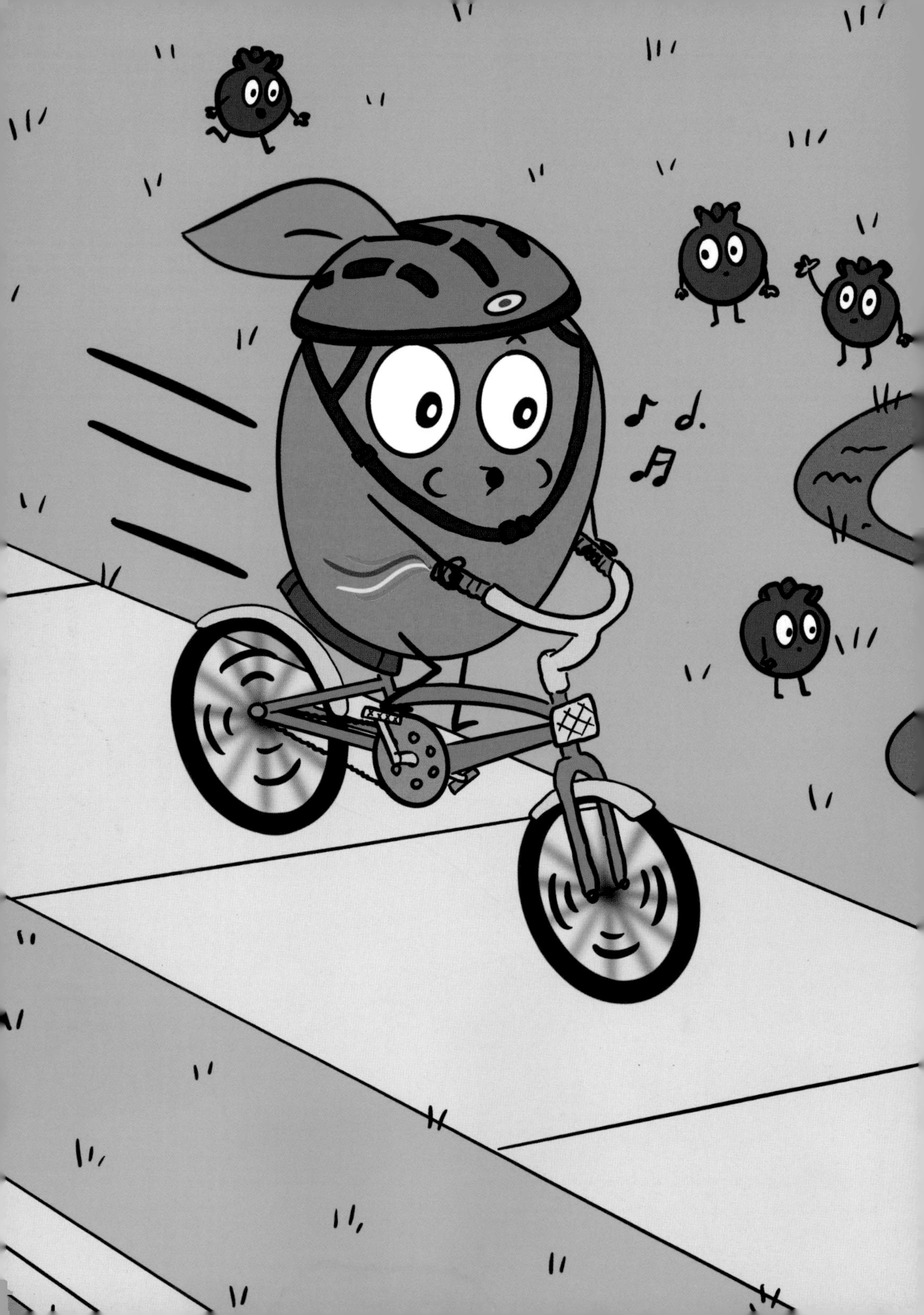

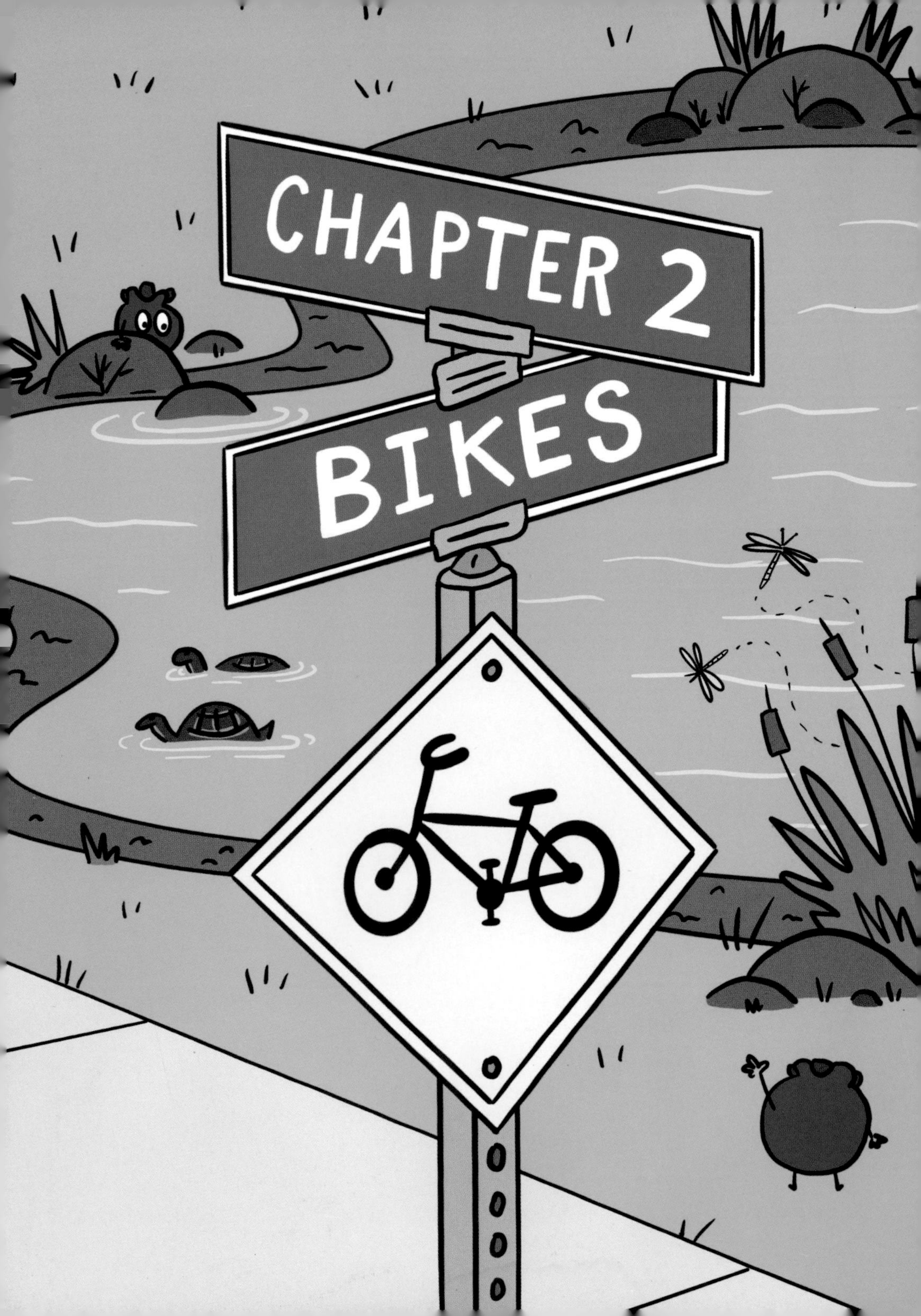
CHAPTER 2
BIKES

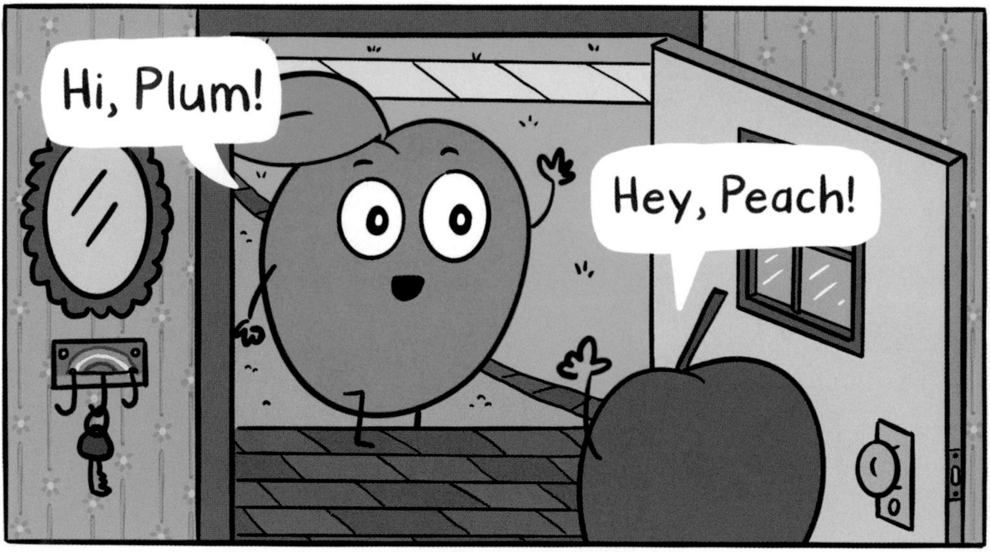
Hi, Plum!
Hey, Peach!

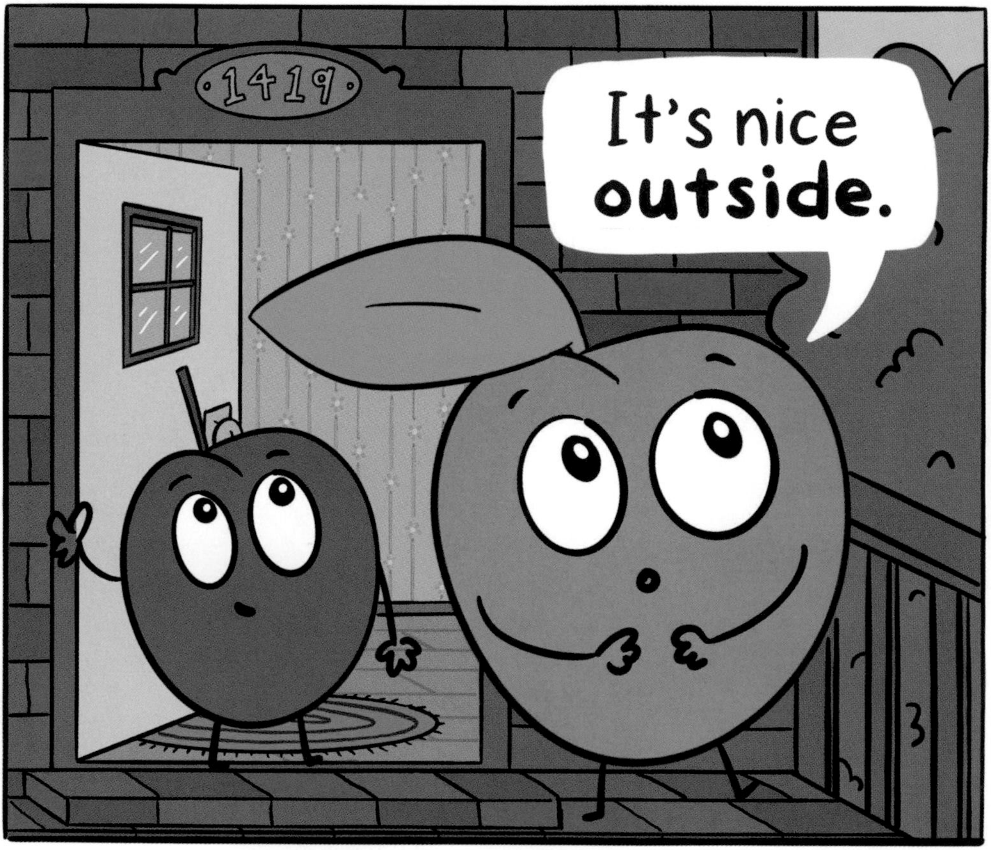
1419
It's nice **outside.**

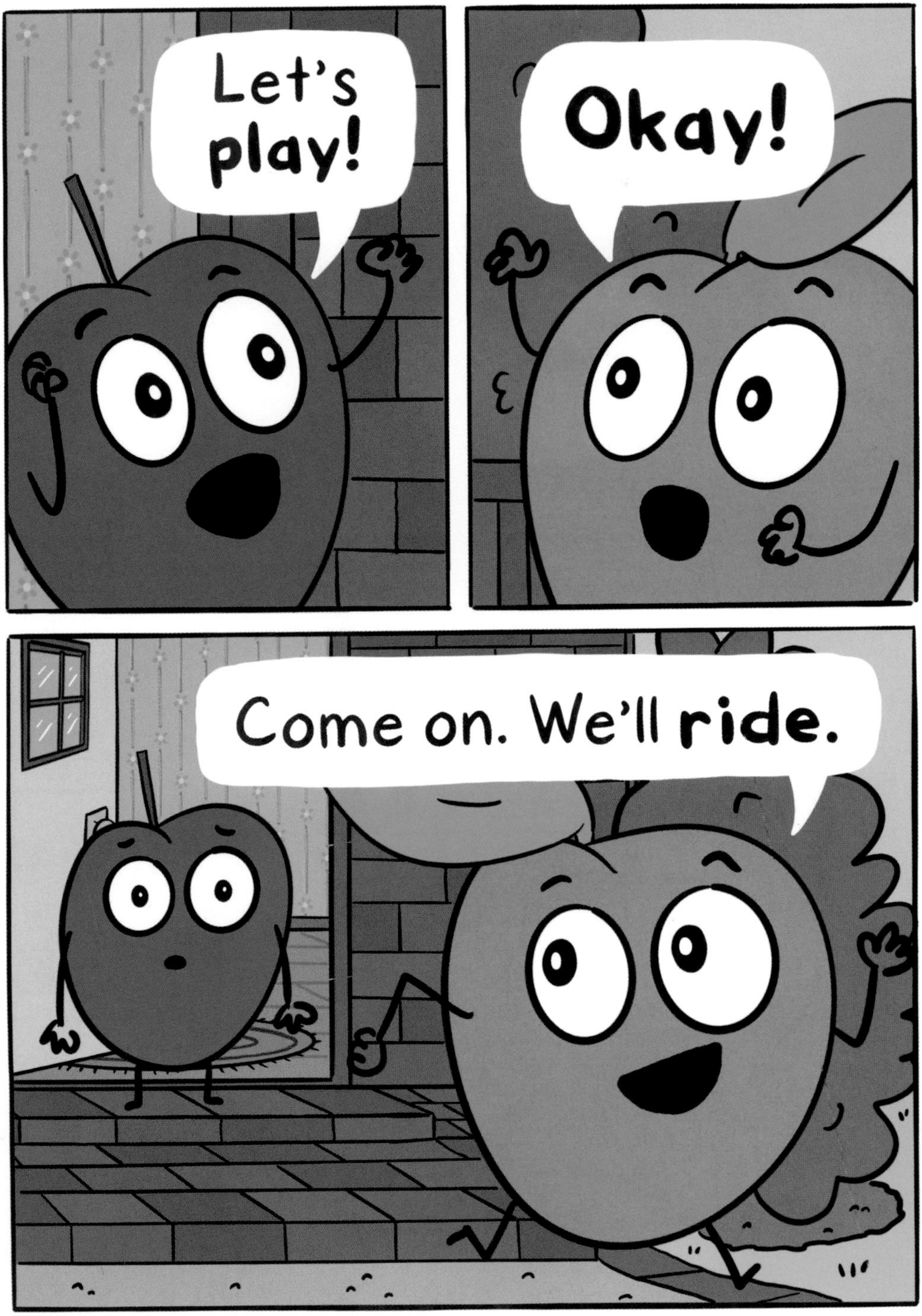
Let's play!
Okay!
Come on. We'll ride.

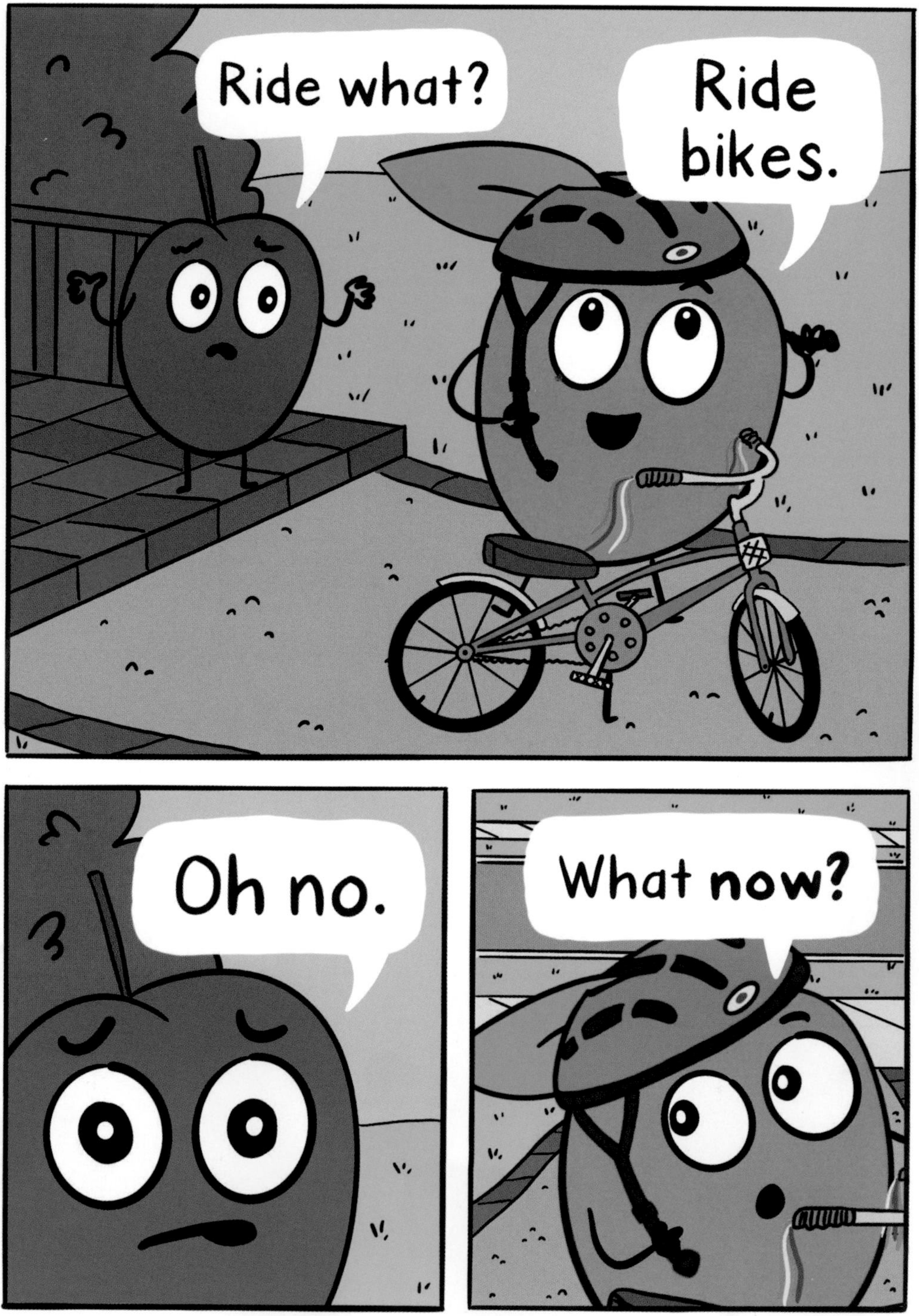
Ride what?
Ride bikes.
Oh no.
What now?

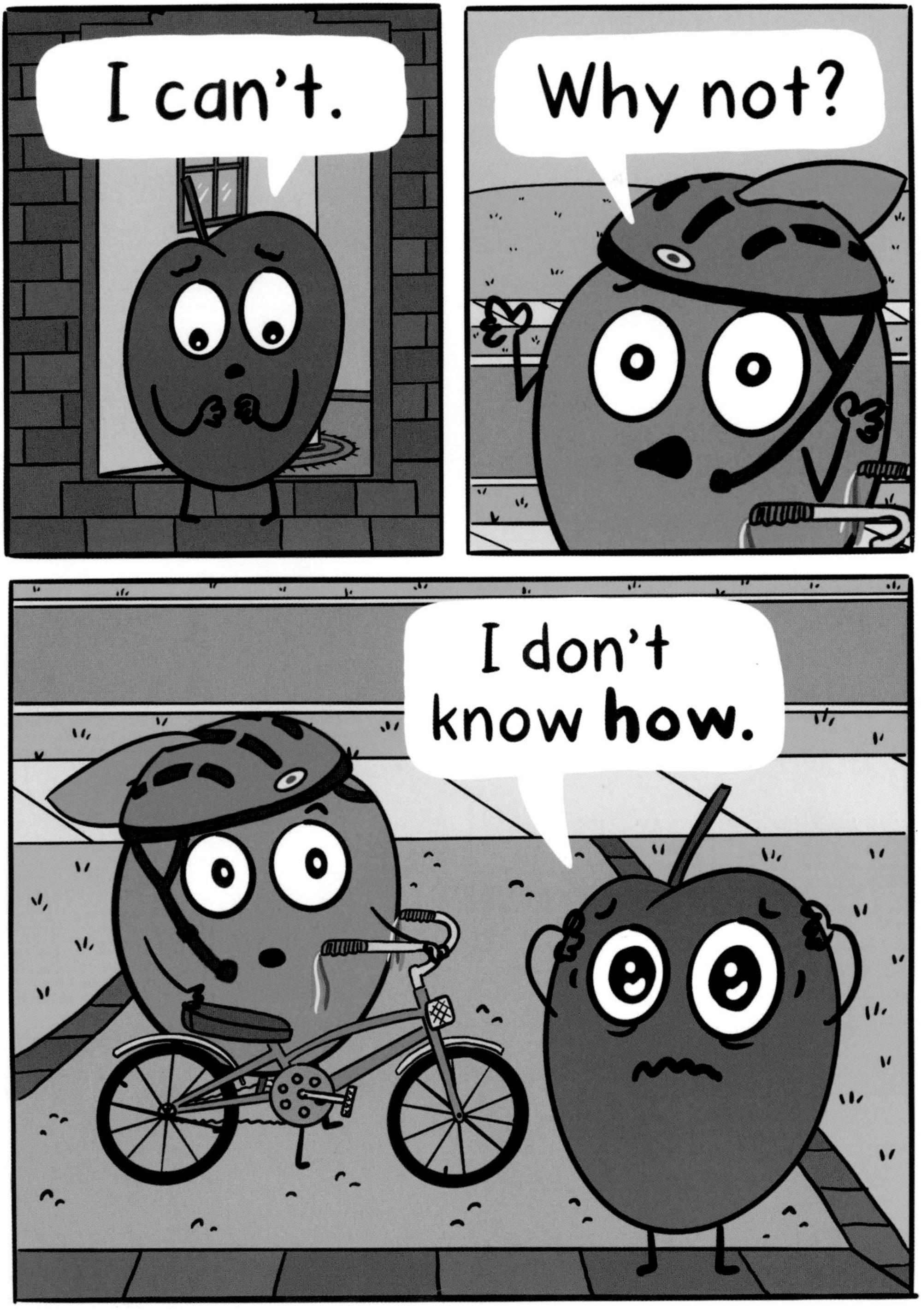
I can't.
Why not?
I don't know how.

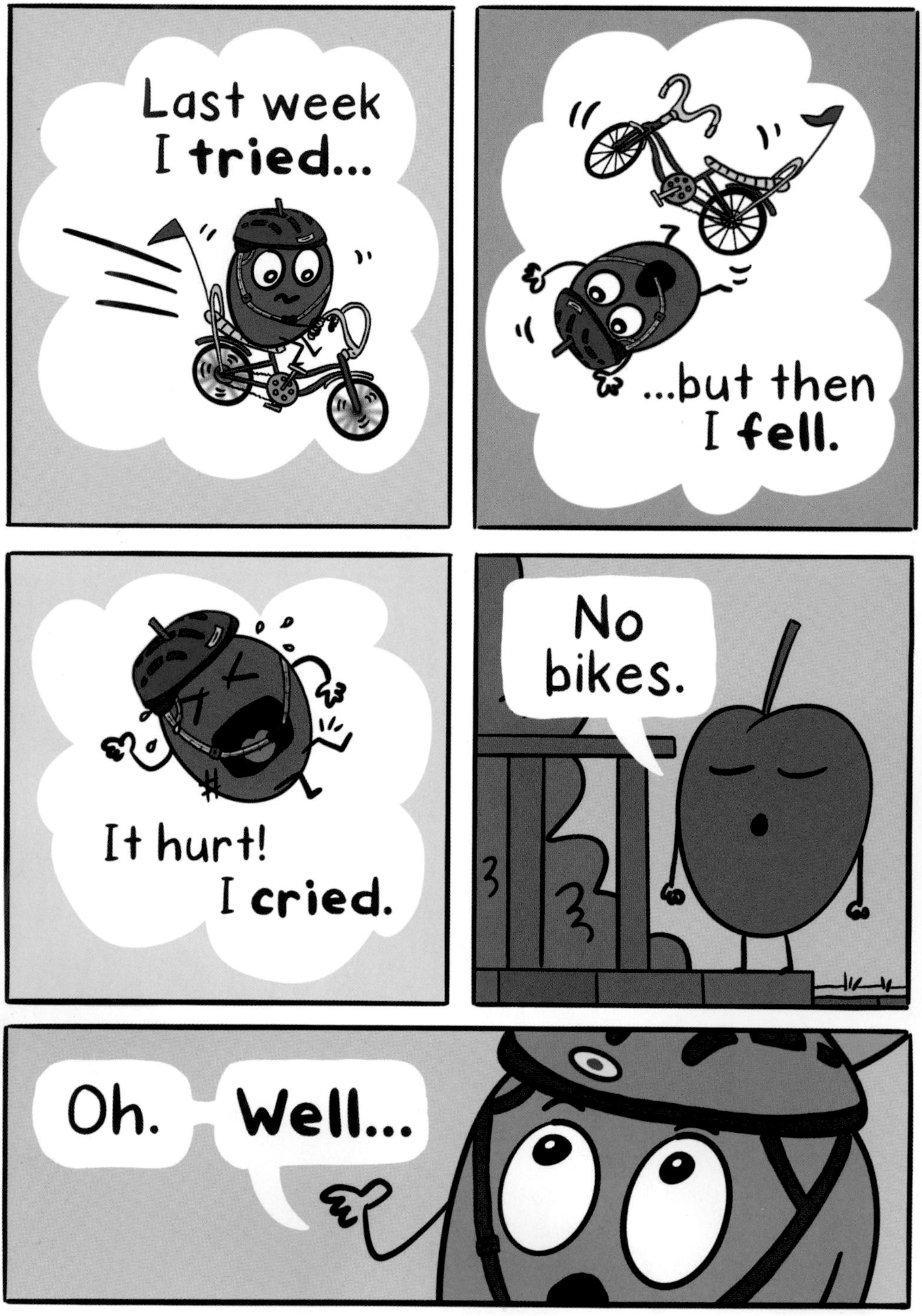
Last week I tried...
...but then I fell.
It hurt! I cried.
No bikes.
Oh.
Well...

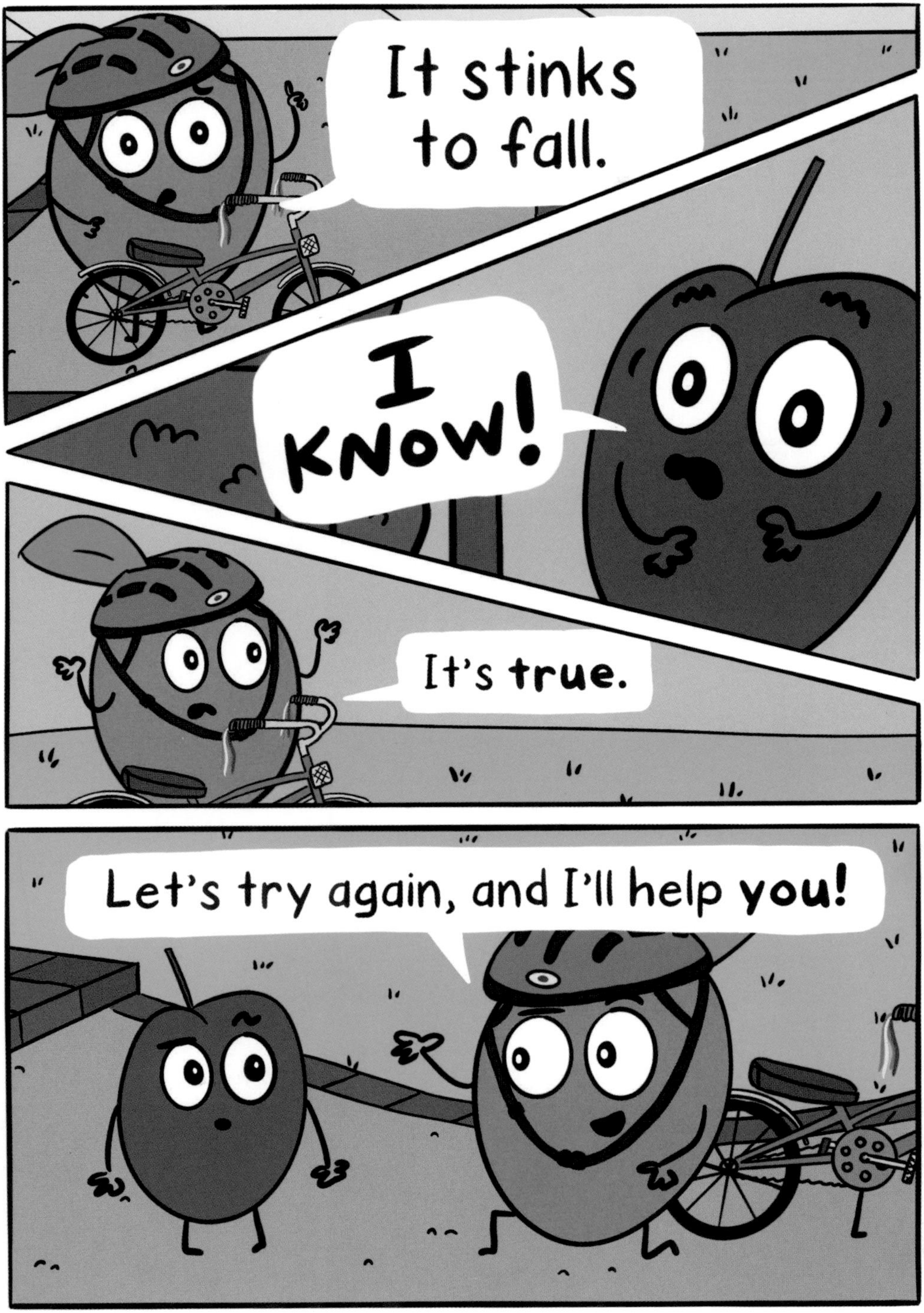
It stinks to fall.
I KNOW!
It's true.
Let's try again, and I'll help you!

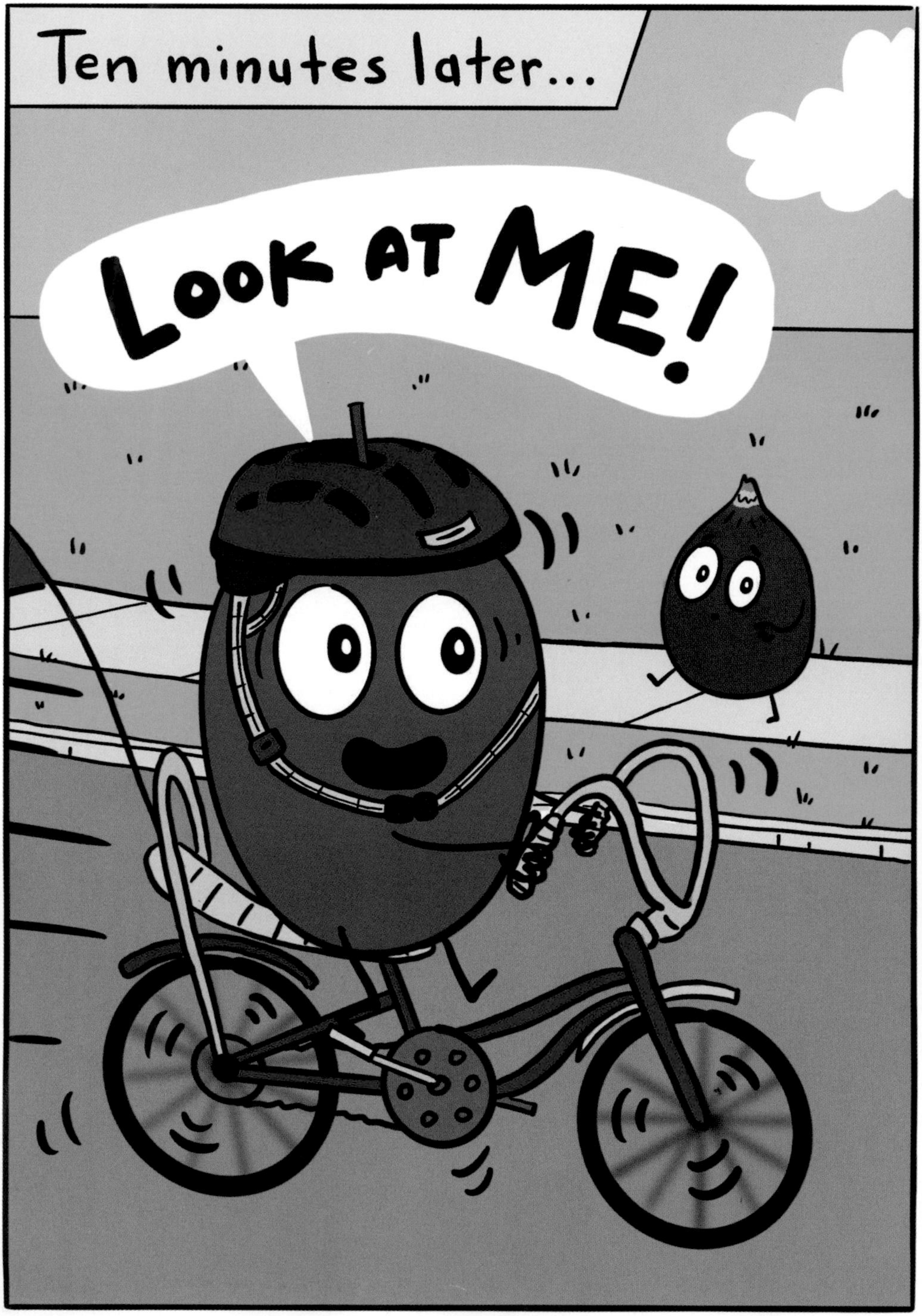
Ten minutes later...
LOOK AT ME!

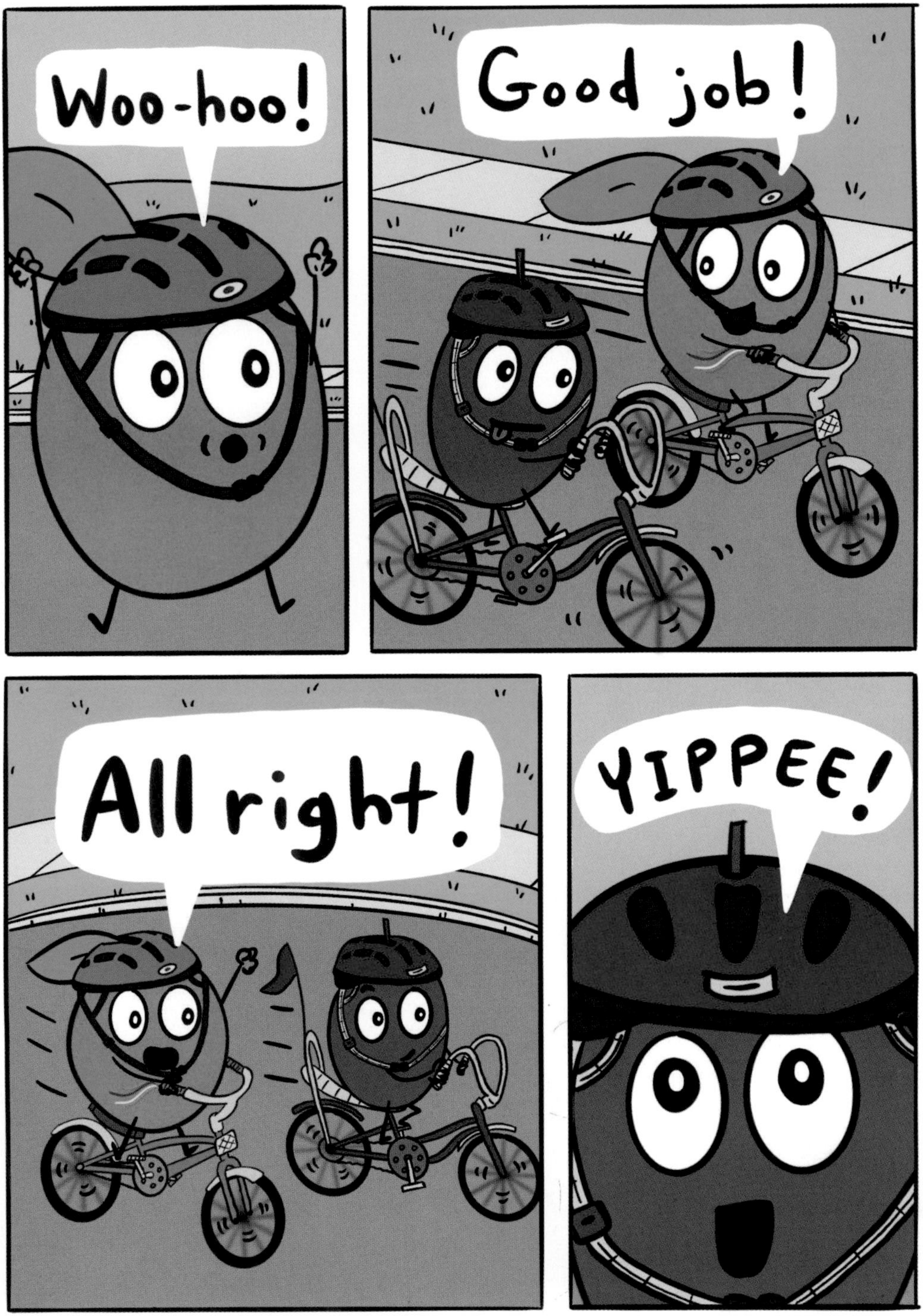
Woo-hoo!
Good job!
All right!
YIPPEE!

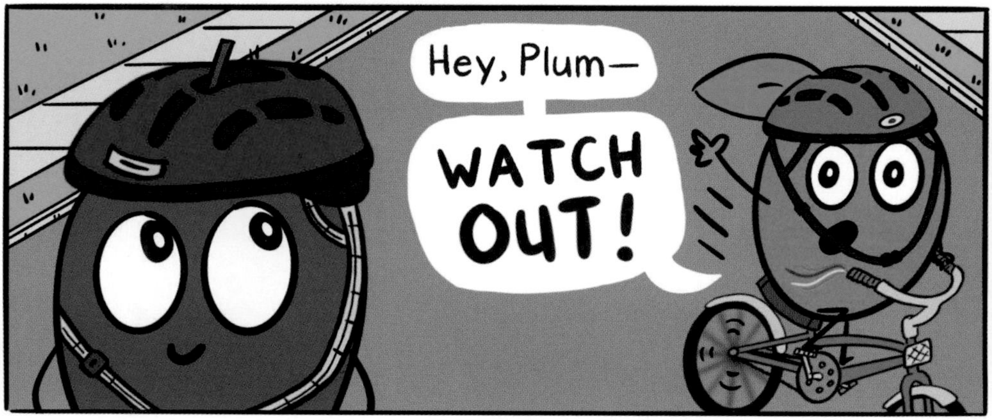
Hey, Plum—
WATCH OUT!

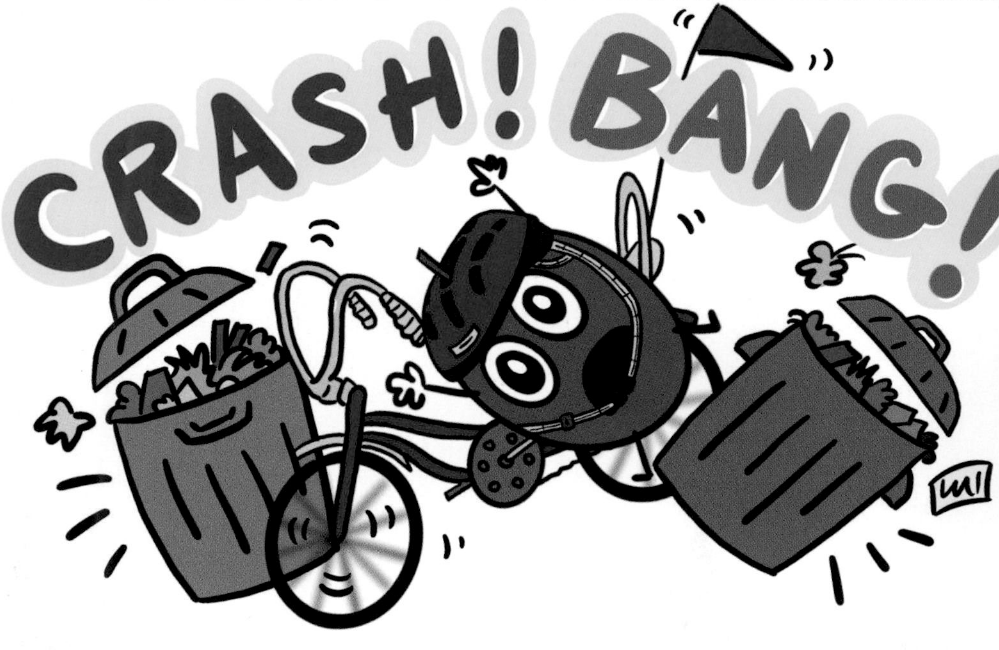
CRASH! BANG!

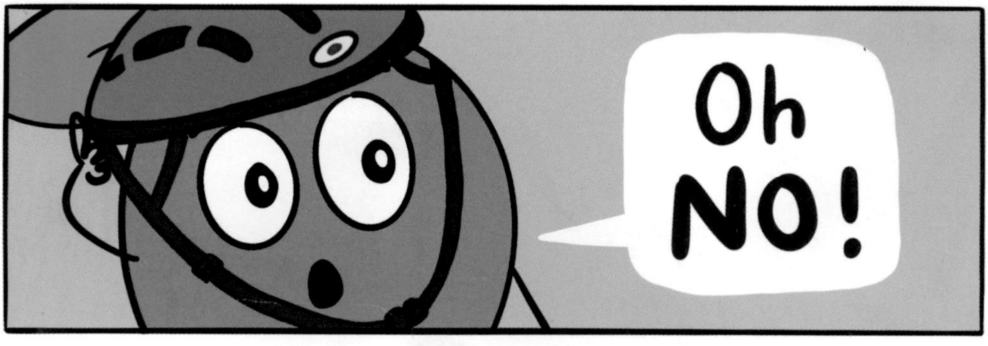
Oh NO!

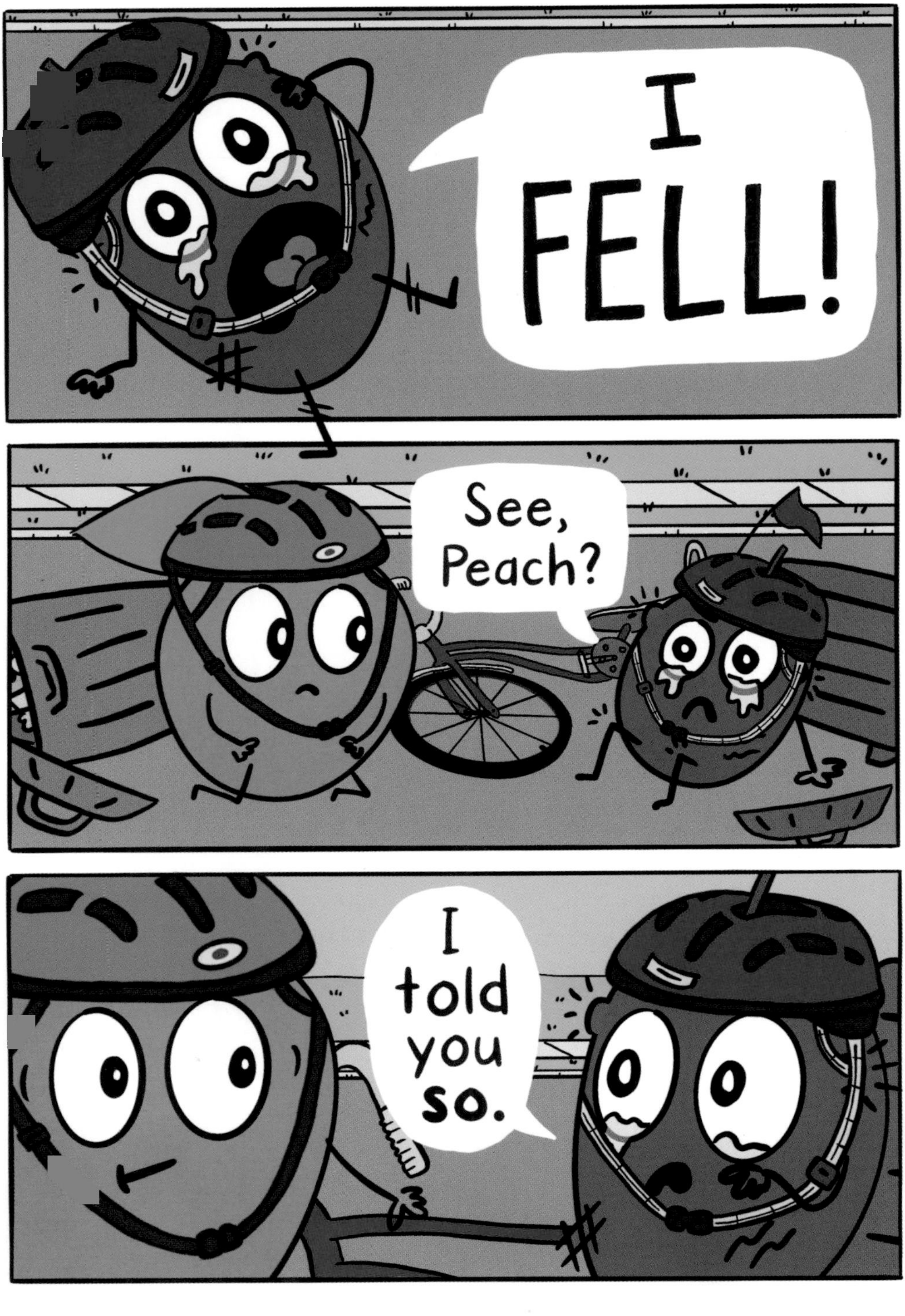
I FELL!
See, Peach?
I told you so.

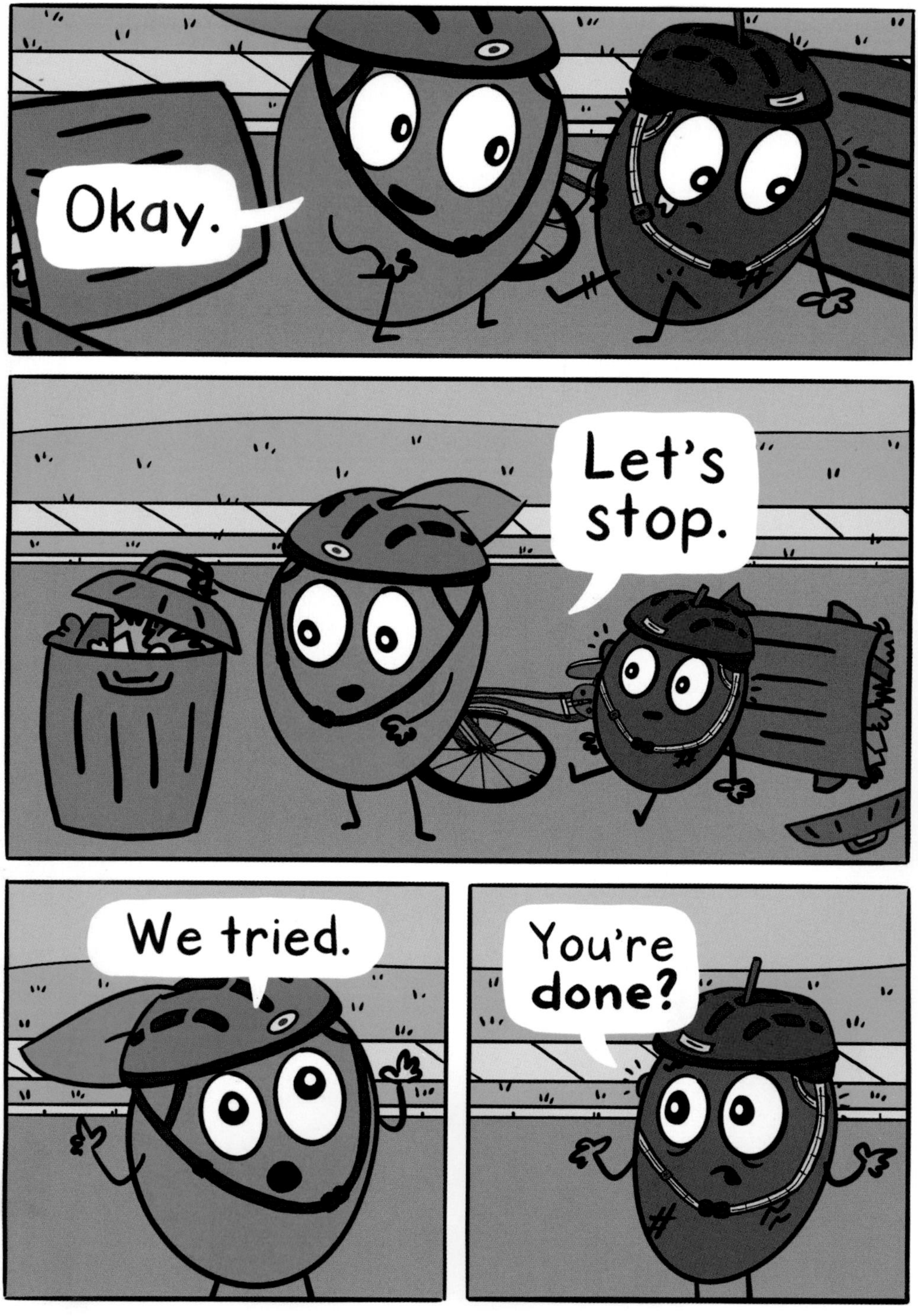
Okay.
Let's stop.
We tried.
You're done?

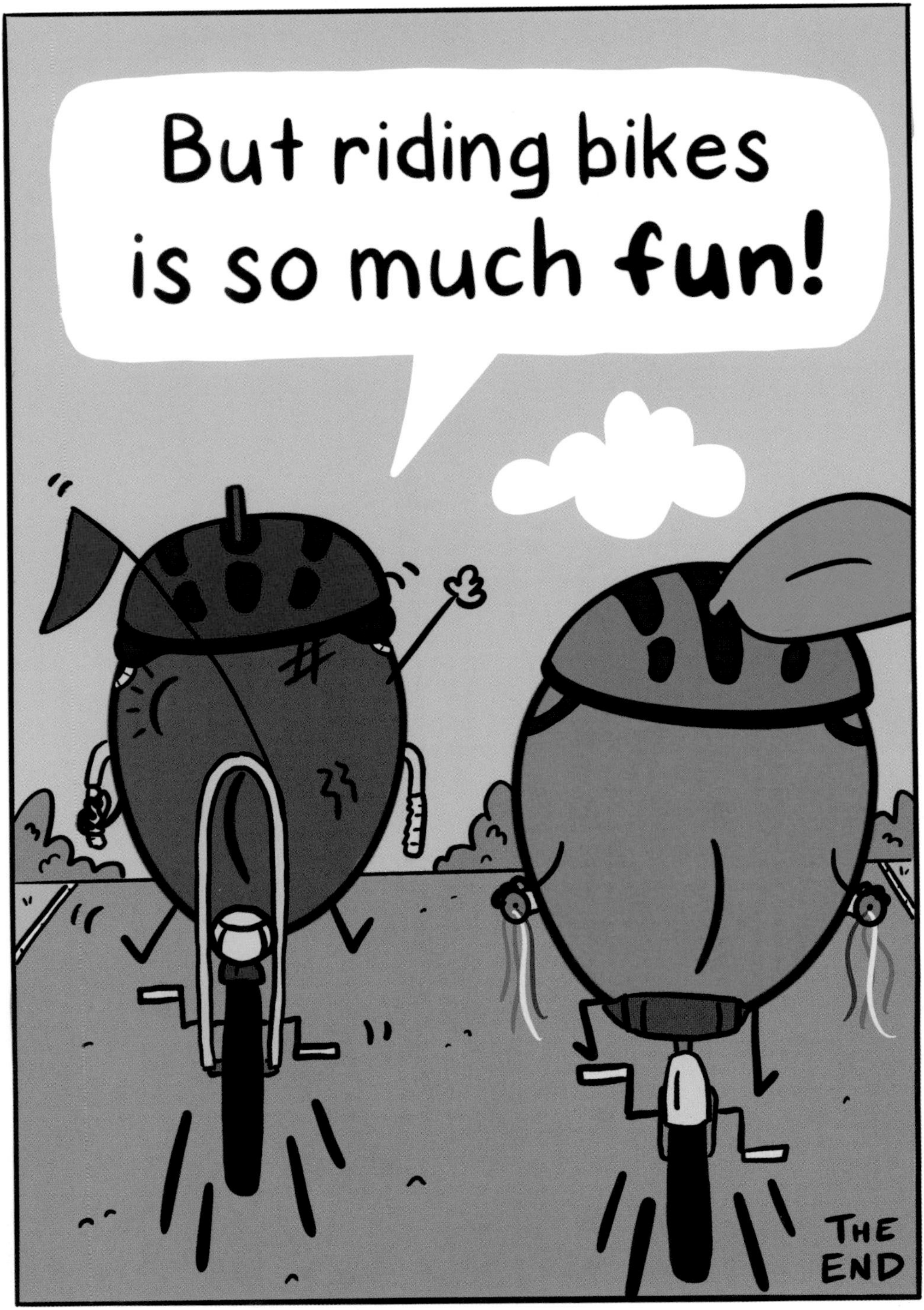
But riding bikes is so much **fun**!
THE END

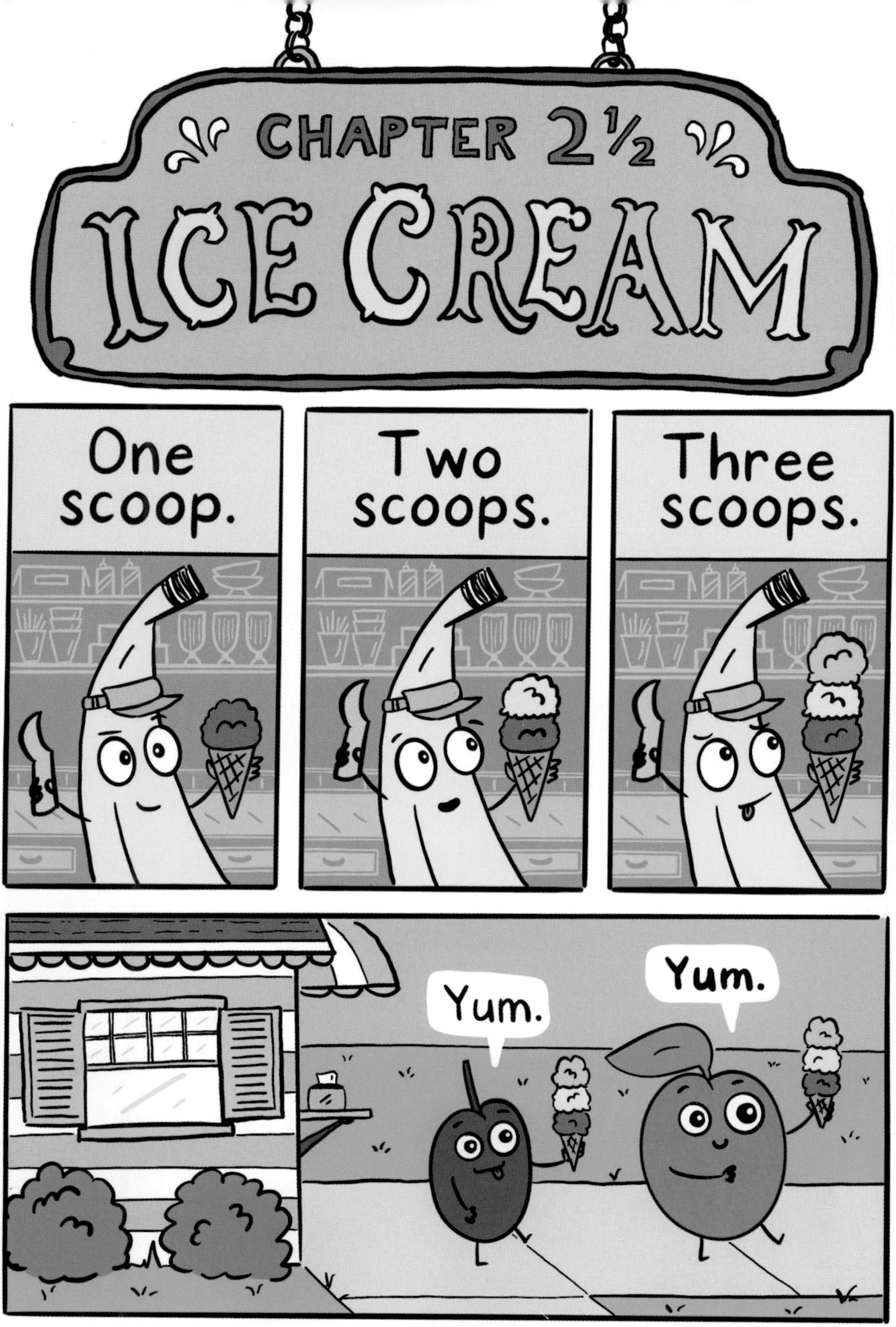
CHAPTER 2½
ICE CREAM
One scoop.
Two scoops.
Three scoops.
Yum.
Yum.

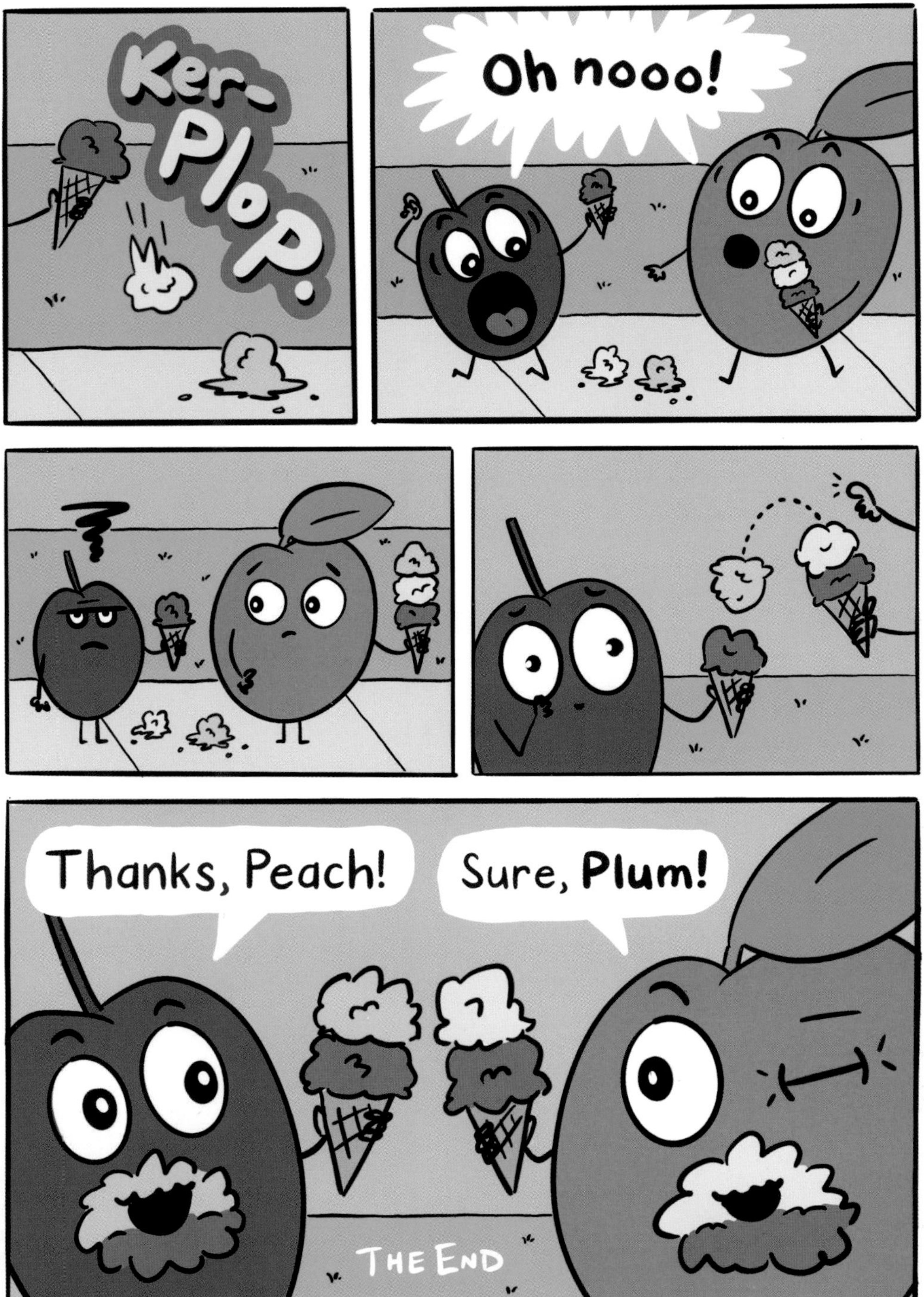
Ker-Plop.
Oh nooo!
Thanks, Peach!
Sure, Plum!
THE END

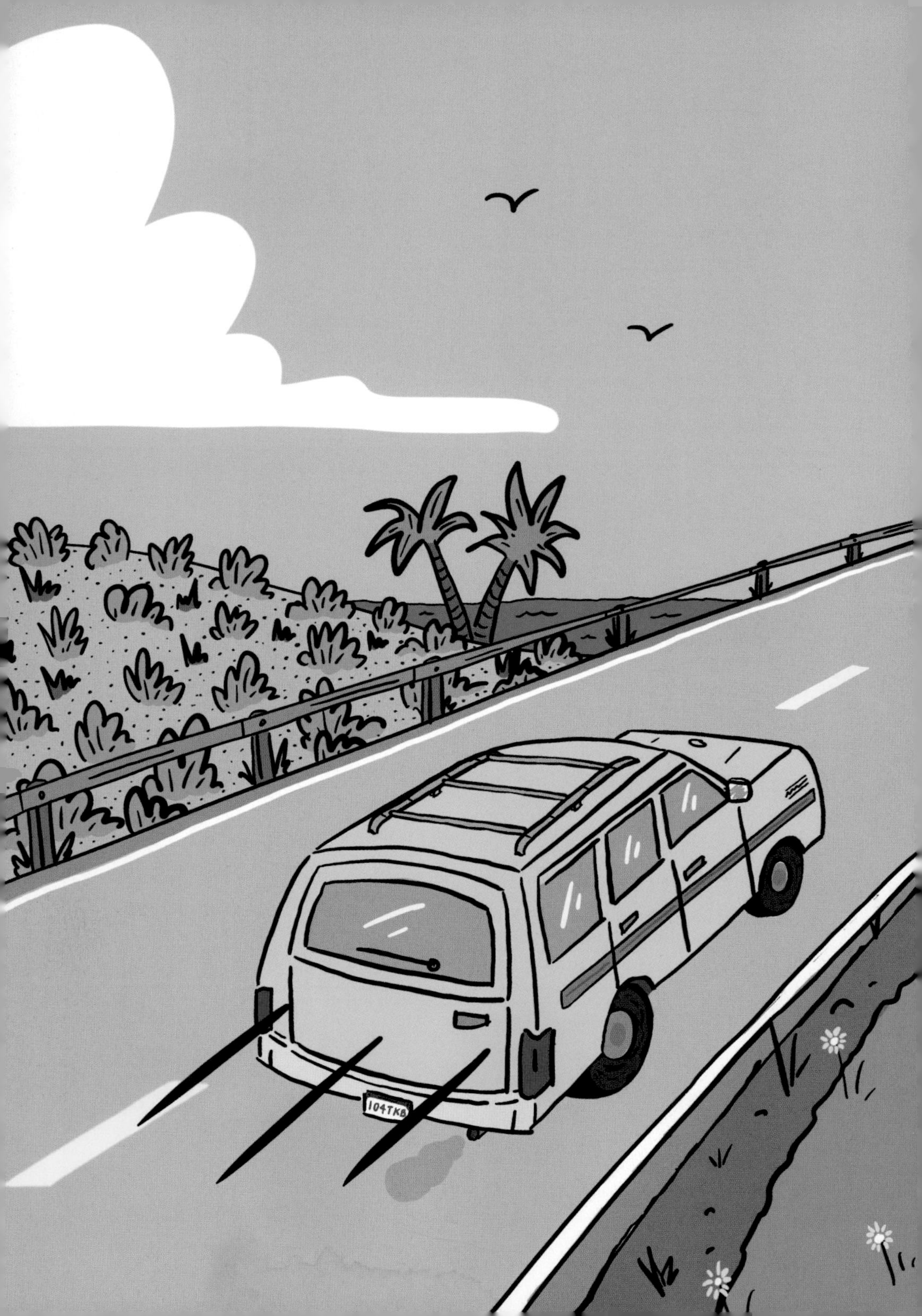
104TKB

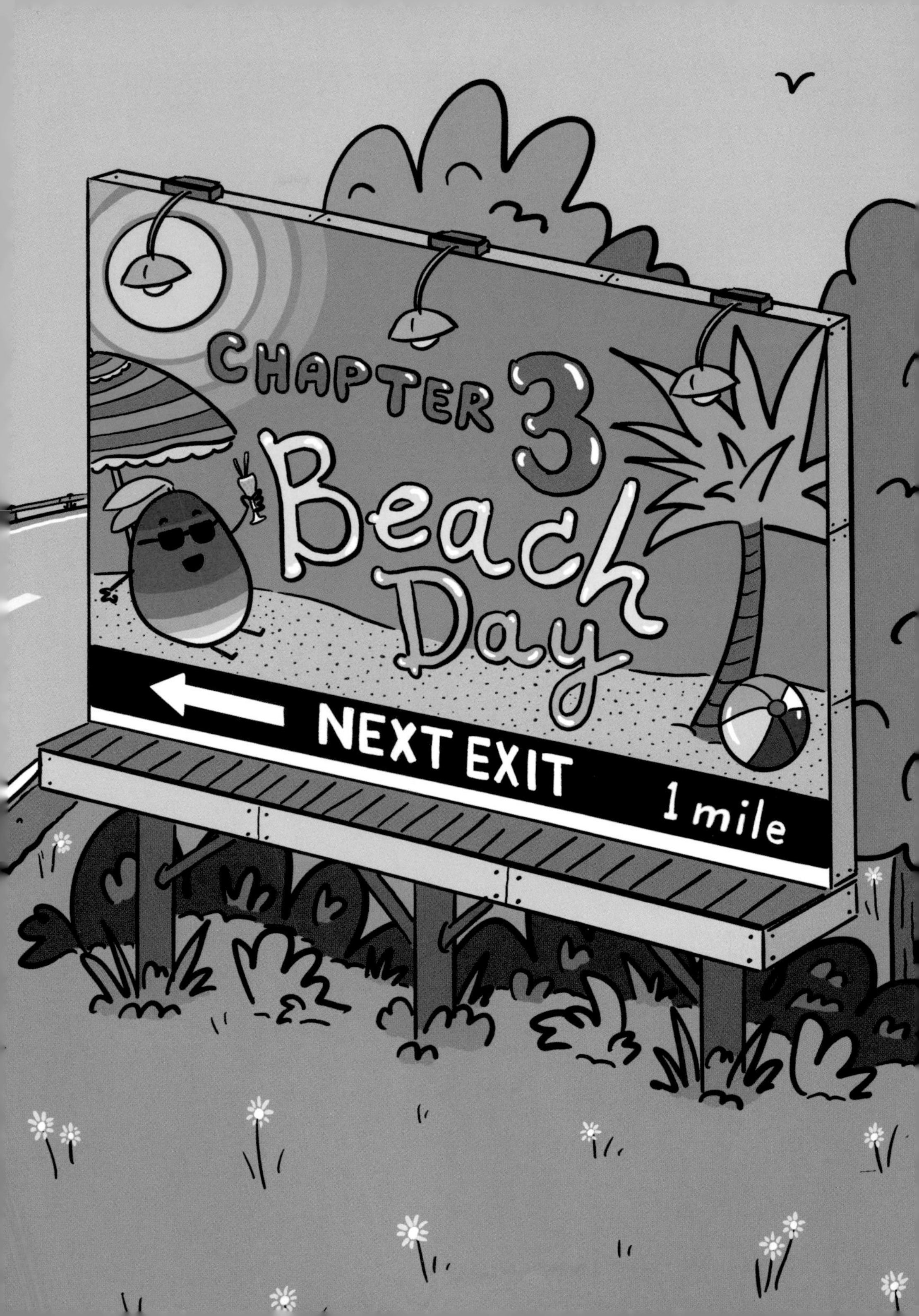
CHAPTER 3
Beach Day
NEXT EXIT
1 mile

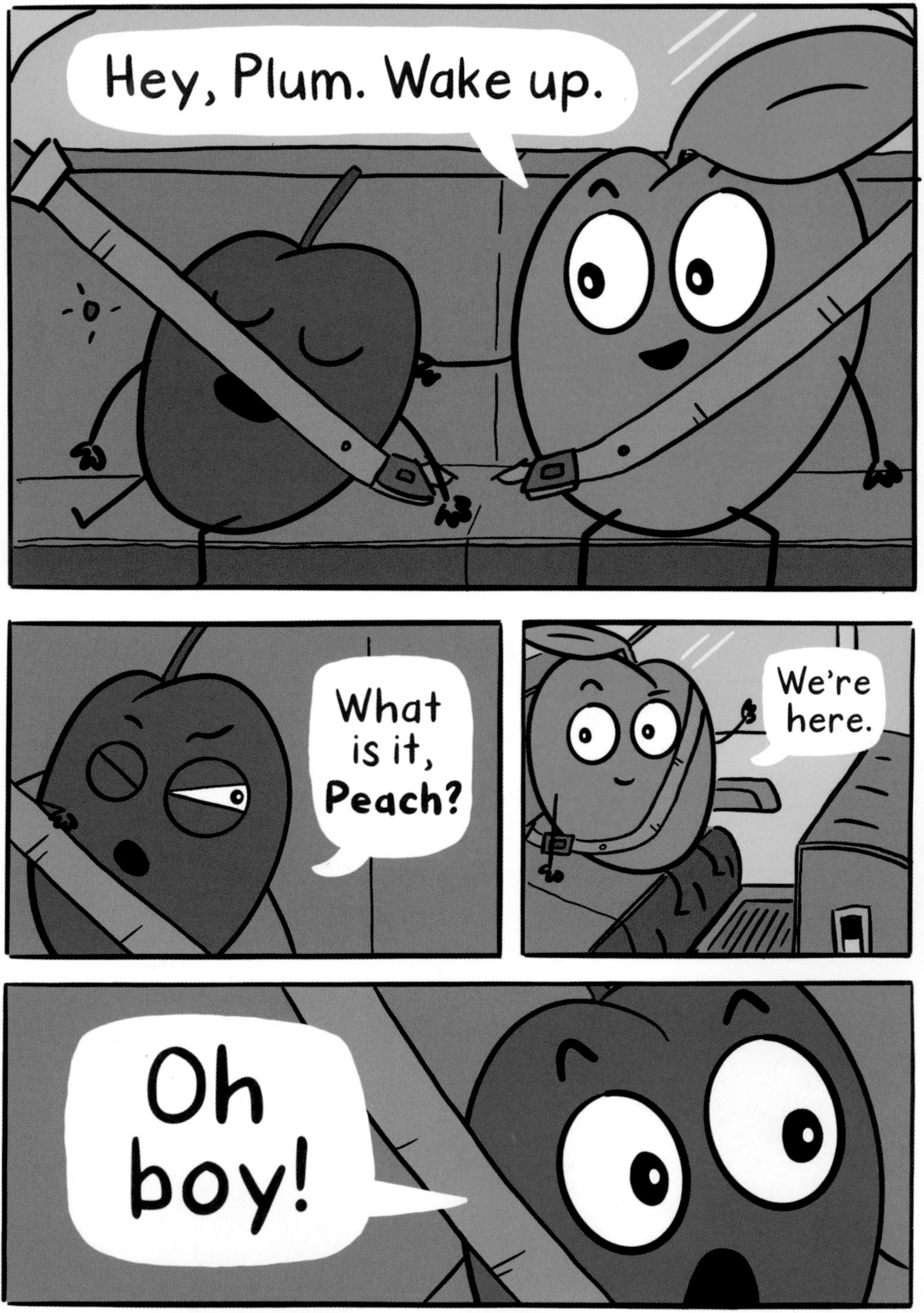
Hey, Plum. Wake up.
What is it, Peach?
We're here.
Oh boy!

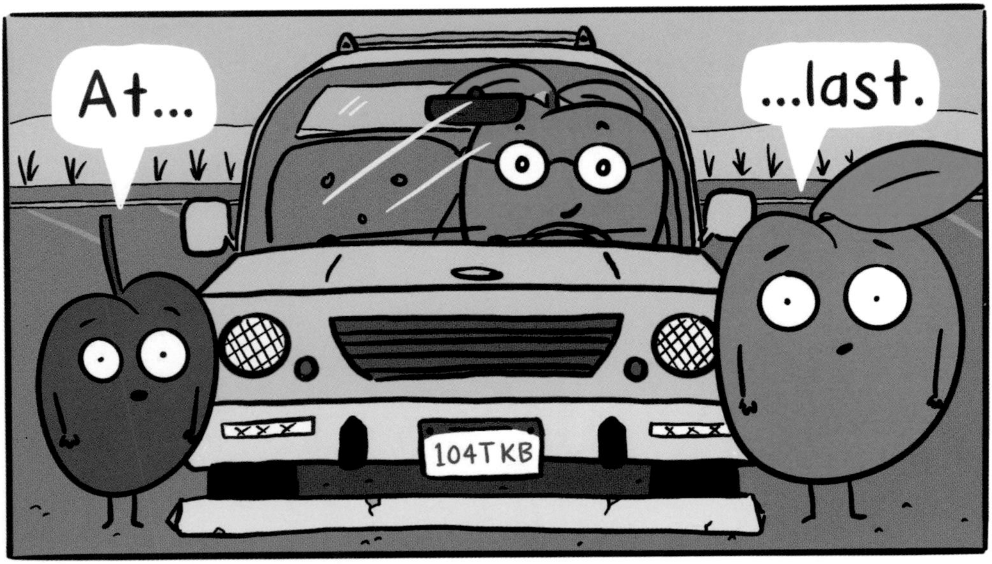
At...
...last.
104TKB

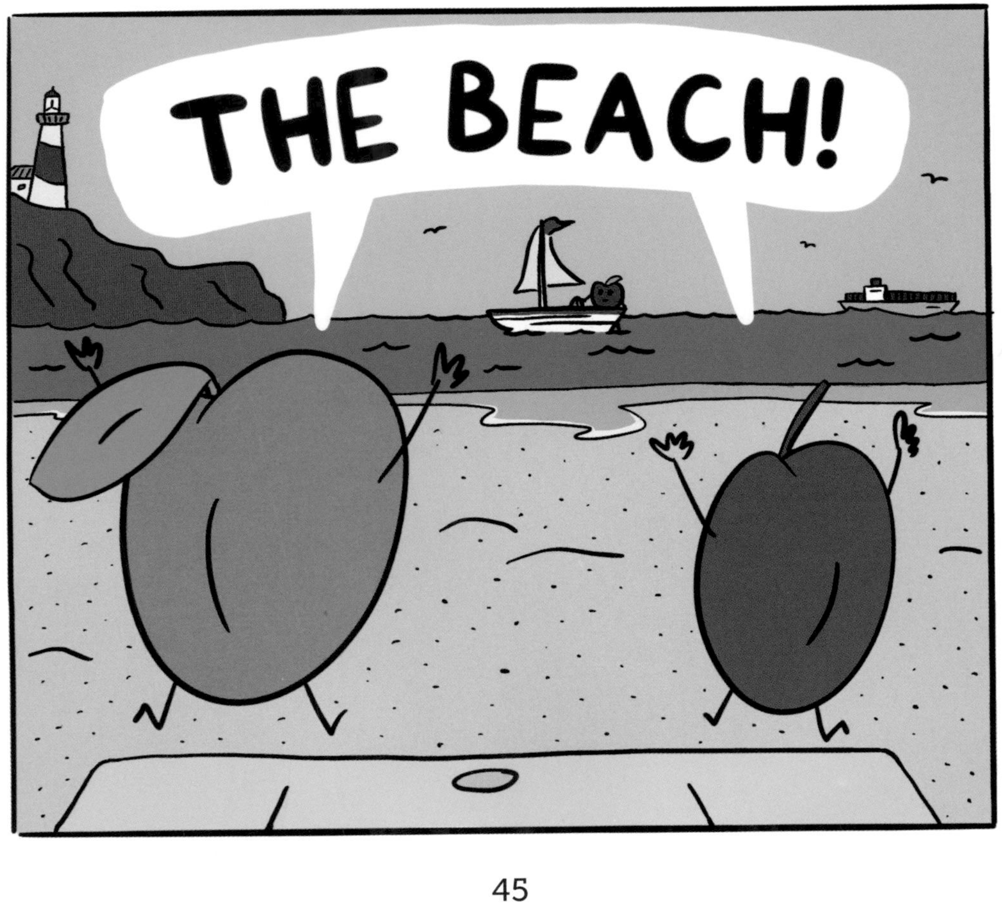
THE BEACH!

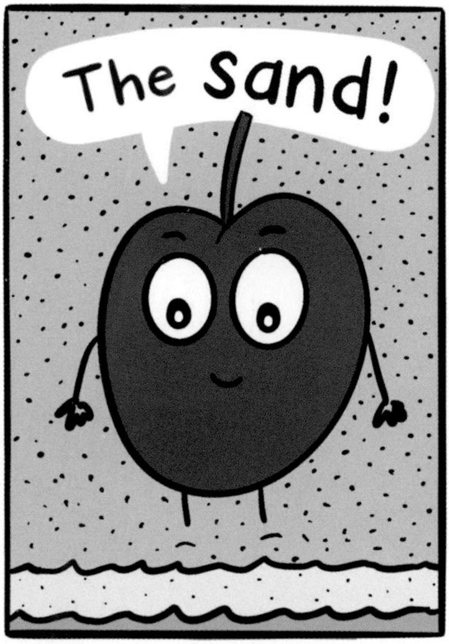
The sand!

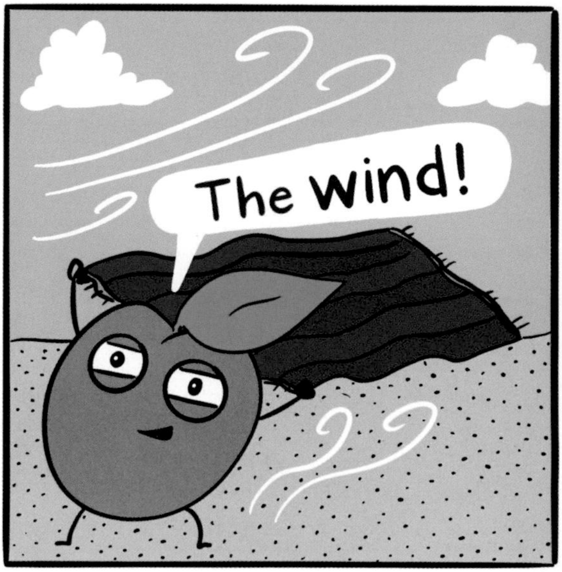
The wind!

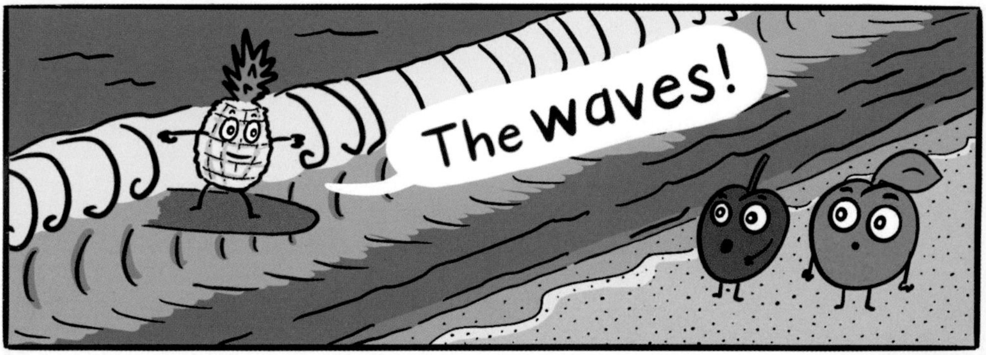
The waves!

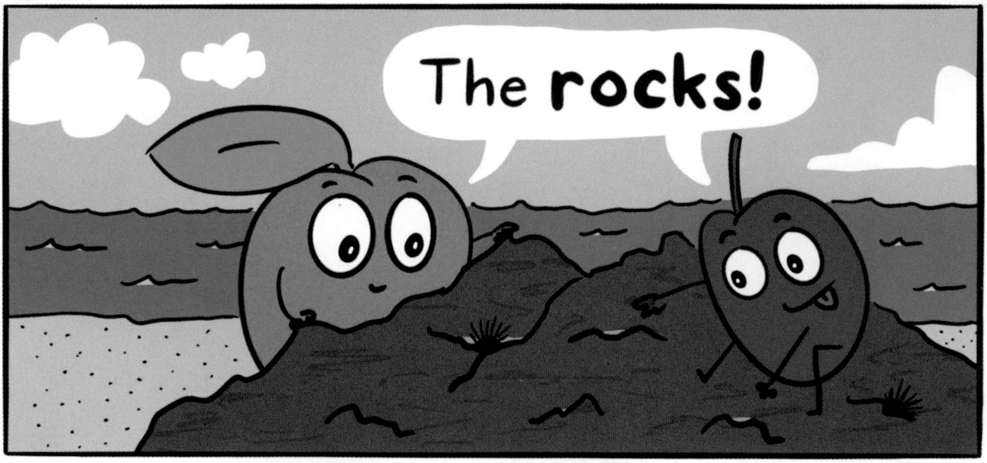
The rocks!

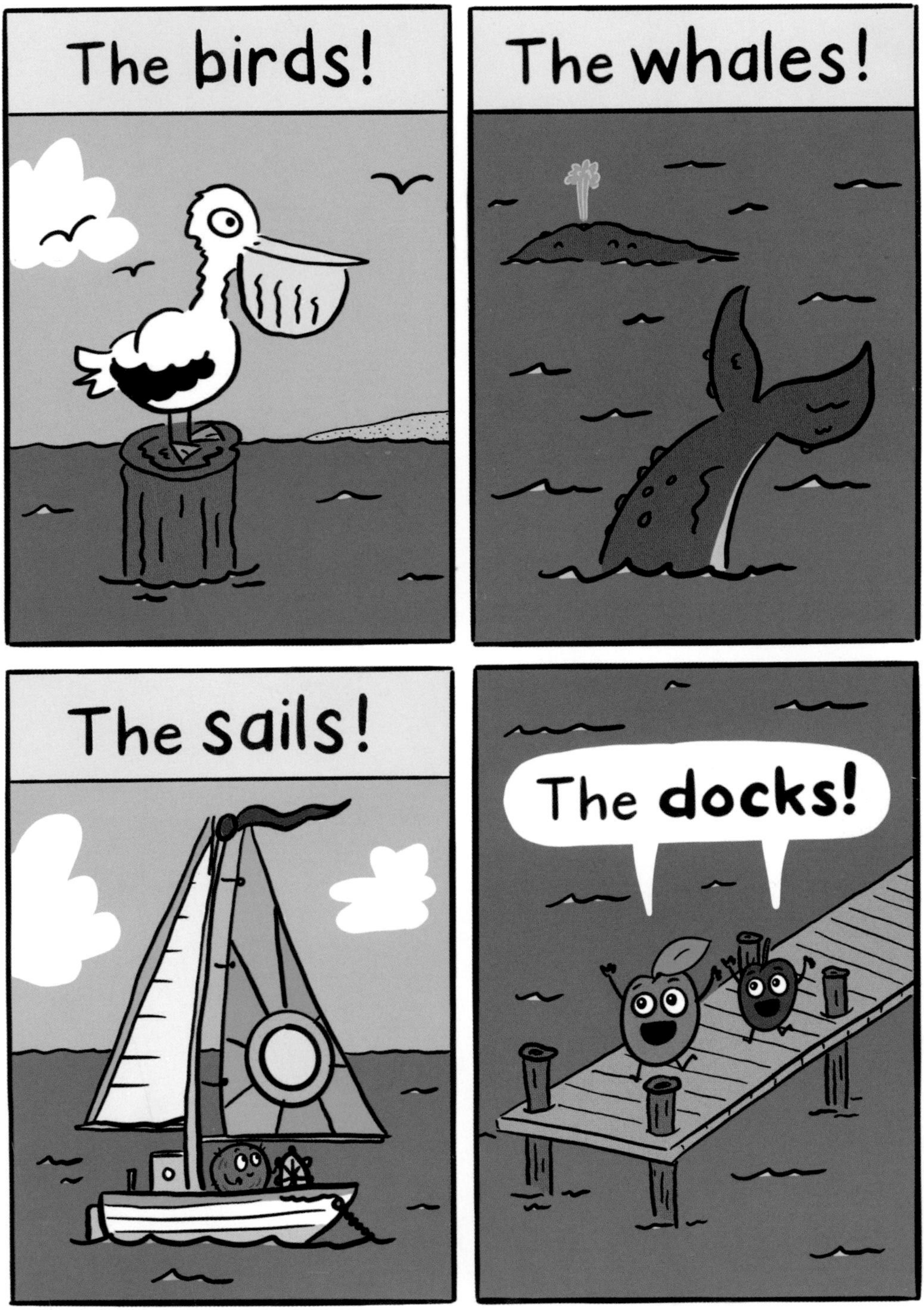
The birds!
The whales!
The sails!
The docks!

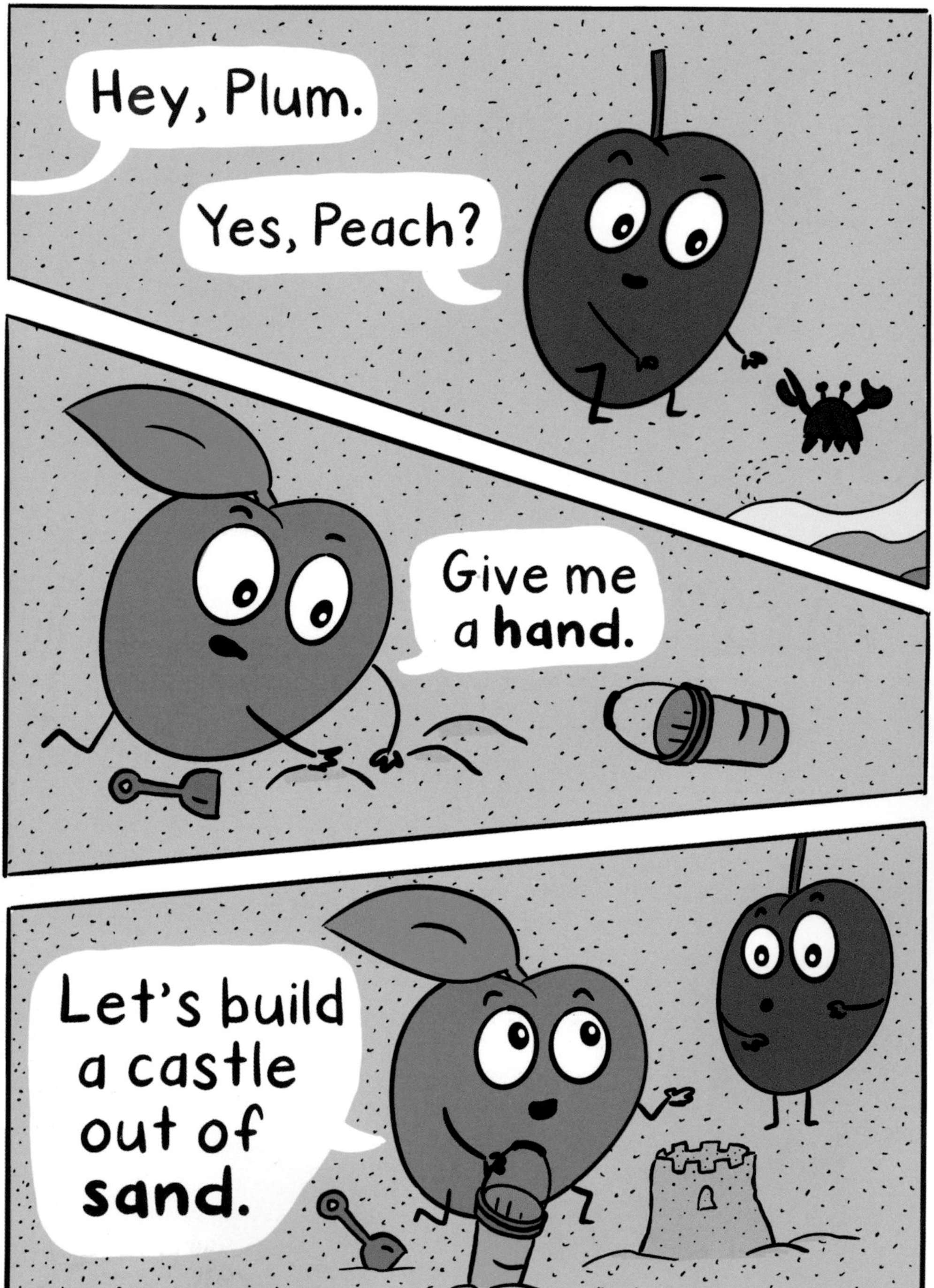
Hey, Plum.
Yes, Peach?
Give me a **hand**.
Let's build a castle out of **sand**.

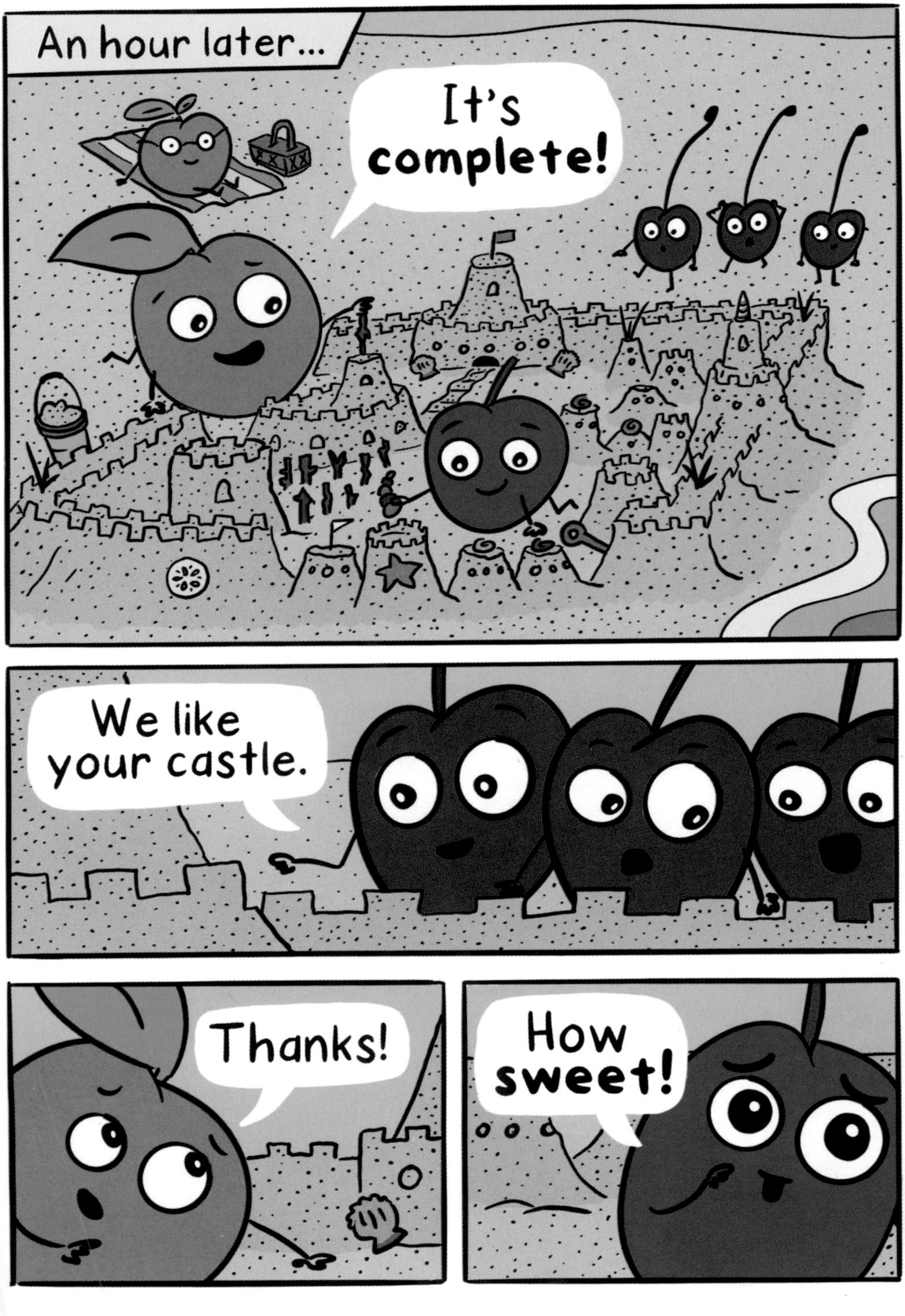
An hour later...
It's complete!
We like your castle.
Thanks!
How sweet!

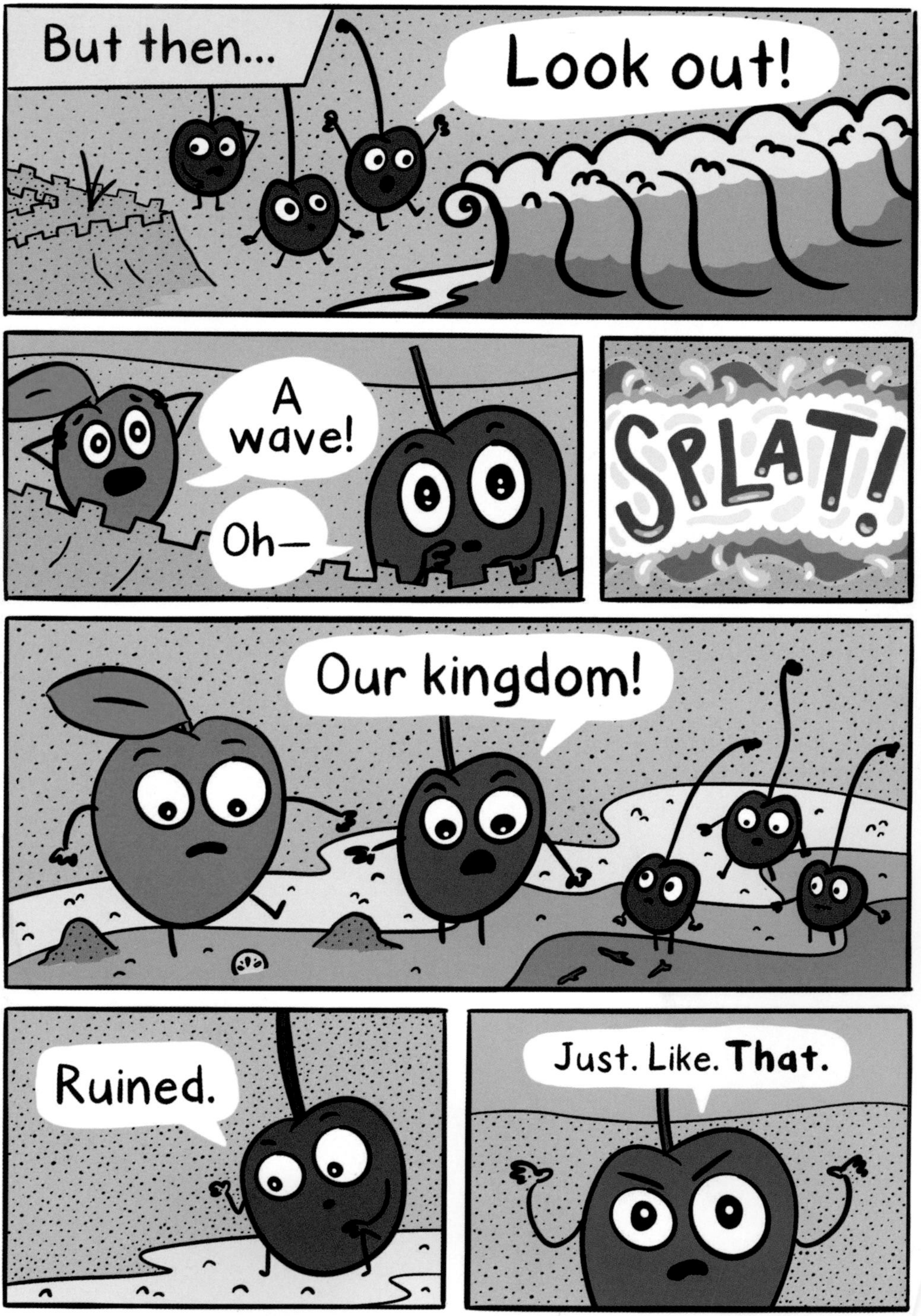
But then...
Look out!
A wave!
Oh—
SPLAT!
Our kingdom!
Ruined.
Just. Like. **That.**

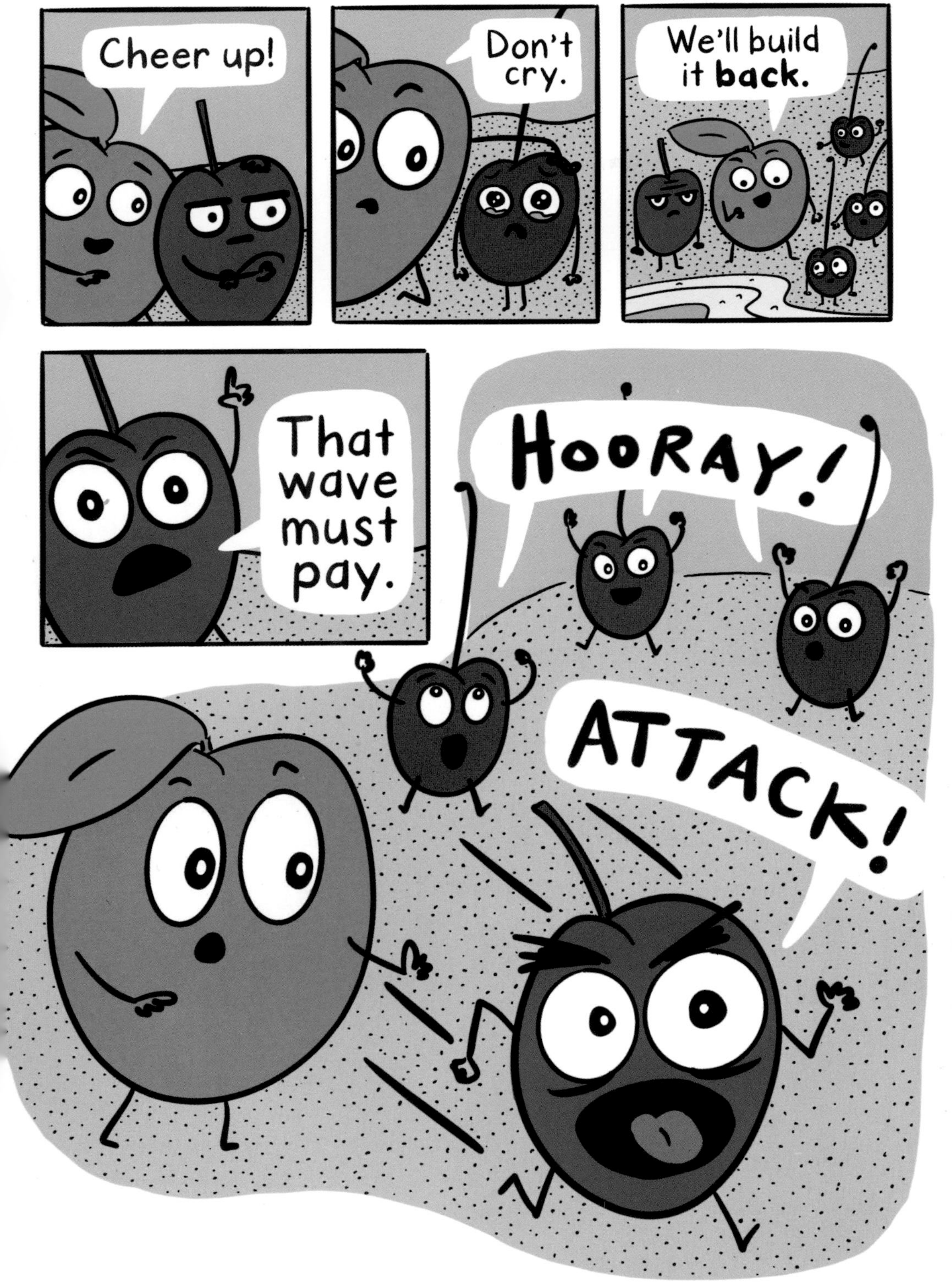
Cheer up!
Don't cry.
We'll build it **back.**
That wave must pay.
HOORAY!
ATTACK!

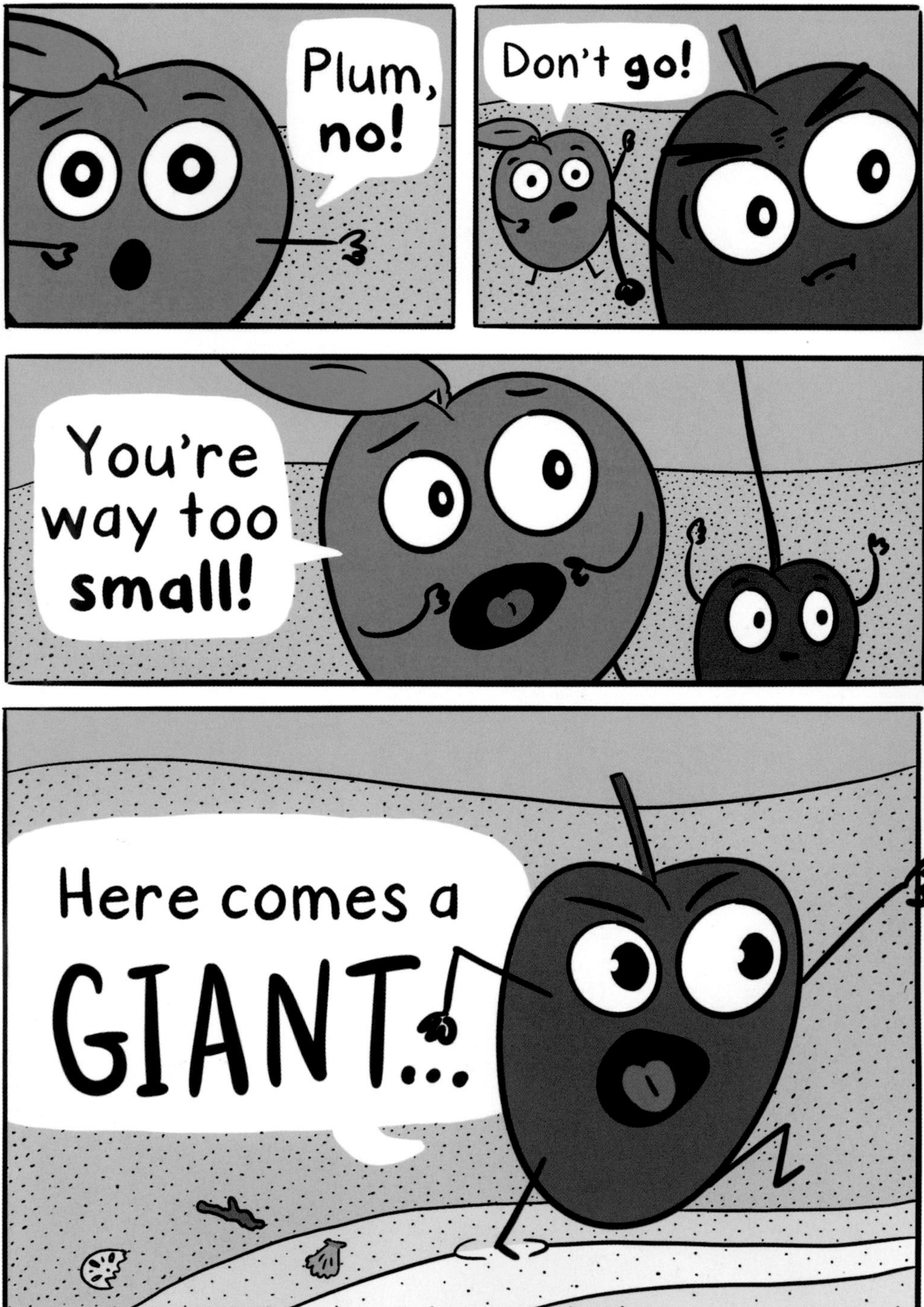
Plum, no!
Don't go!
You're way too small!
Here comes a GIANT...

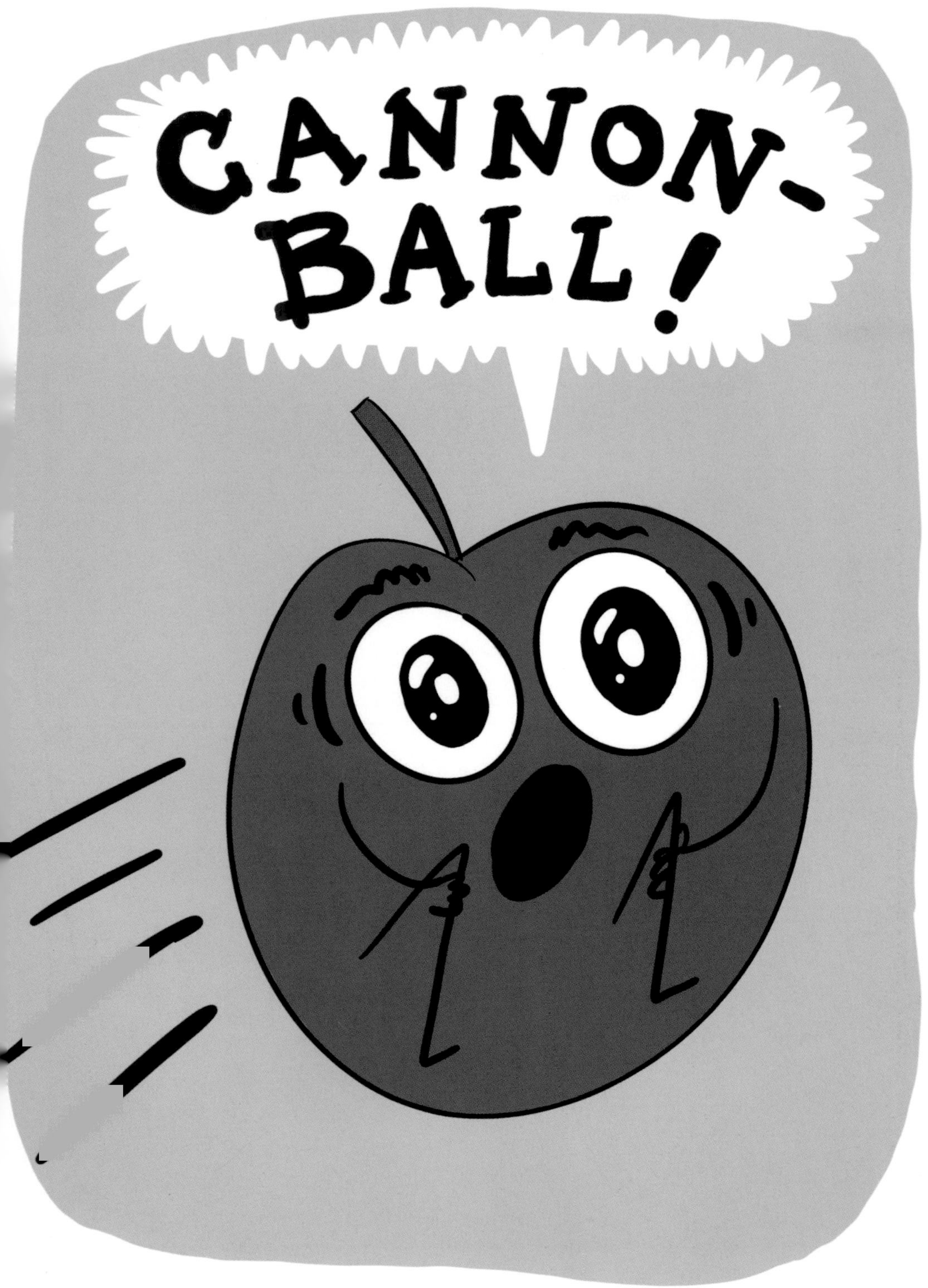
CANNON-
BALL!

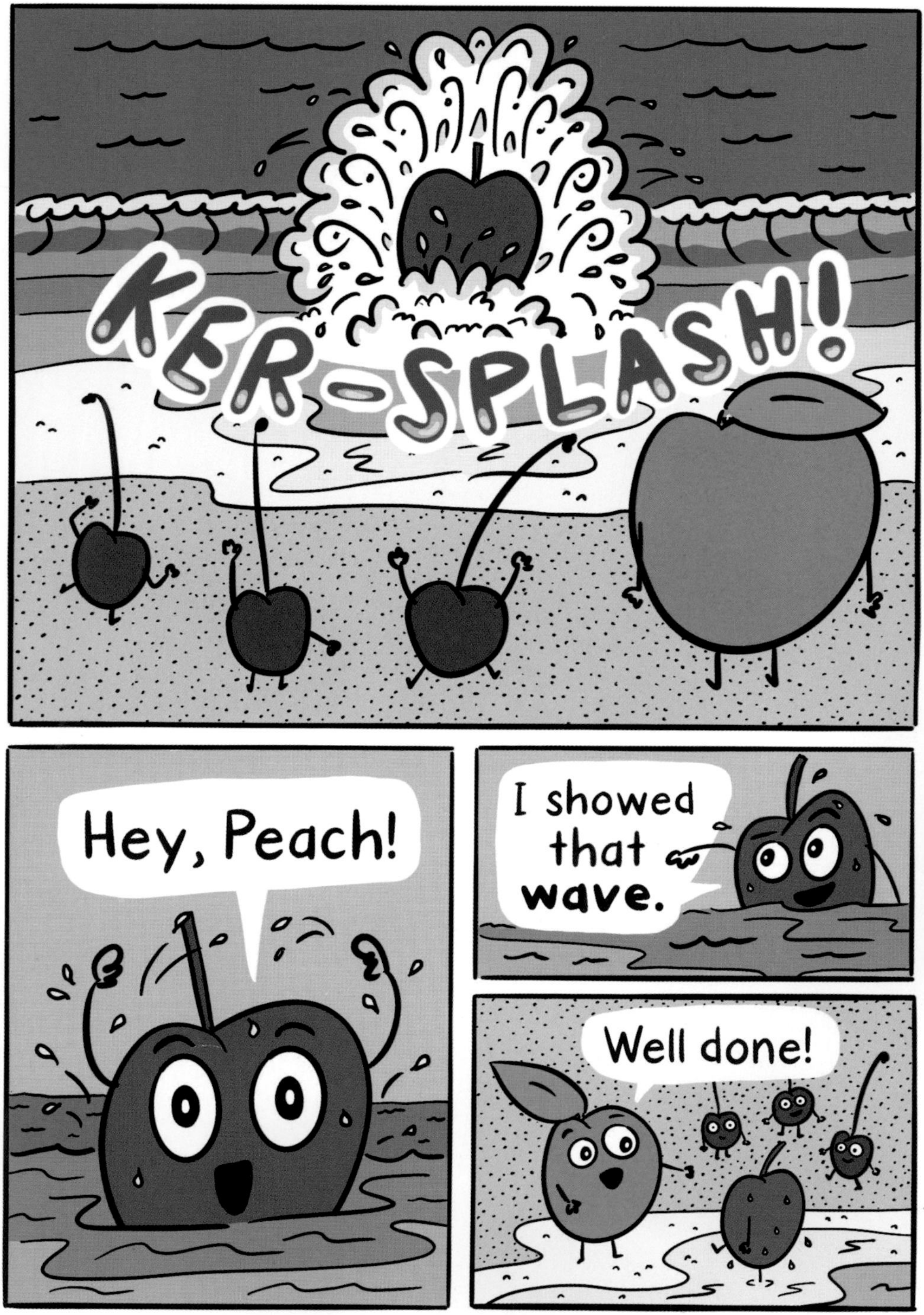
KER-SPLASH!
Hey, Peach!
I showed that **wave.**
Well done!

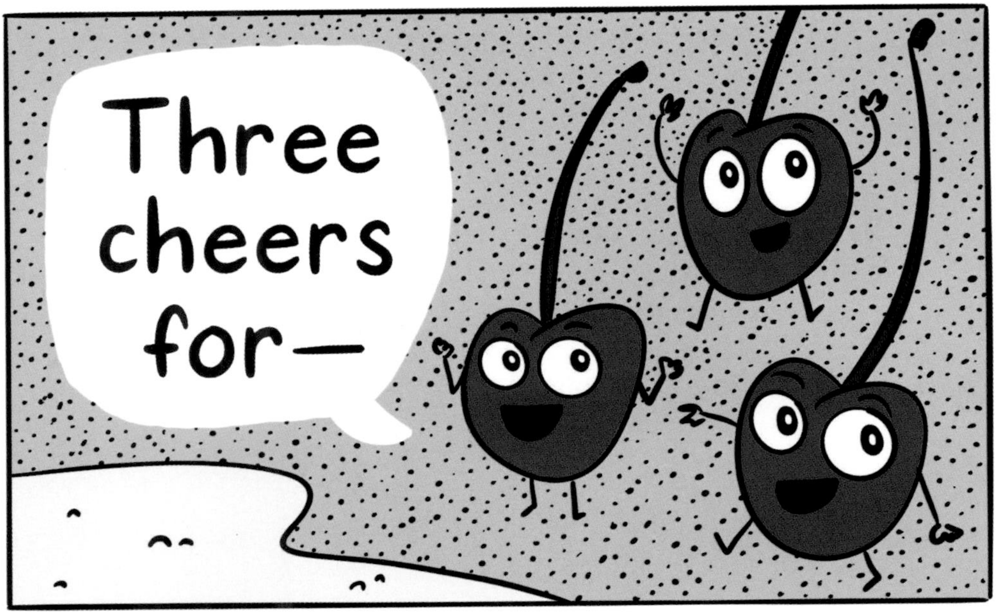
Three cheers for—

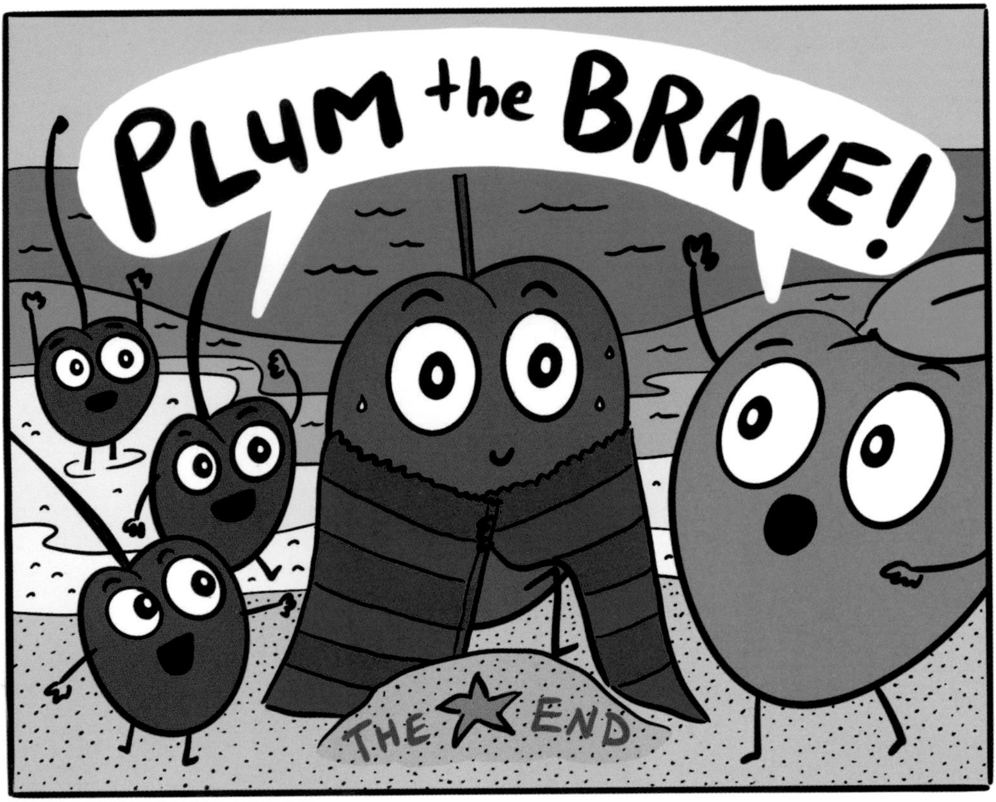
PLUM the BRAVE!
THE END

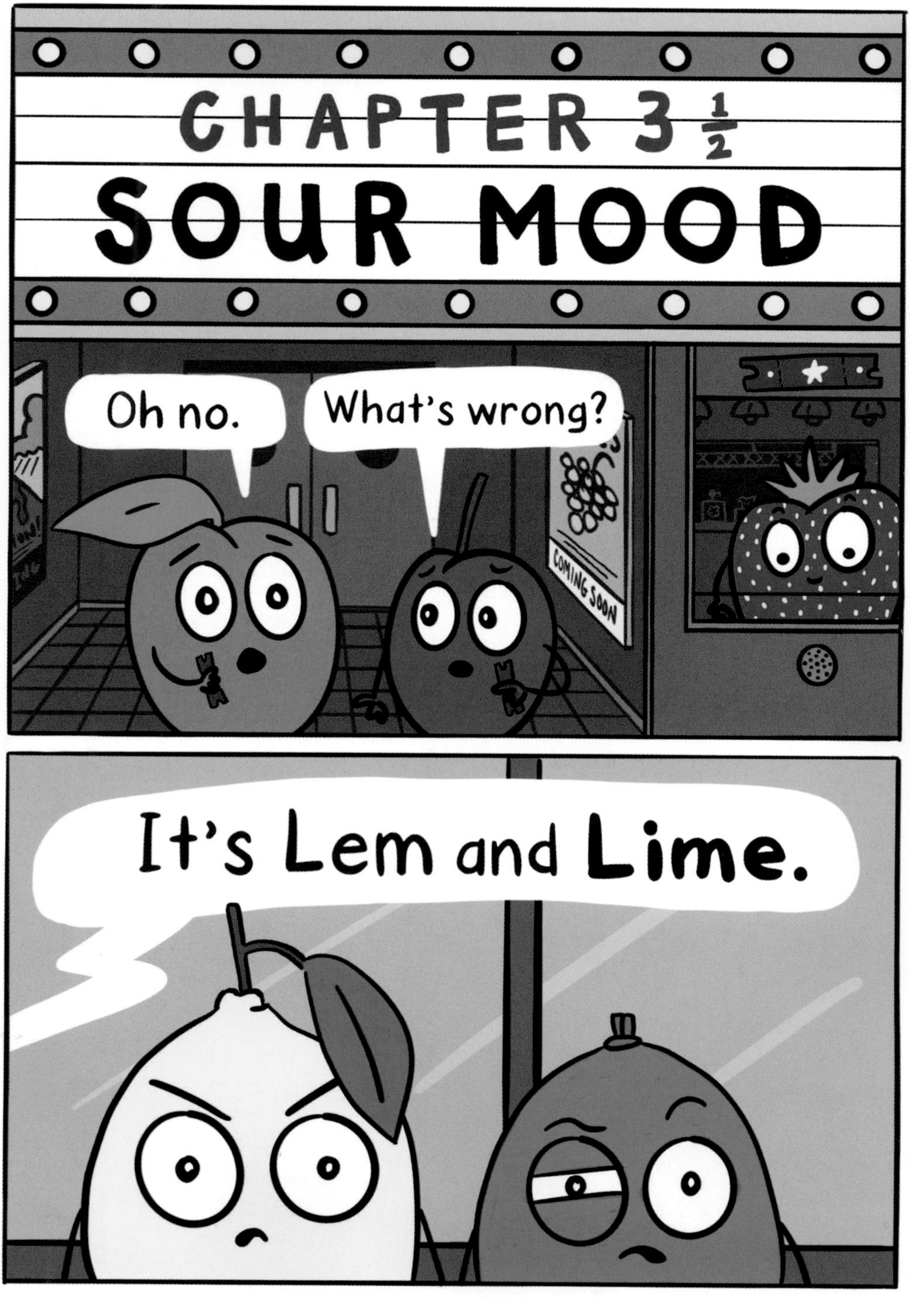
CHAPTER 3 1/2
SOUR MOOD
Oh no.
What's wrong?
COMING SOON
It's Lem and Lime.

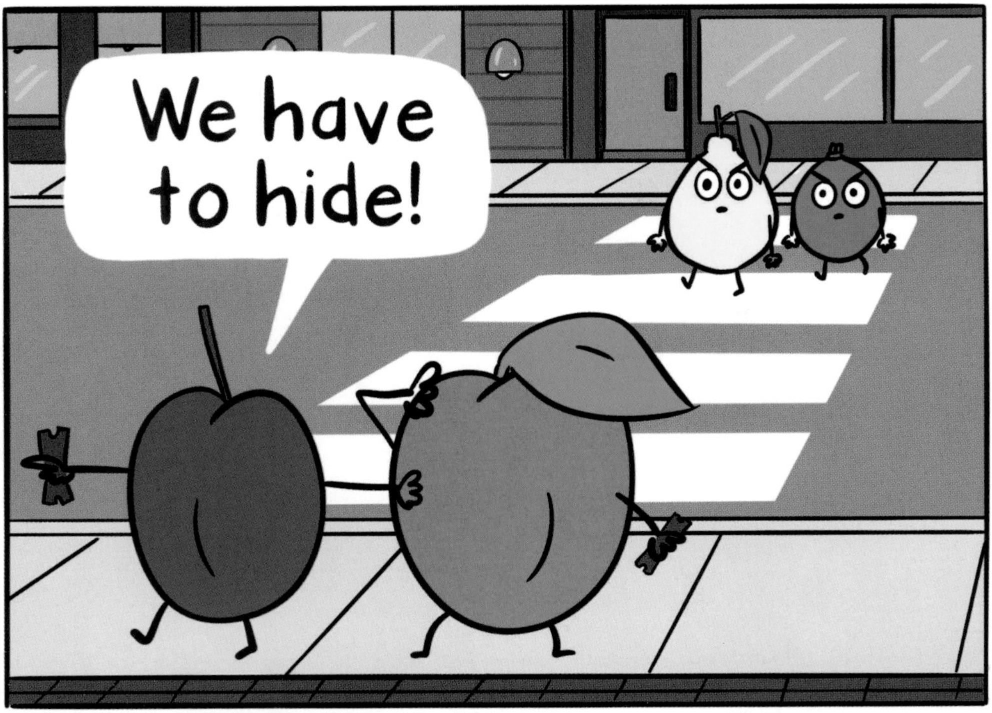
We have to hide!

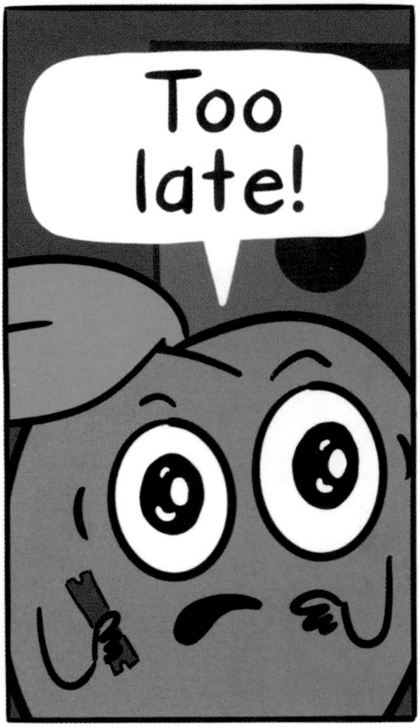
Too late!

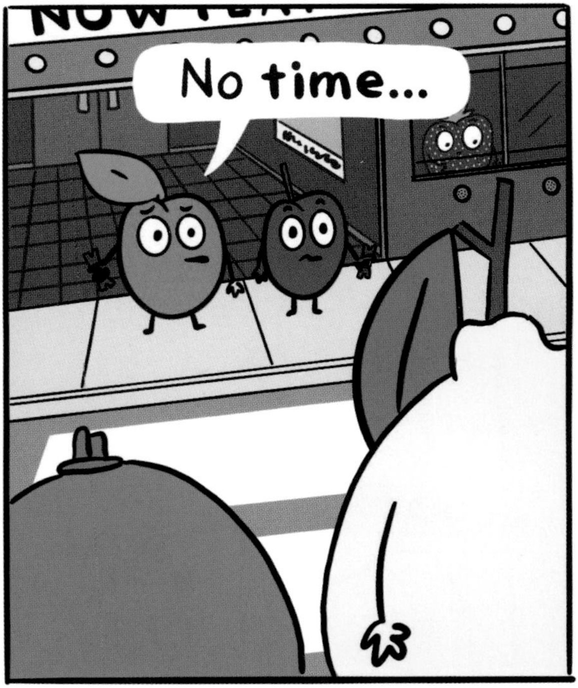
No time...

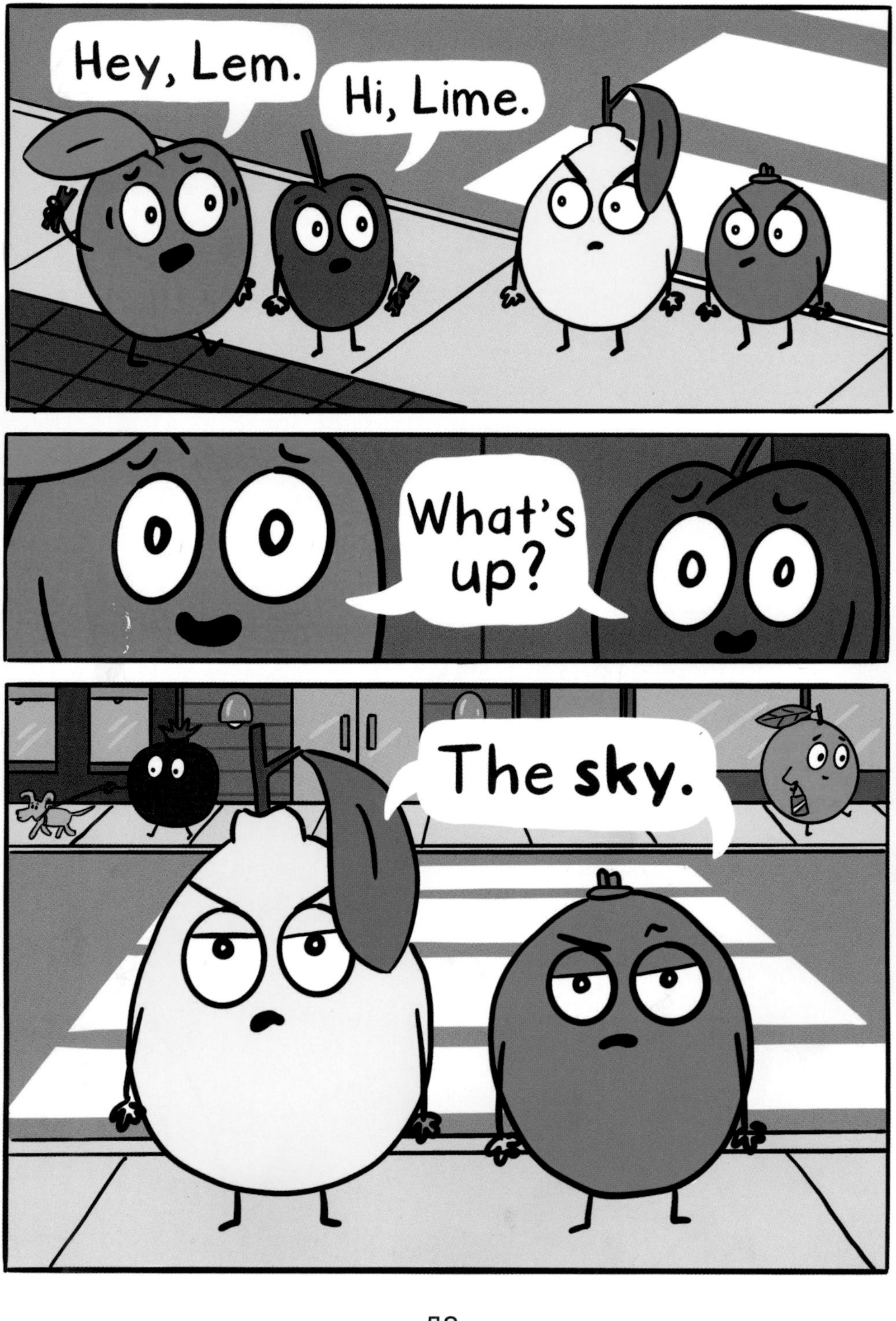
Hey, Lem.
Hi, Lime.
What's up?
The sky.

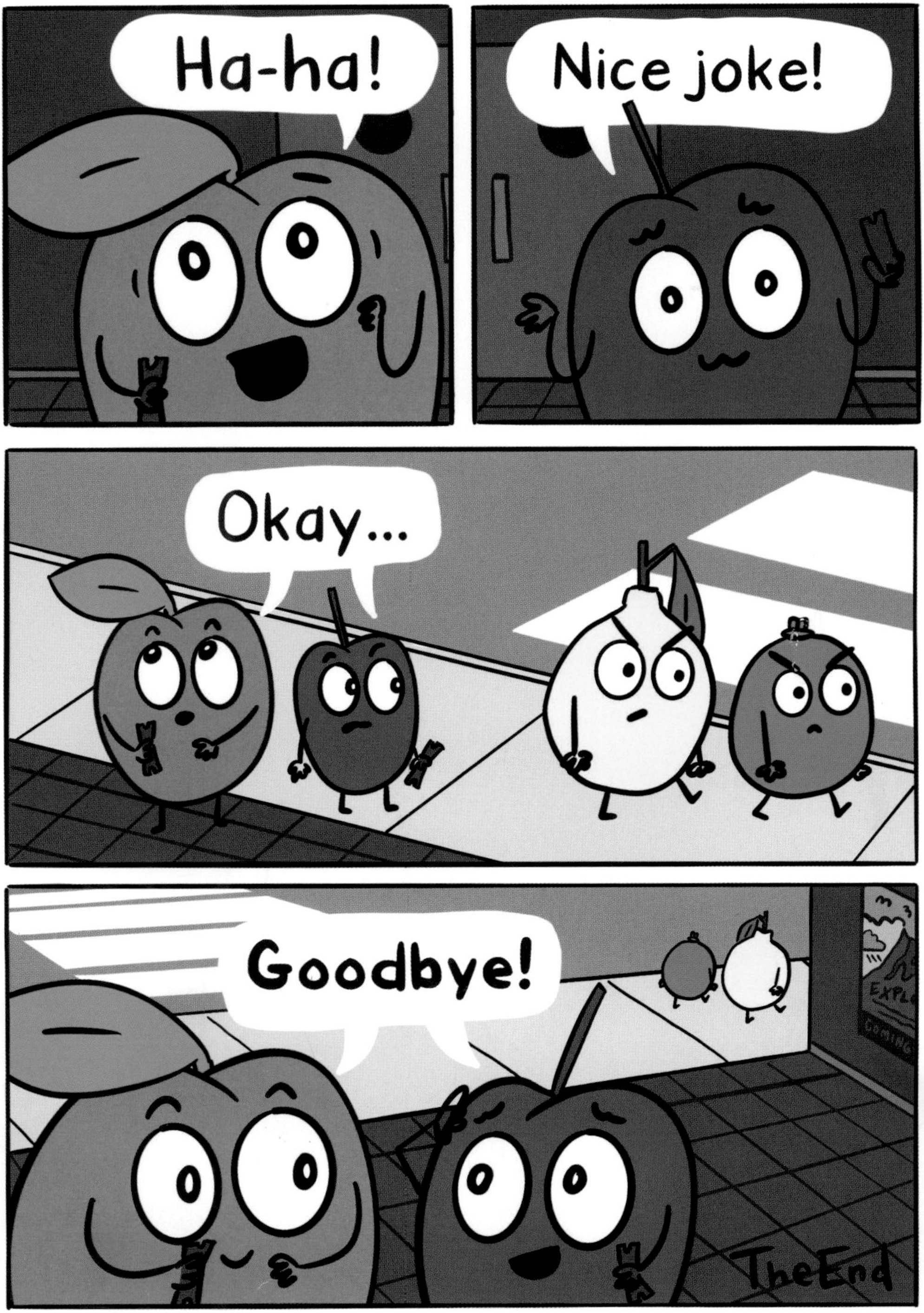
Ha-ha!
Nice joke!
Okay...
Goodbye!
The End

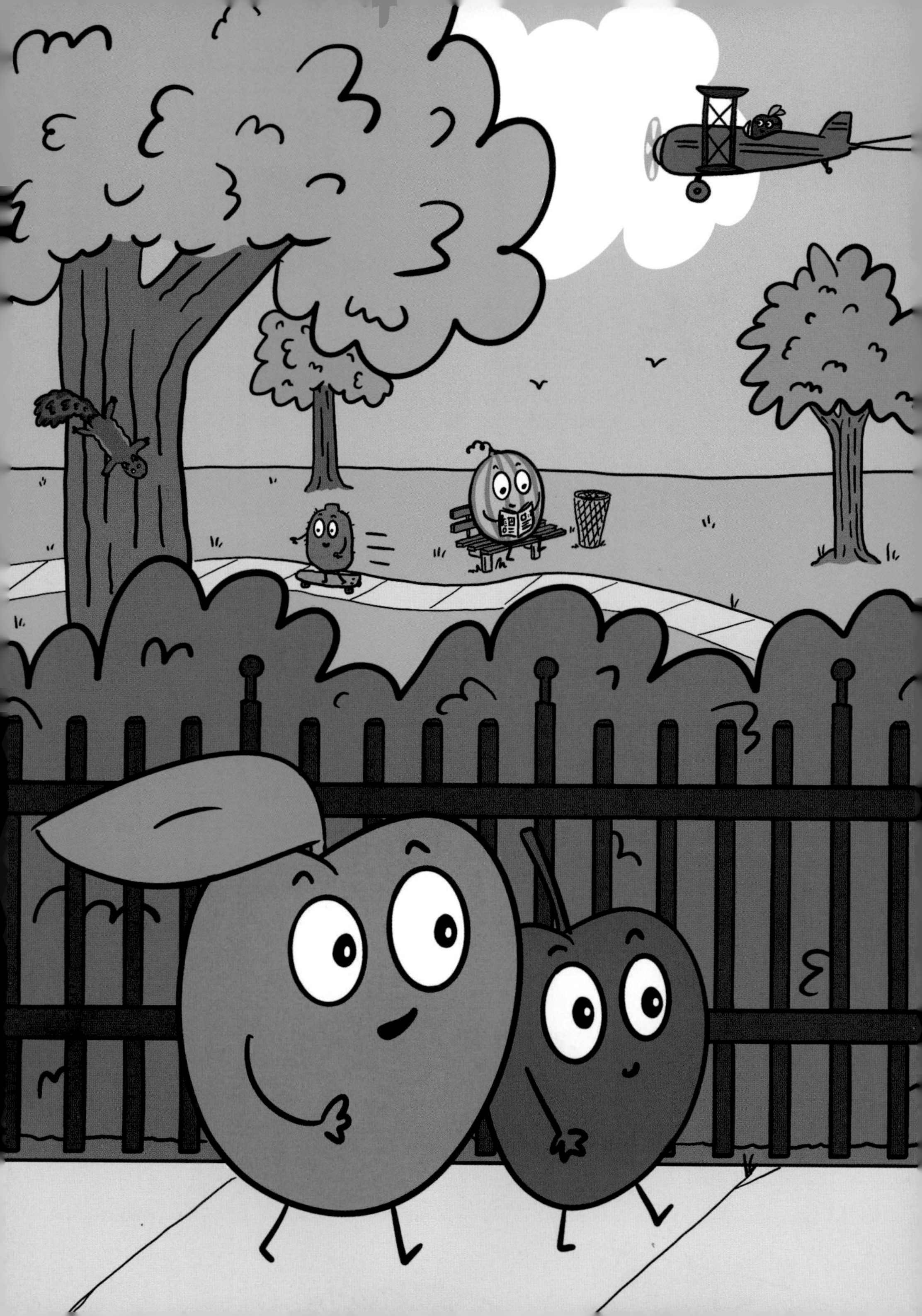

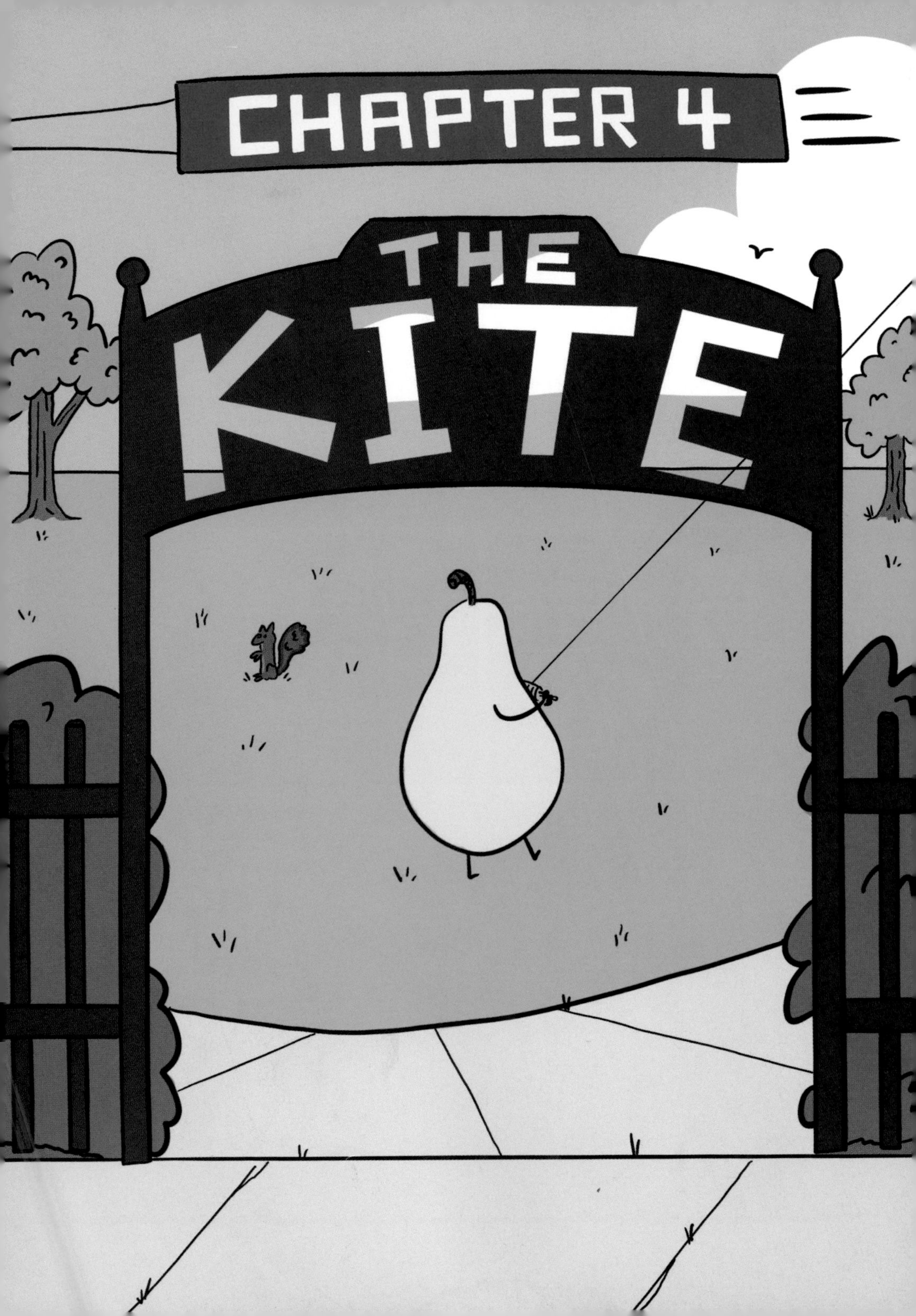
CHAPTER 4
THE KITE

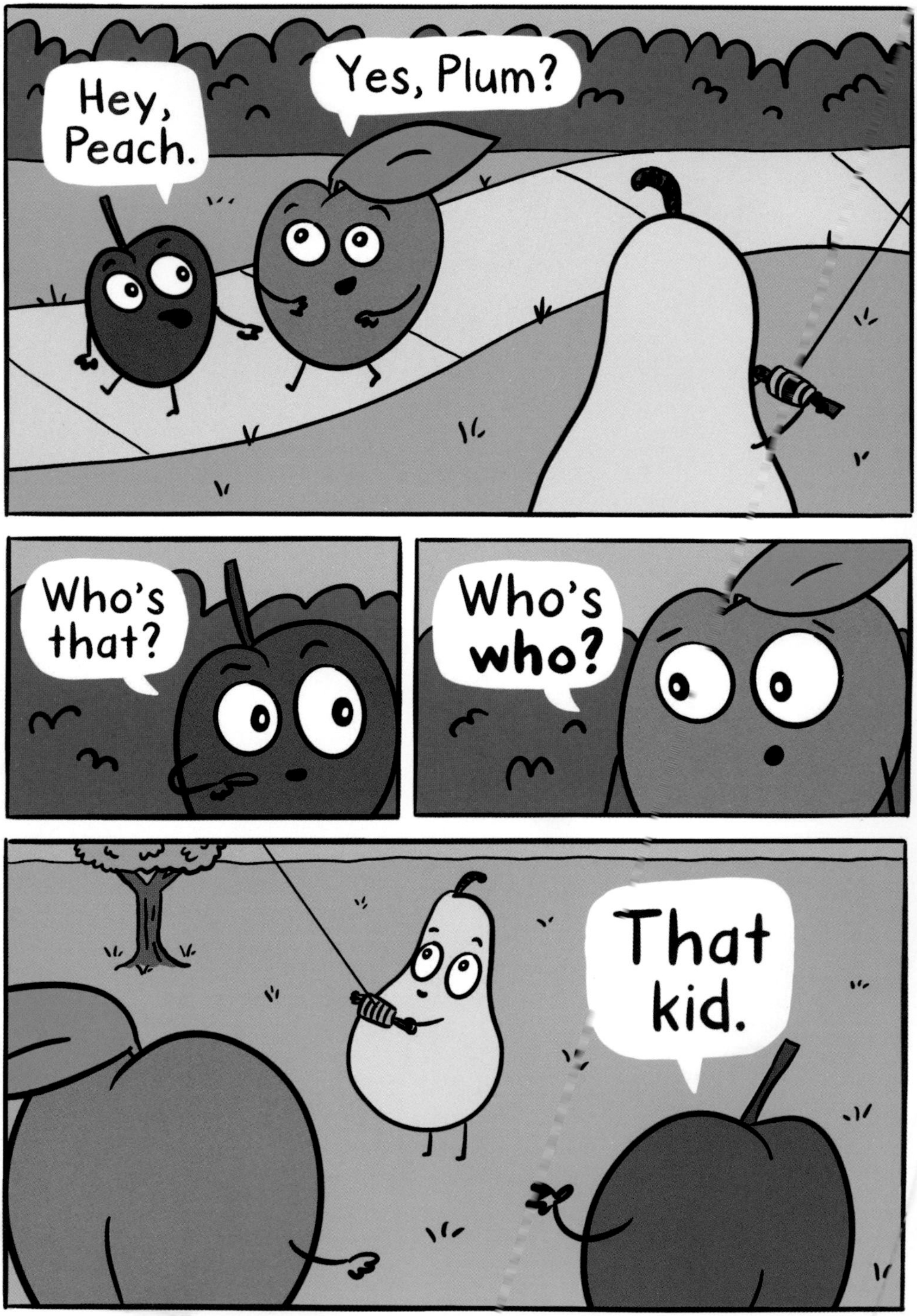
Hey, Peach.
Yes, Plum?
Who's that?
Who's **who?**
That kid.

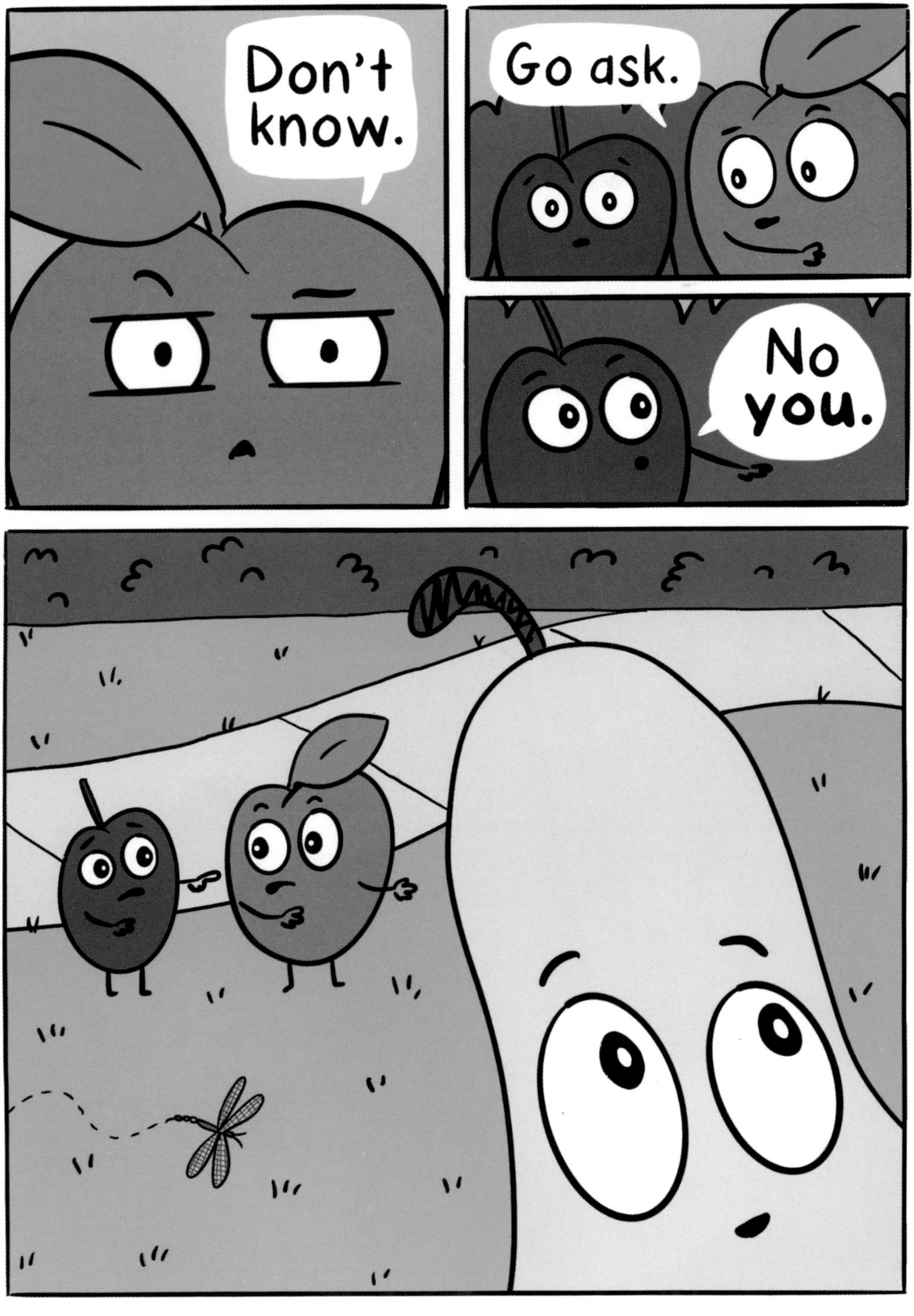
Don't know.
Go ask.
No you.

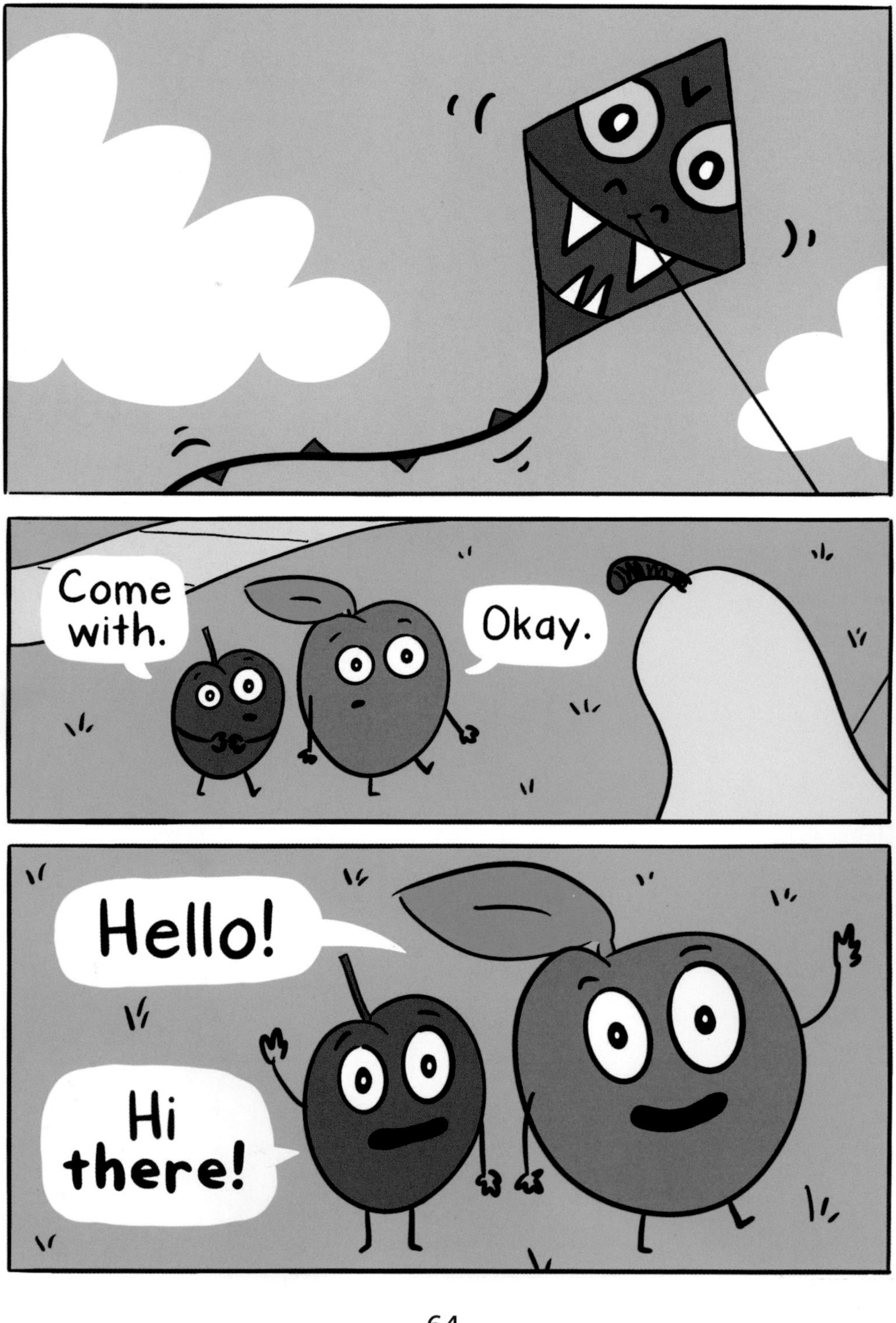
Come with.
Okay.
Hello!
Hi there!

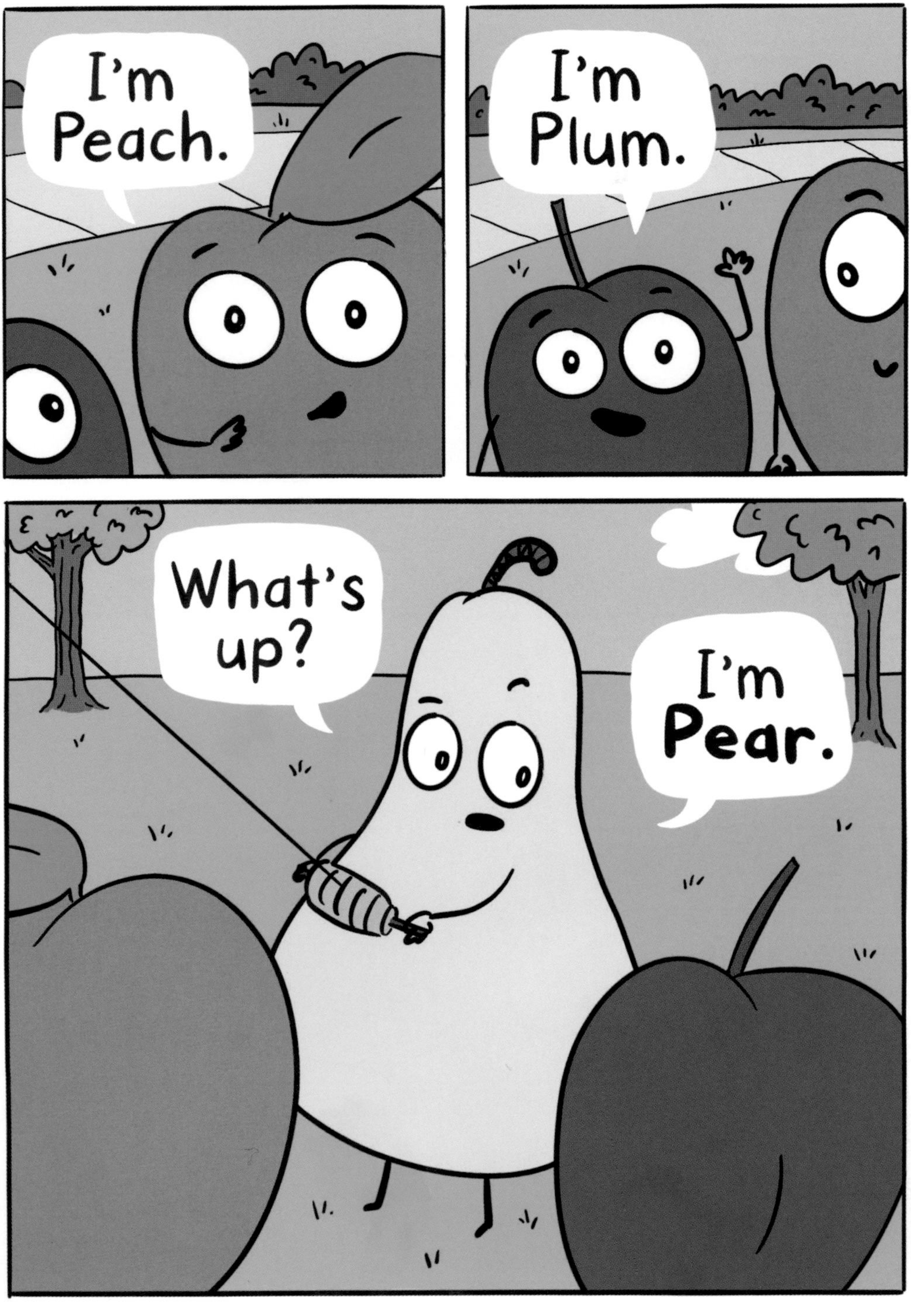
I'm Peach.
I'm Plum.
What's up?
I'm **Pear.**

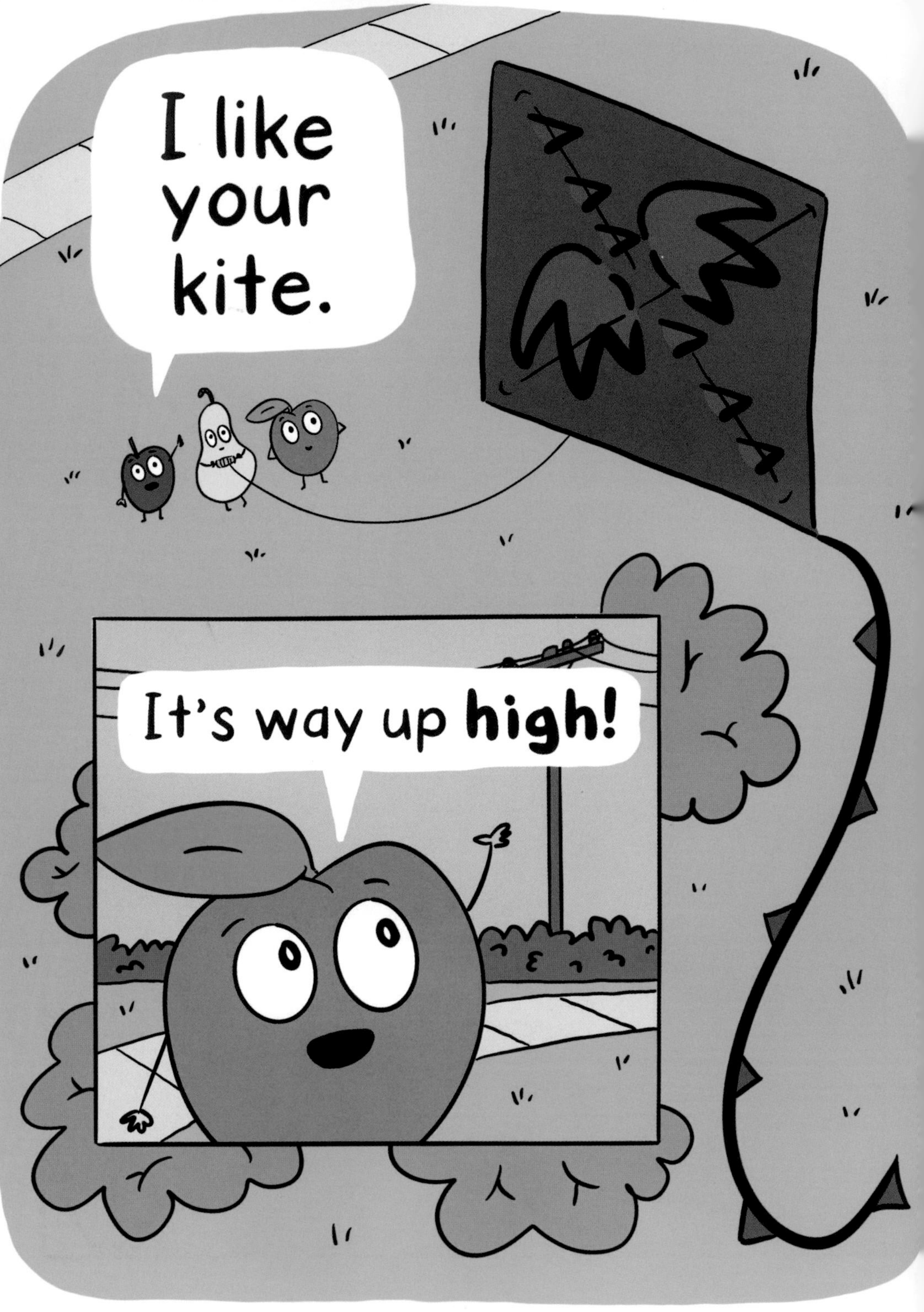
I like your kite.
It's way up **high**!

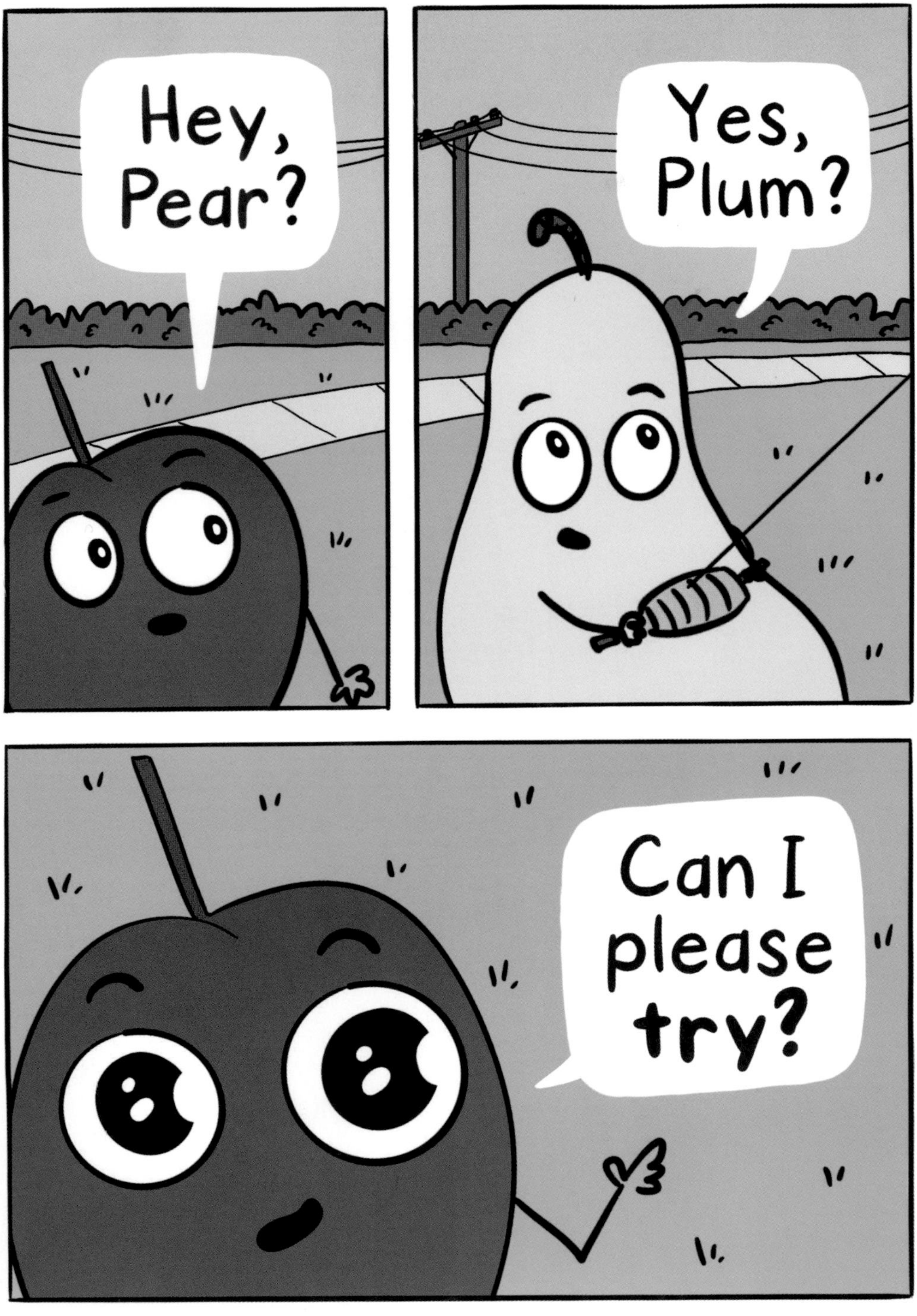
Hey, Pear?
Yes, Plum?
Can I please **try**?

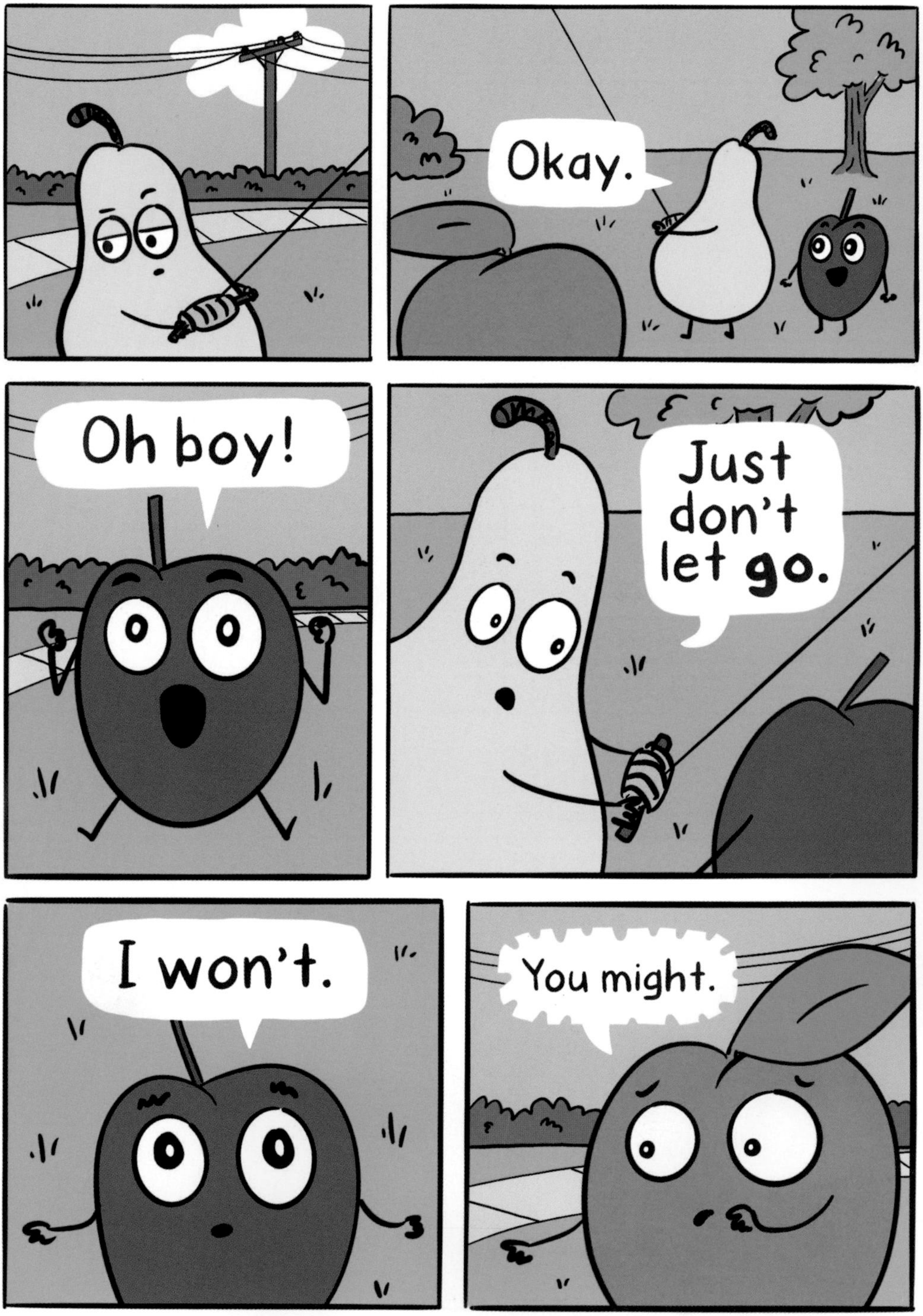
Okay.
Oh boy!
Just don't let go.
I won't.
You might.

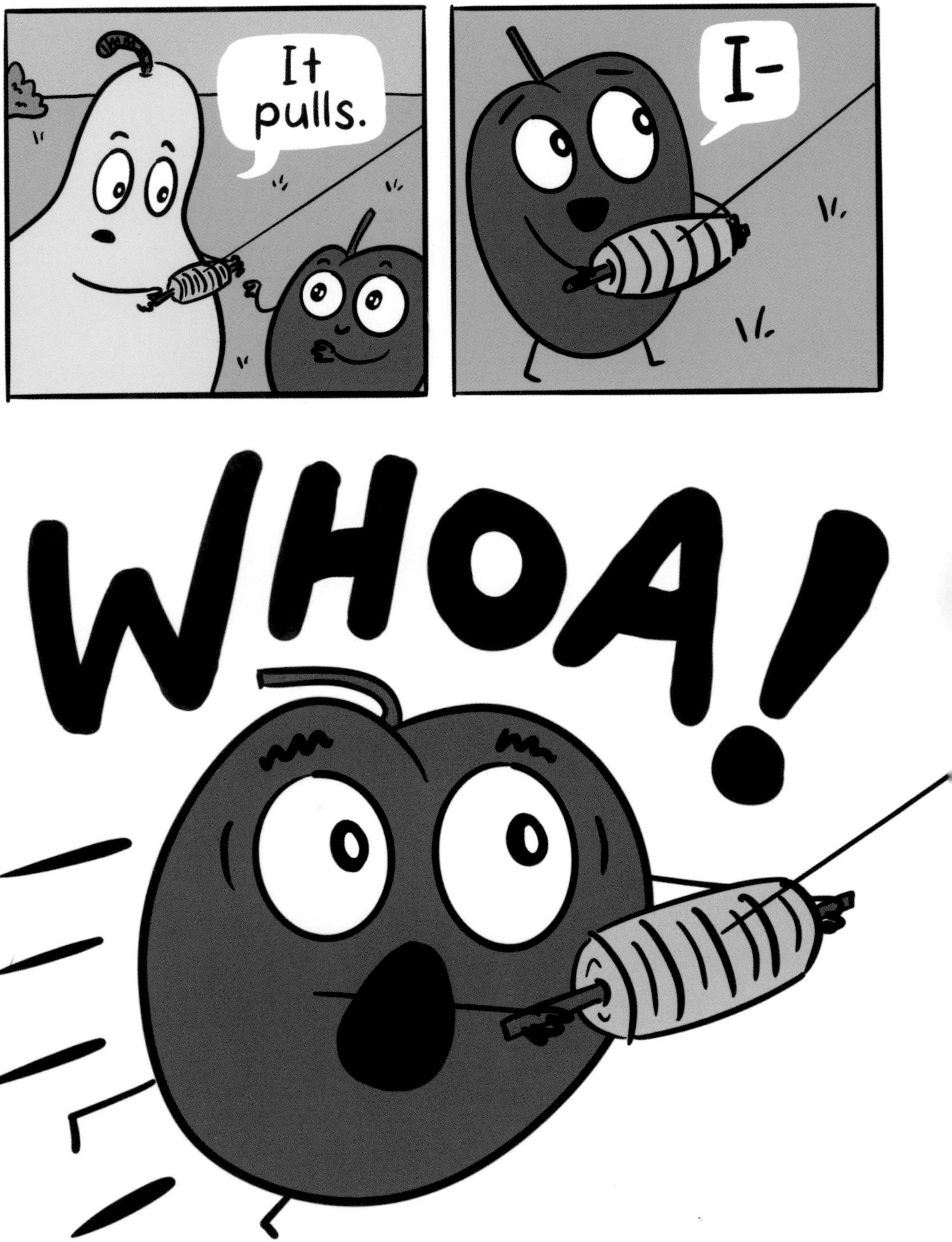
It pulls.
I-
WHOA!

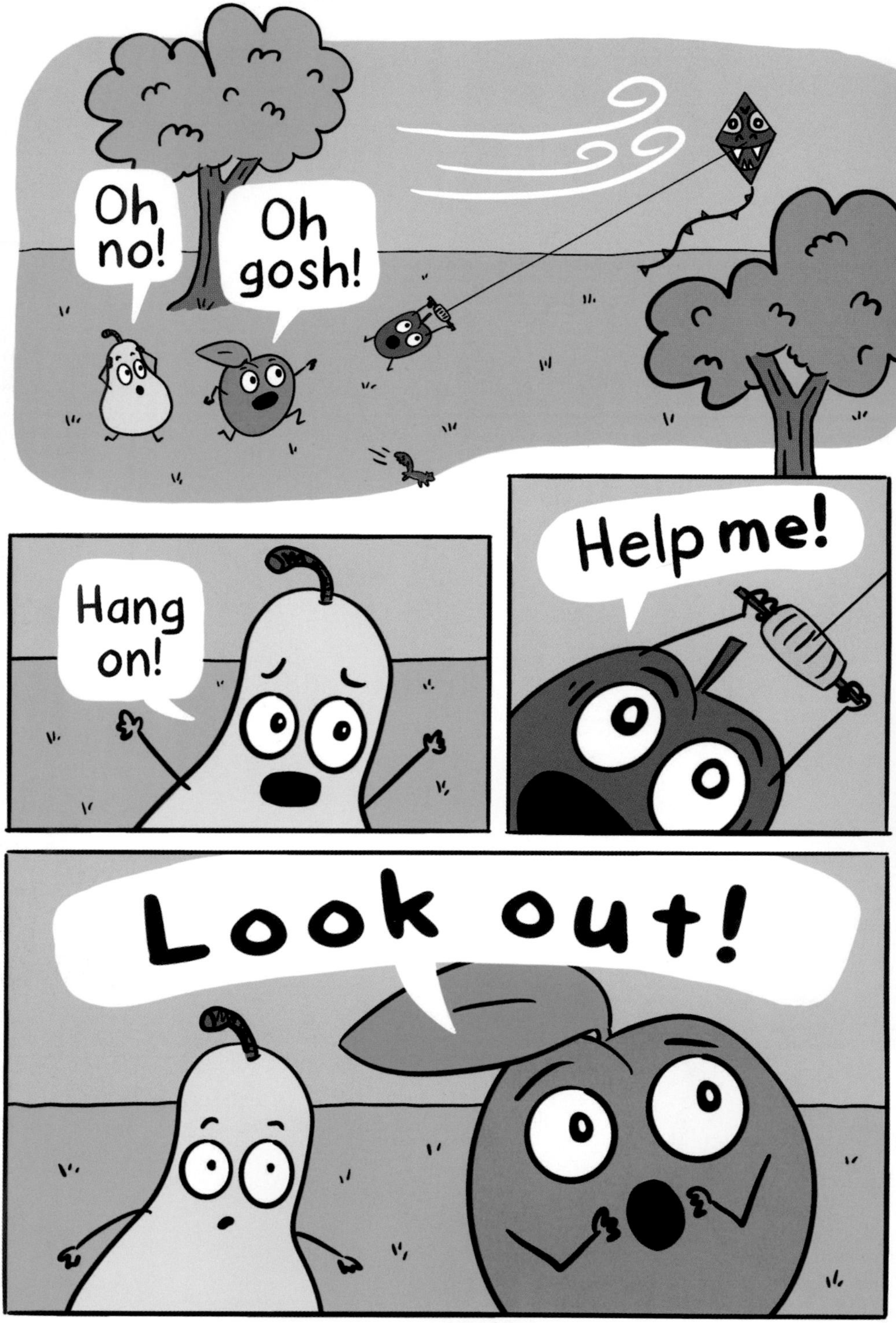
Oh no!
Oh gosh!
Hang on!
Help me!
Look out!

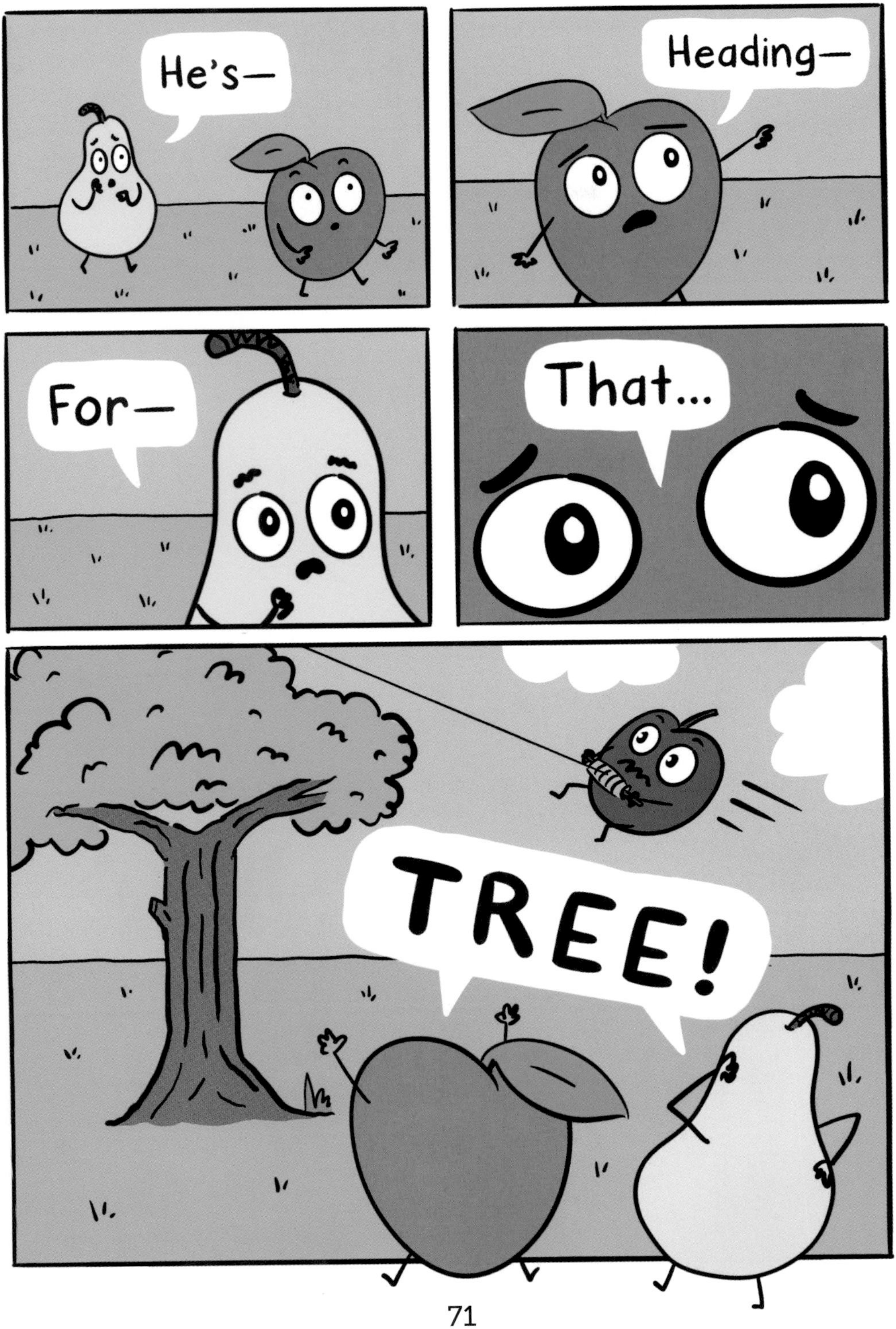
He's—
Heading—
For—
That...
TREE!

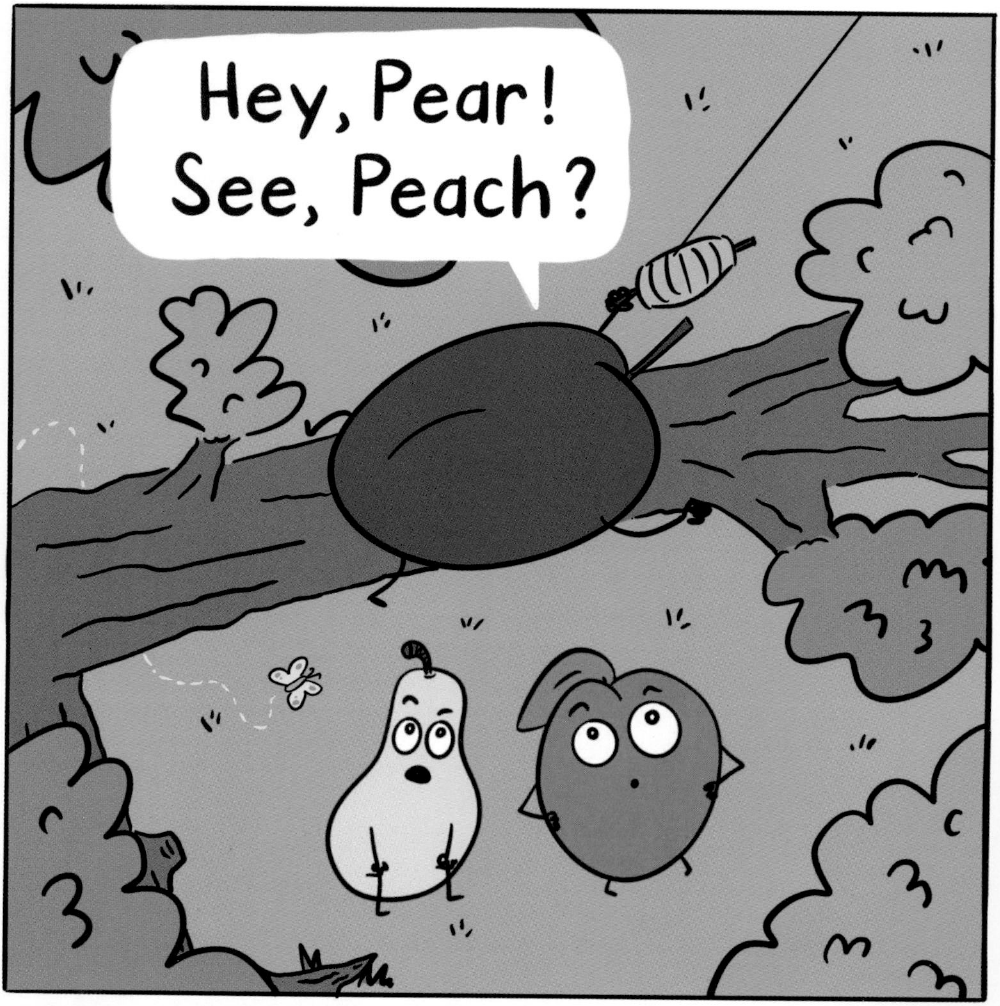
Hey, Pear! See, Peach?

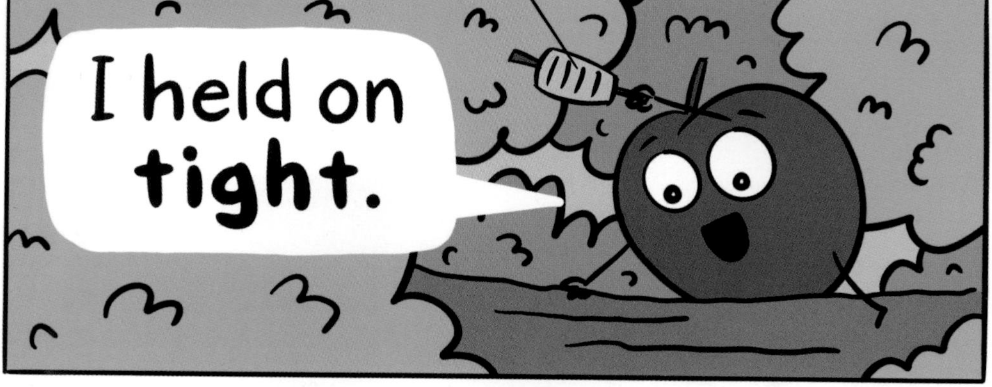
I held on **tight**.

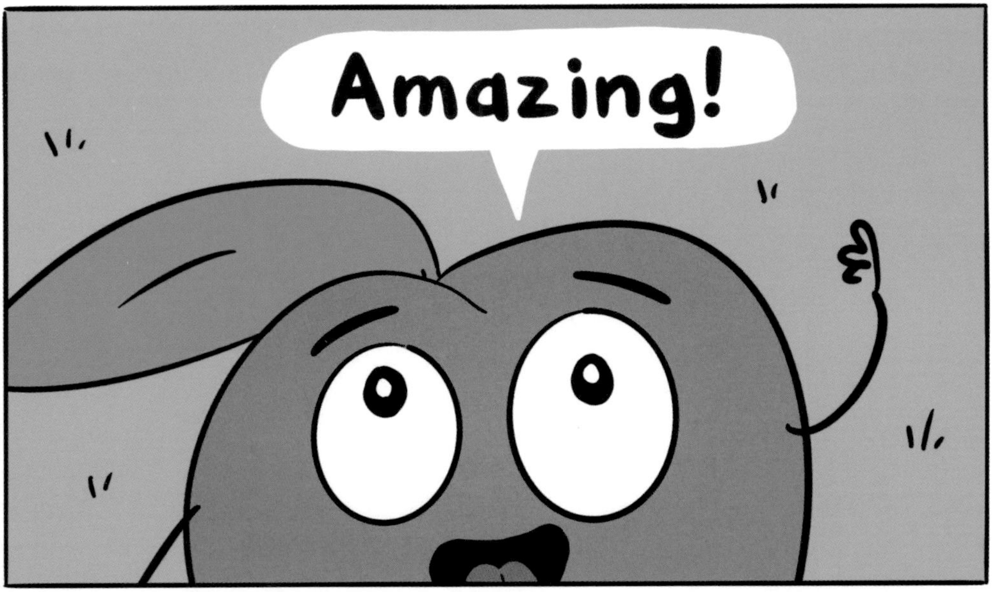
Amazing!

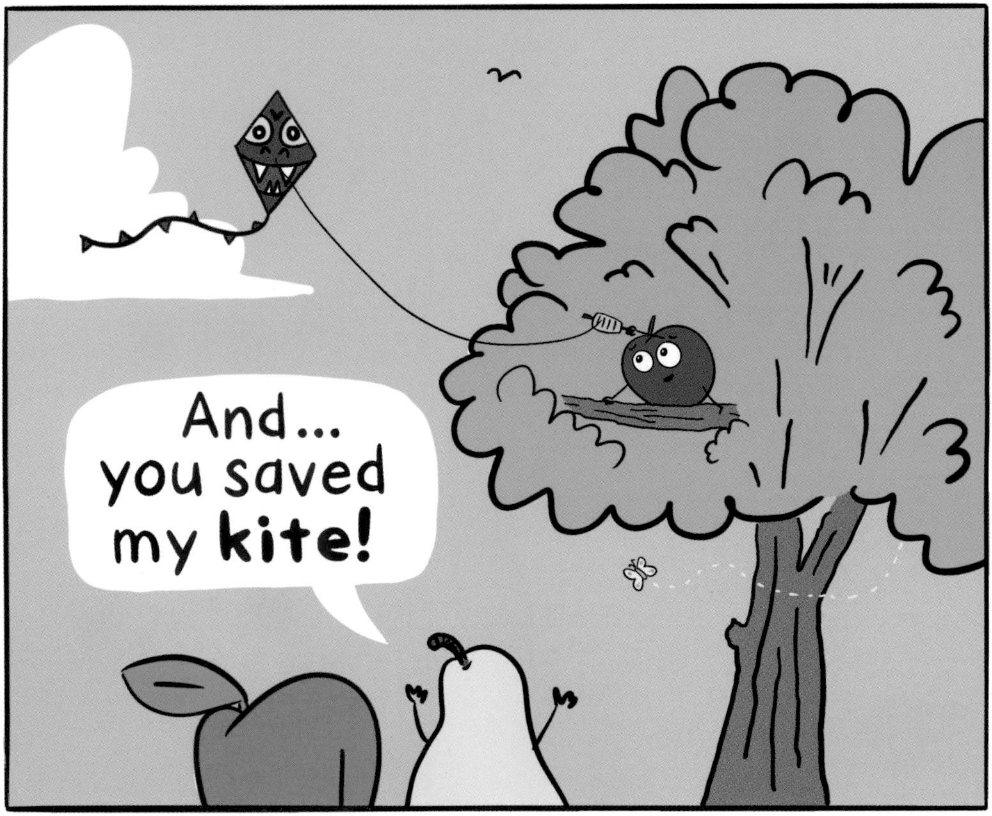
And...
you saved
my **kite**!

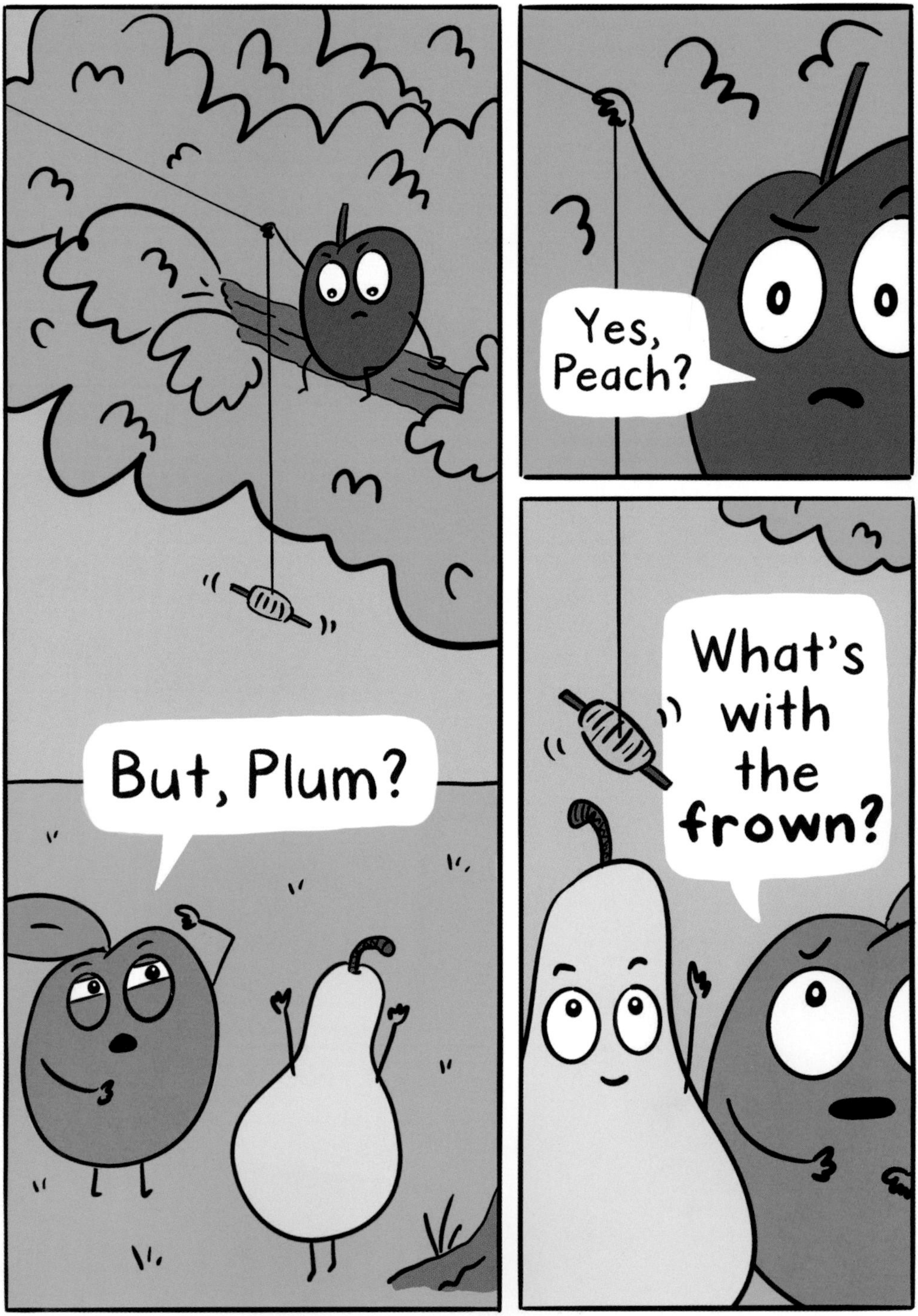
But, Plum?
Yes, Peach?
What's with the **frown?**

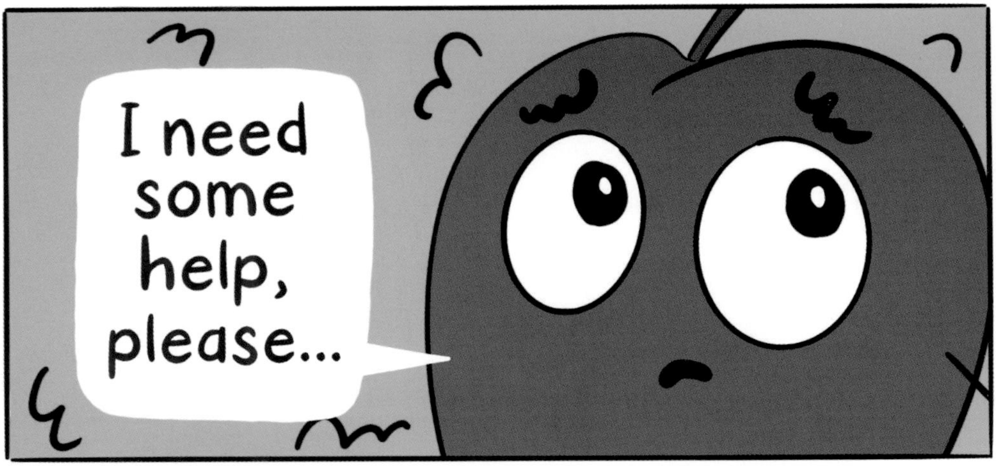
I need some help, please...

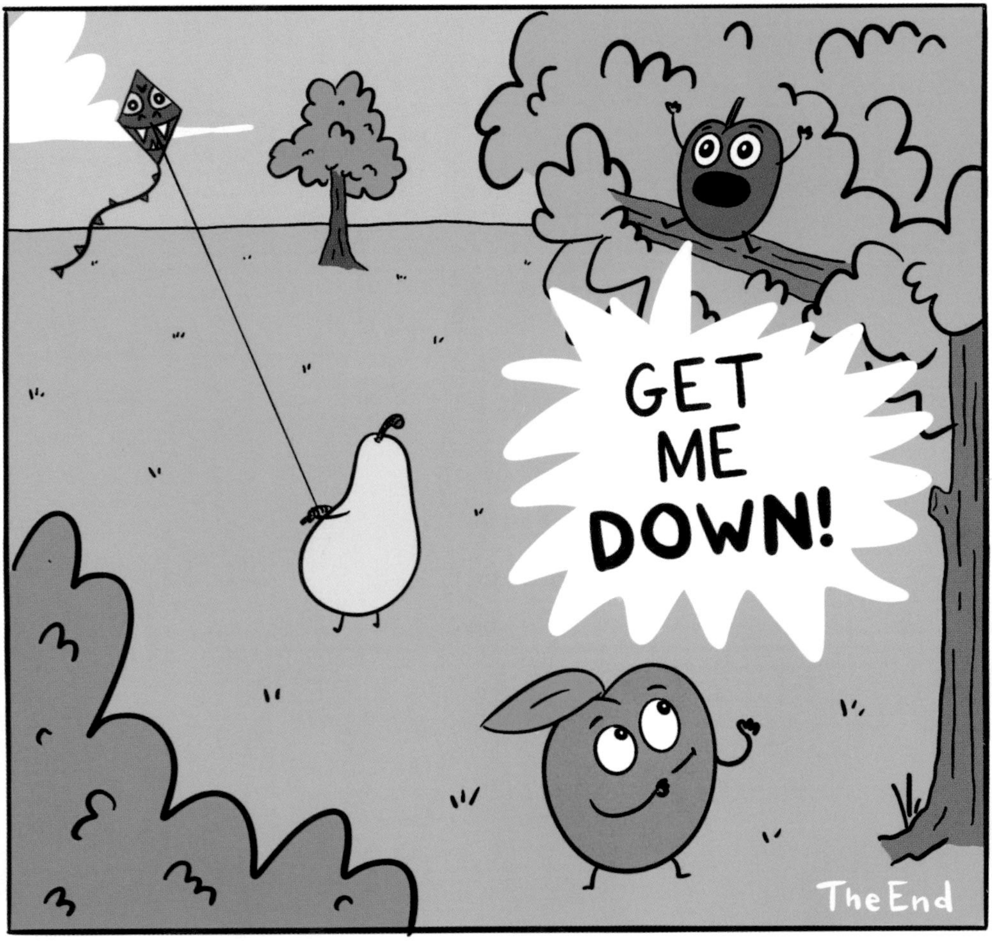
GET ME DOWN!
The End

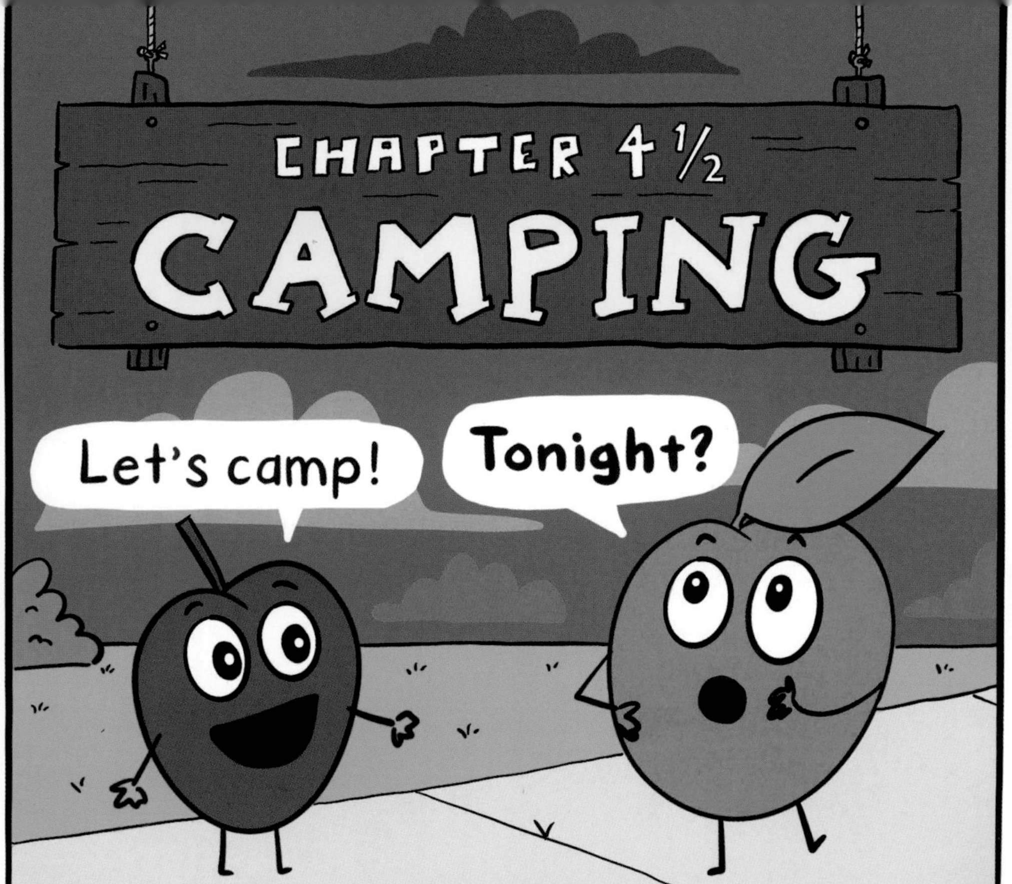
CHAPTER 4 1/2
CAMPING
Let's camp!
Tonight?

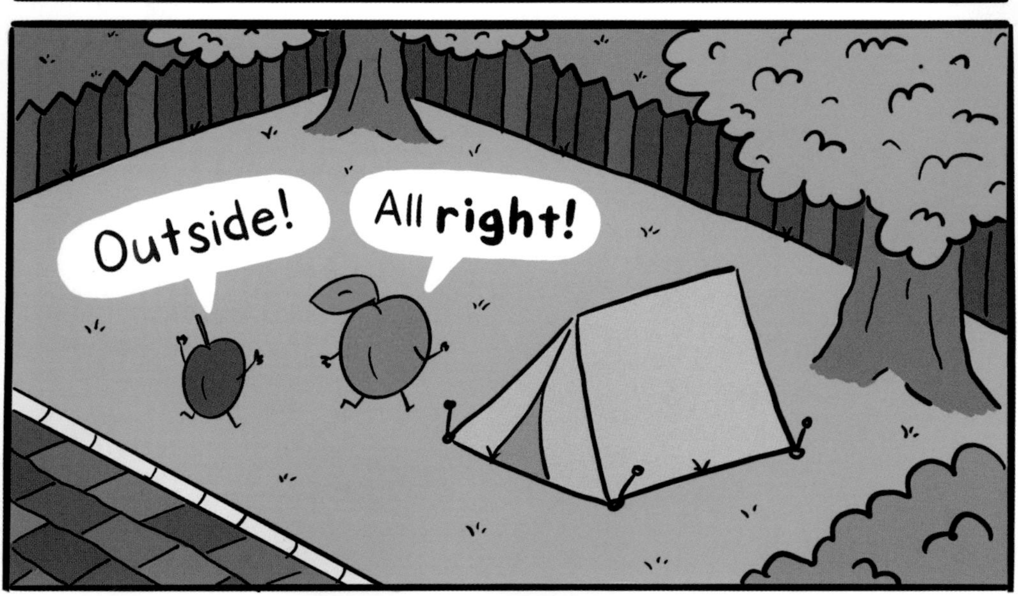
Outside!
All right!

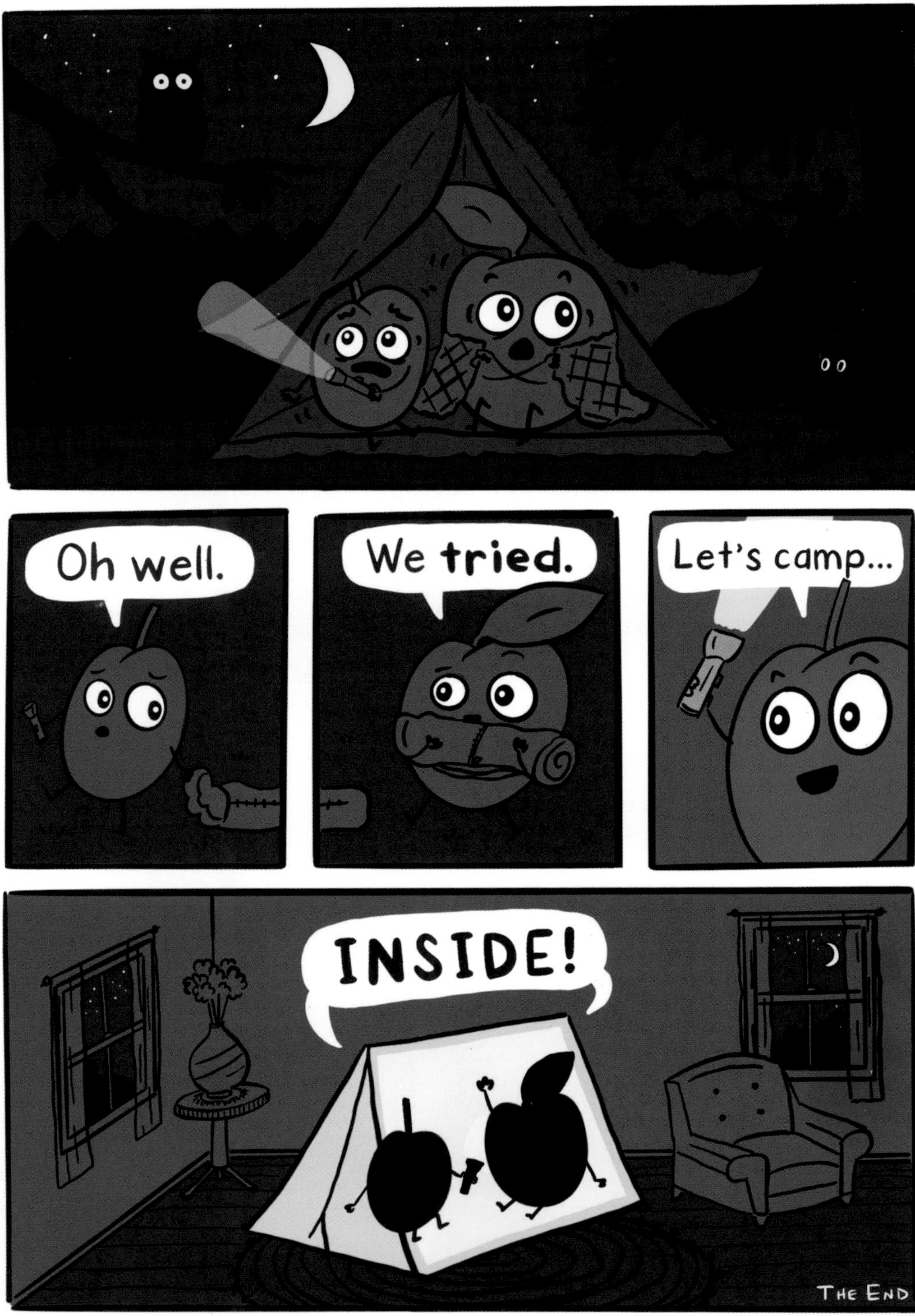
Oh well.
We tried.
Let's camp...
INSIDE!
THE END

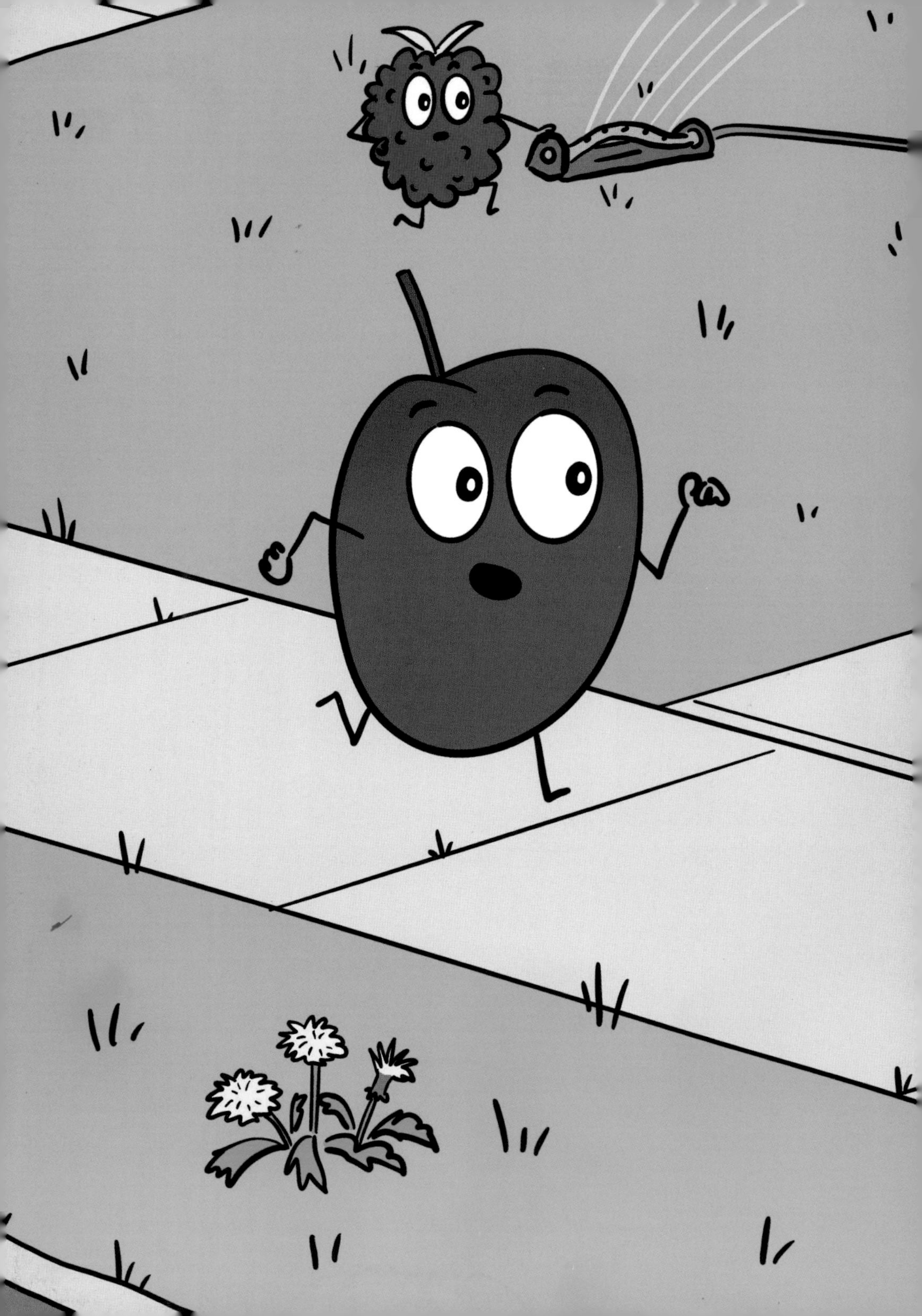

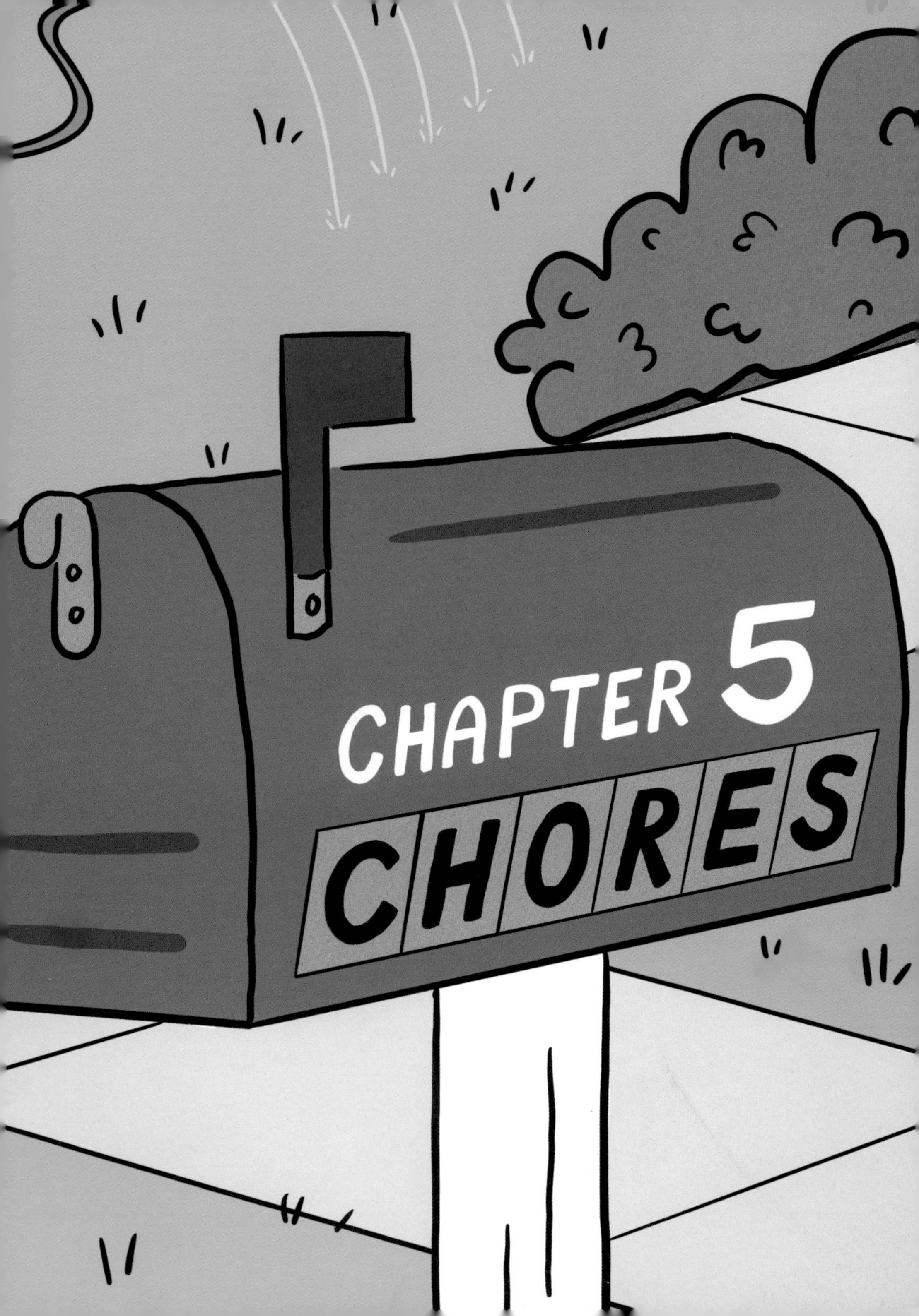
CHAPTER 5
CHORES

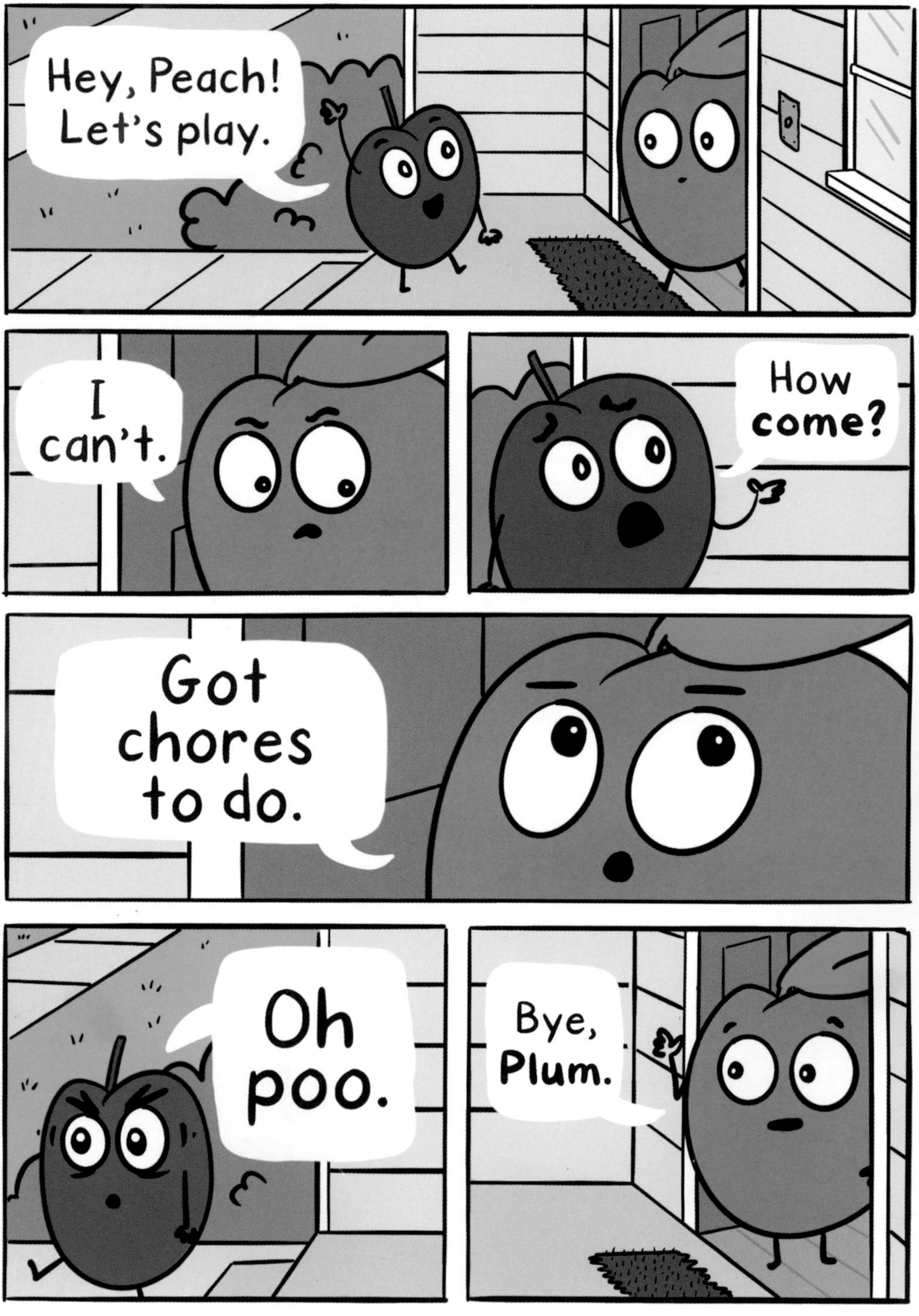
Hey, Peach! Let's play.
I can't.
How come?
Got chores to do.
Oh poo.
Bye, Plum.

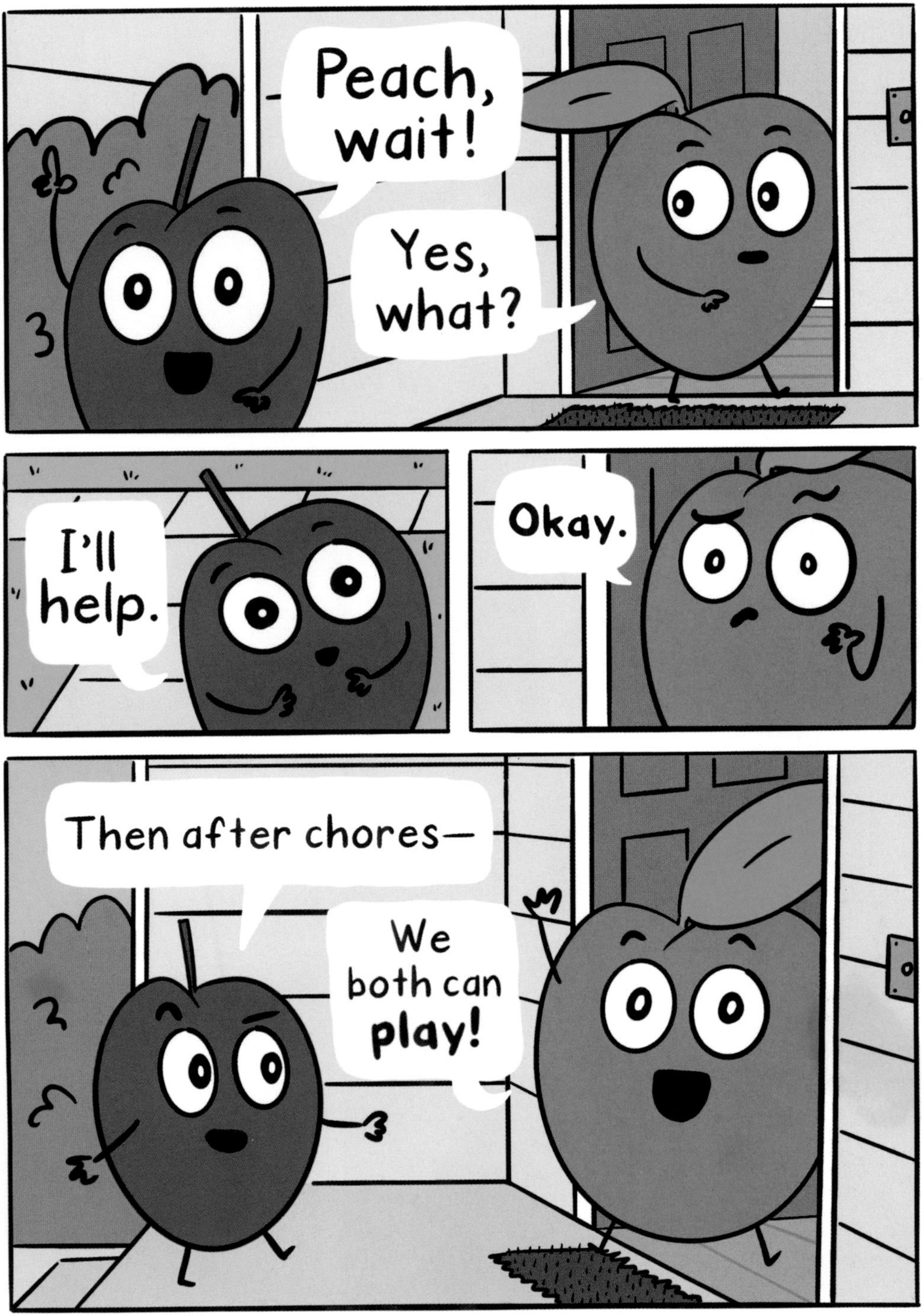
Peach, wait!
Yes, what?
I'll help.
Okay.
Then after chores—
We both can play!

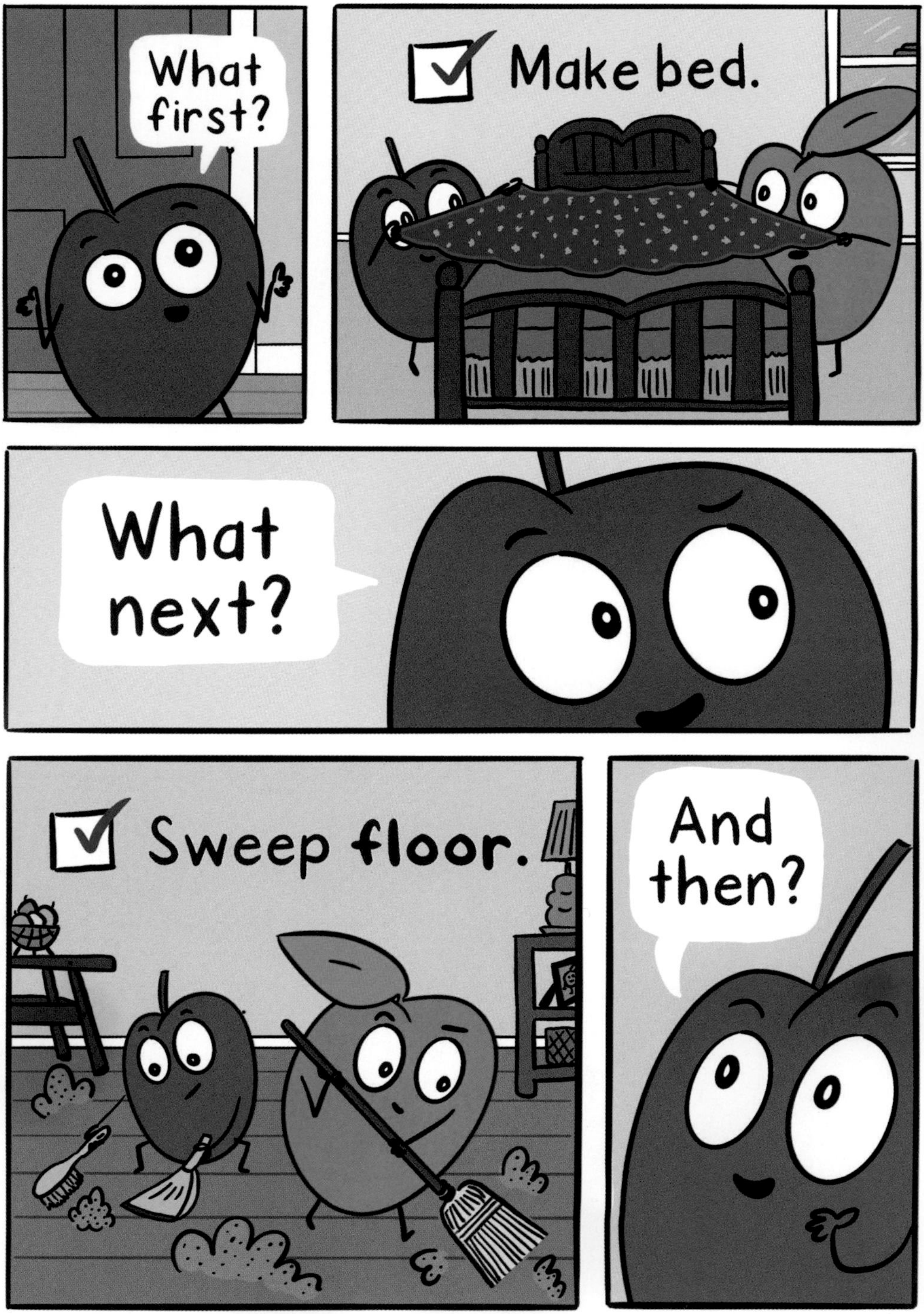
What first?
Make bed.
What next?
Sweep floor.
And then?

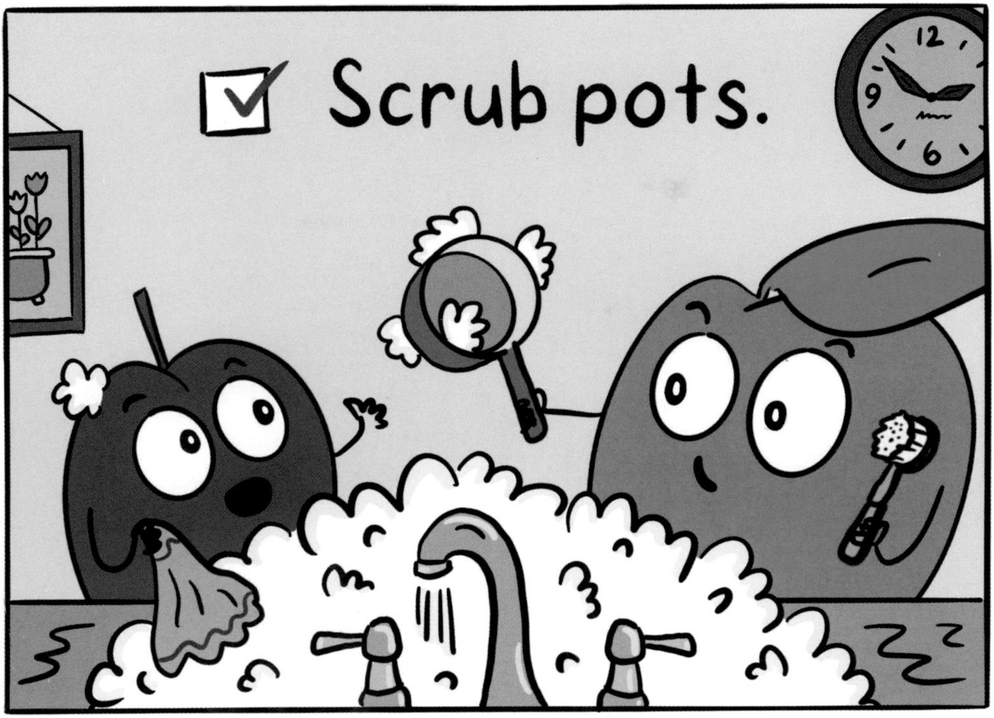
Scrub pots.

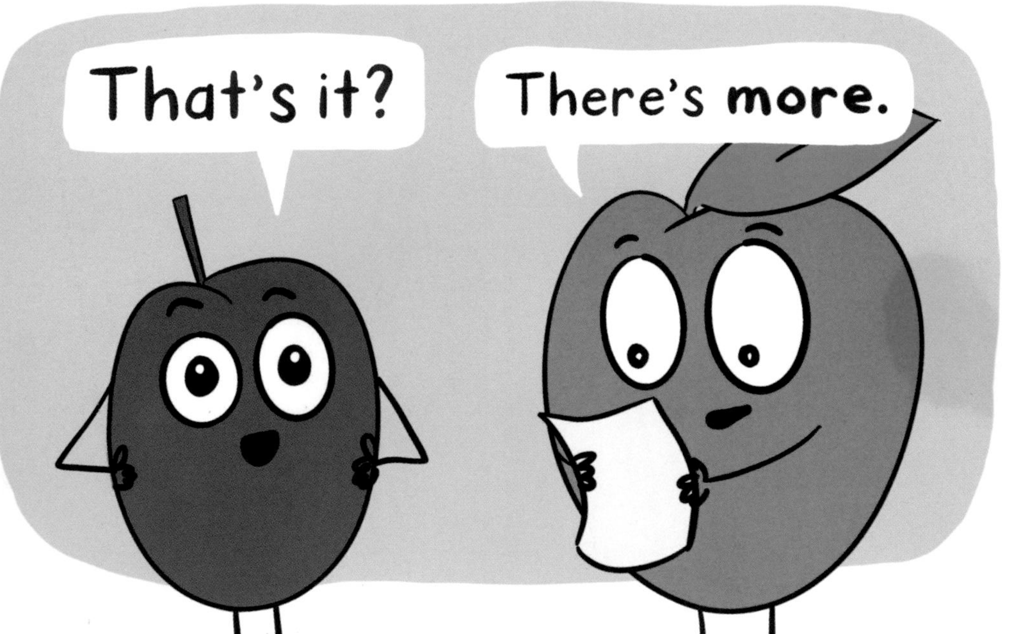
That's it?
There's **more**.

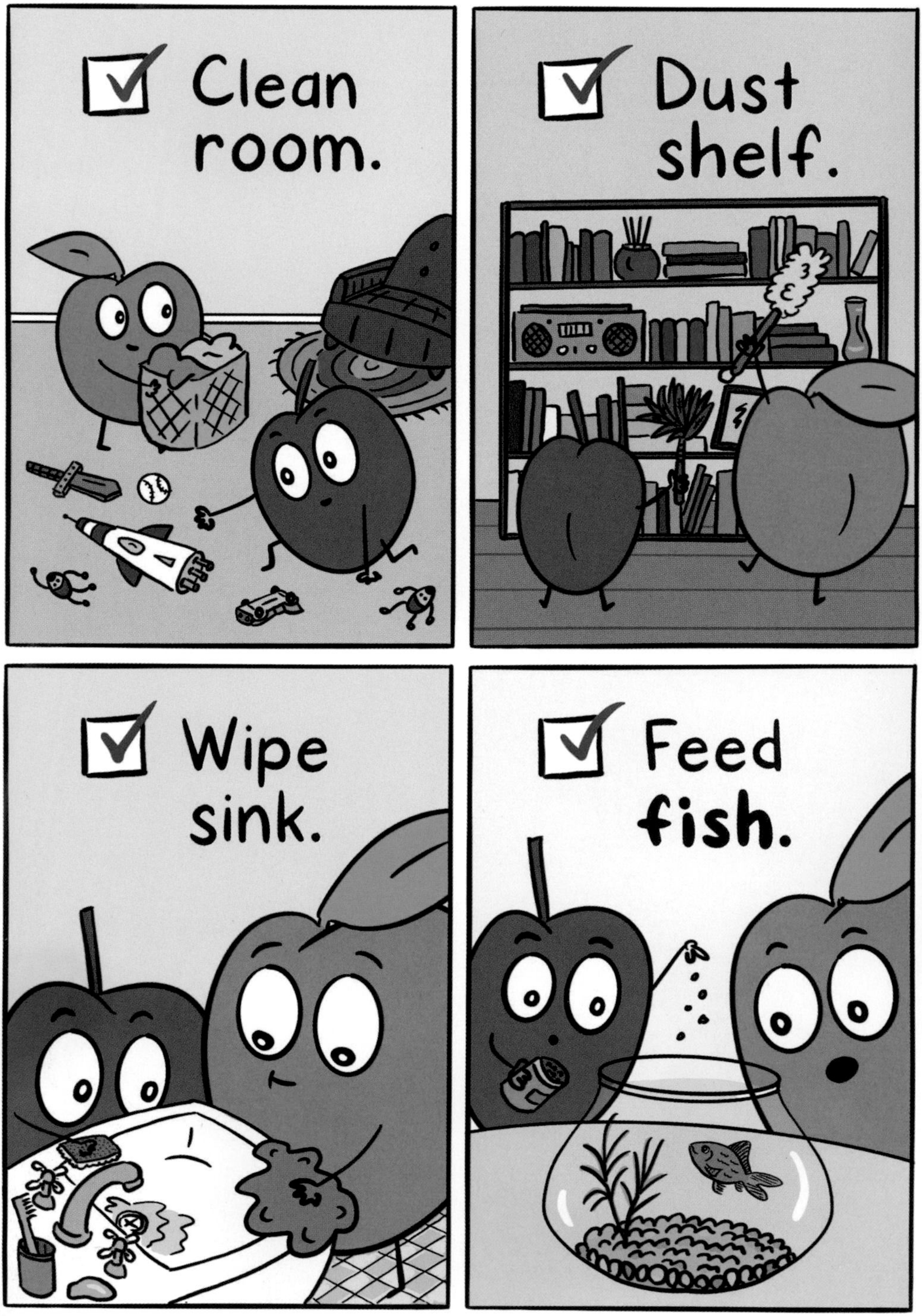
Clean room.
Dust shelf.
Wipe sink.
Feed fish.

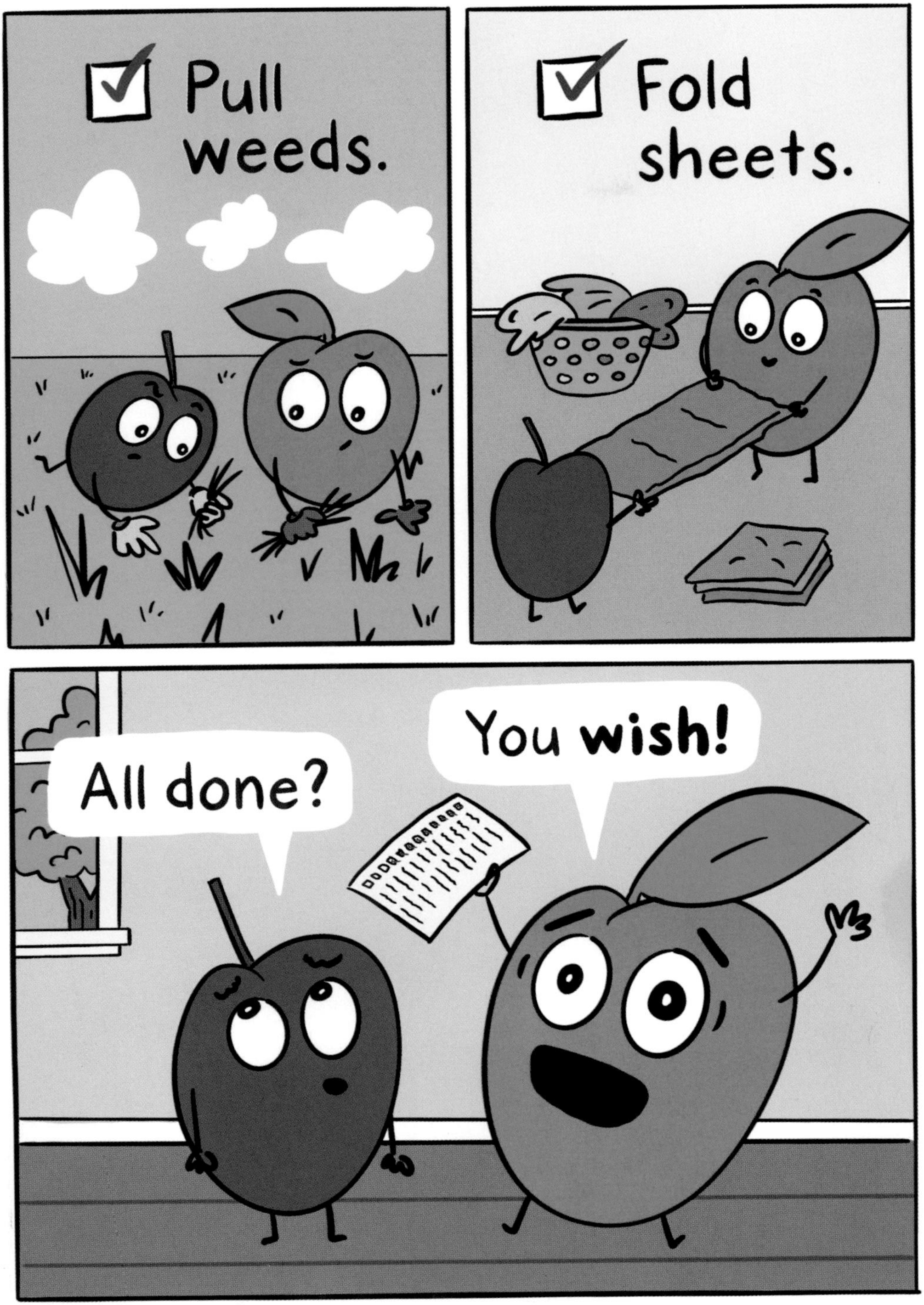

Pull weeds.
Fold sheets.
All done?
You **wish**!

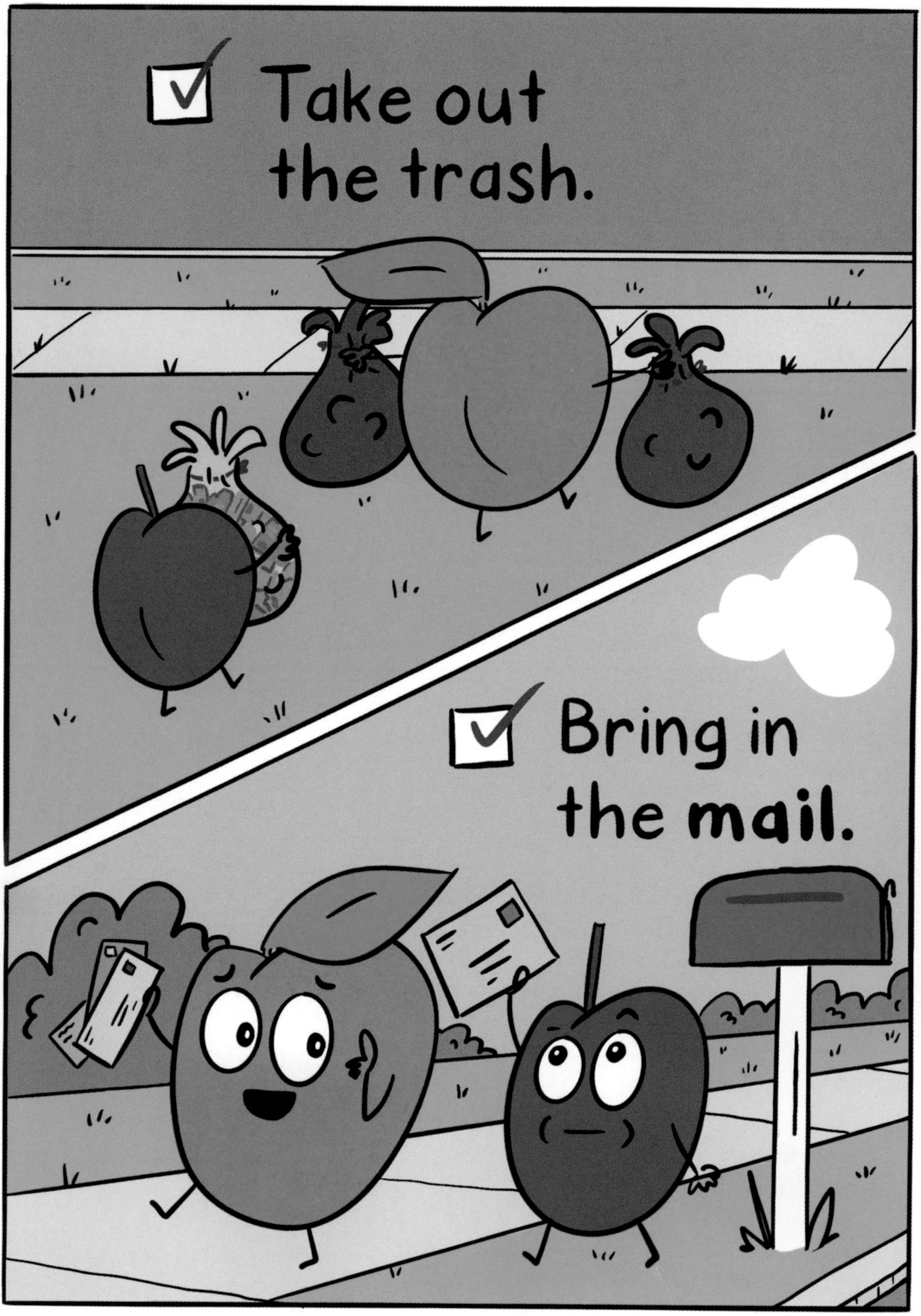
Take out the trash.
Bring in the mail.

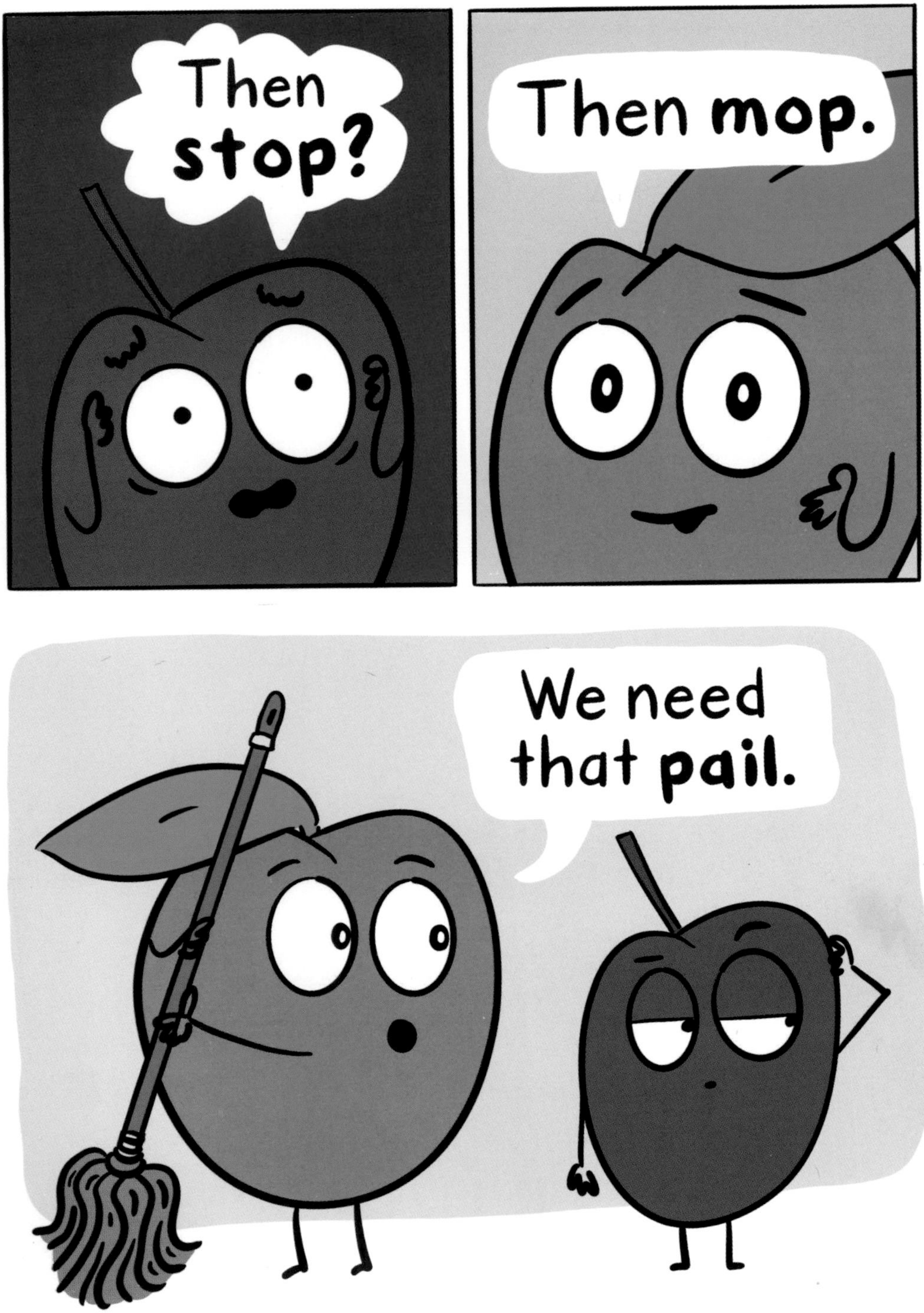
Then stop?
Then mop.
We need that pail.

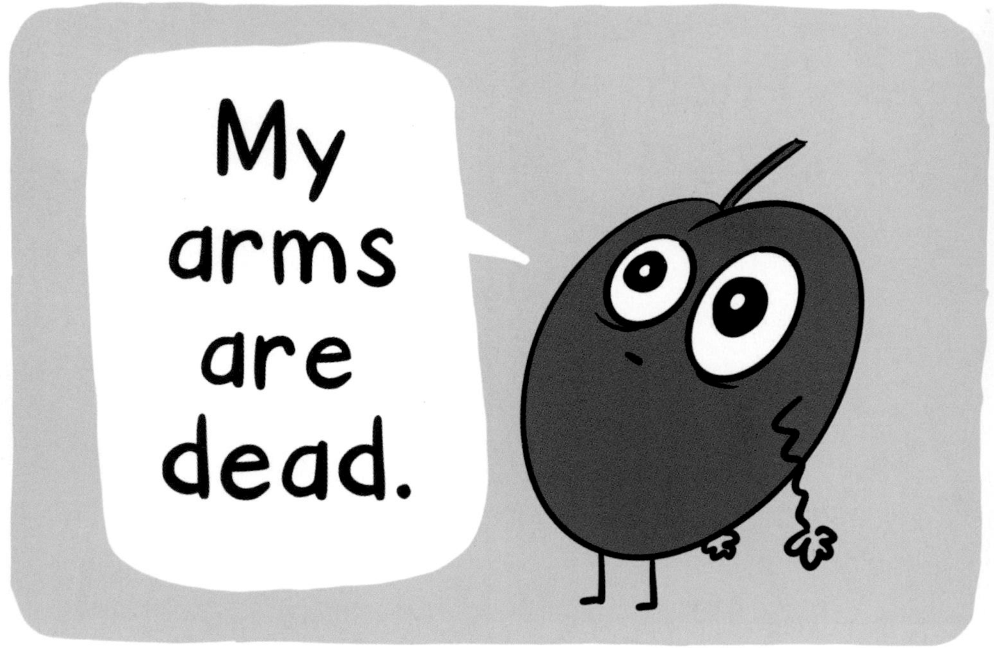
My arms are dead.

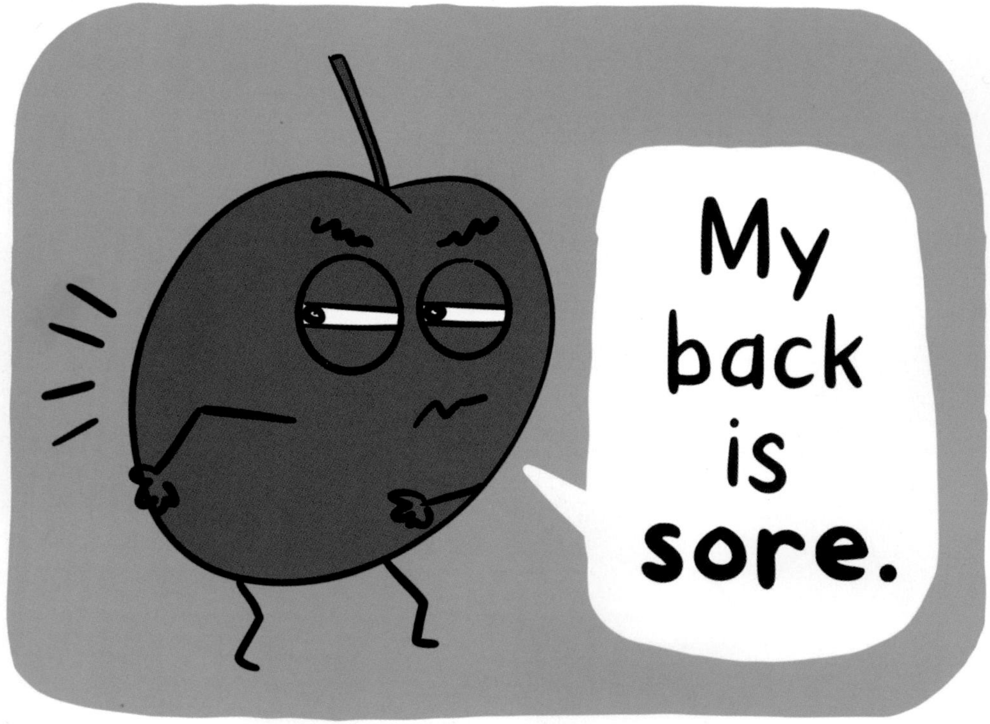
My back is **sore.**

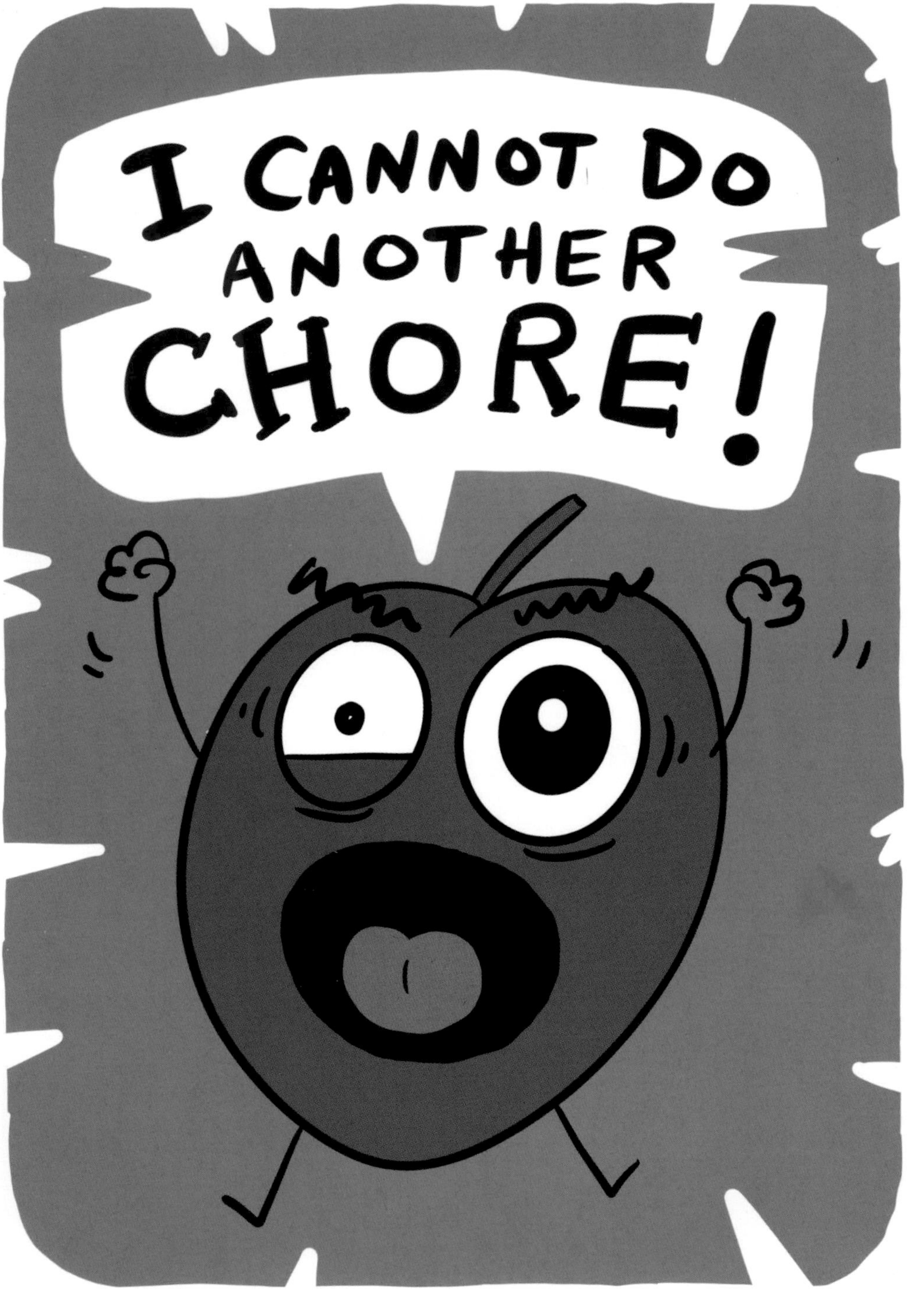
I CANNOT DO ANOTHER CHORE!

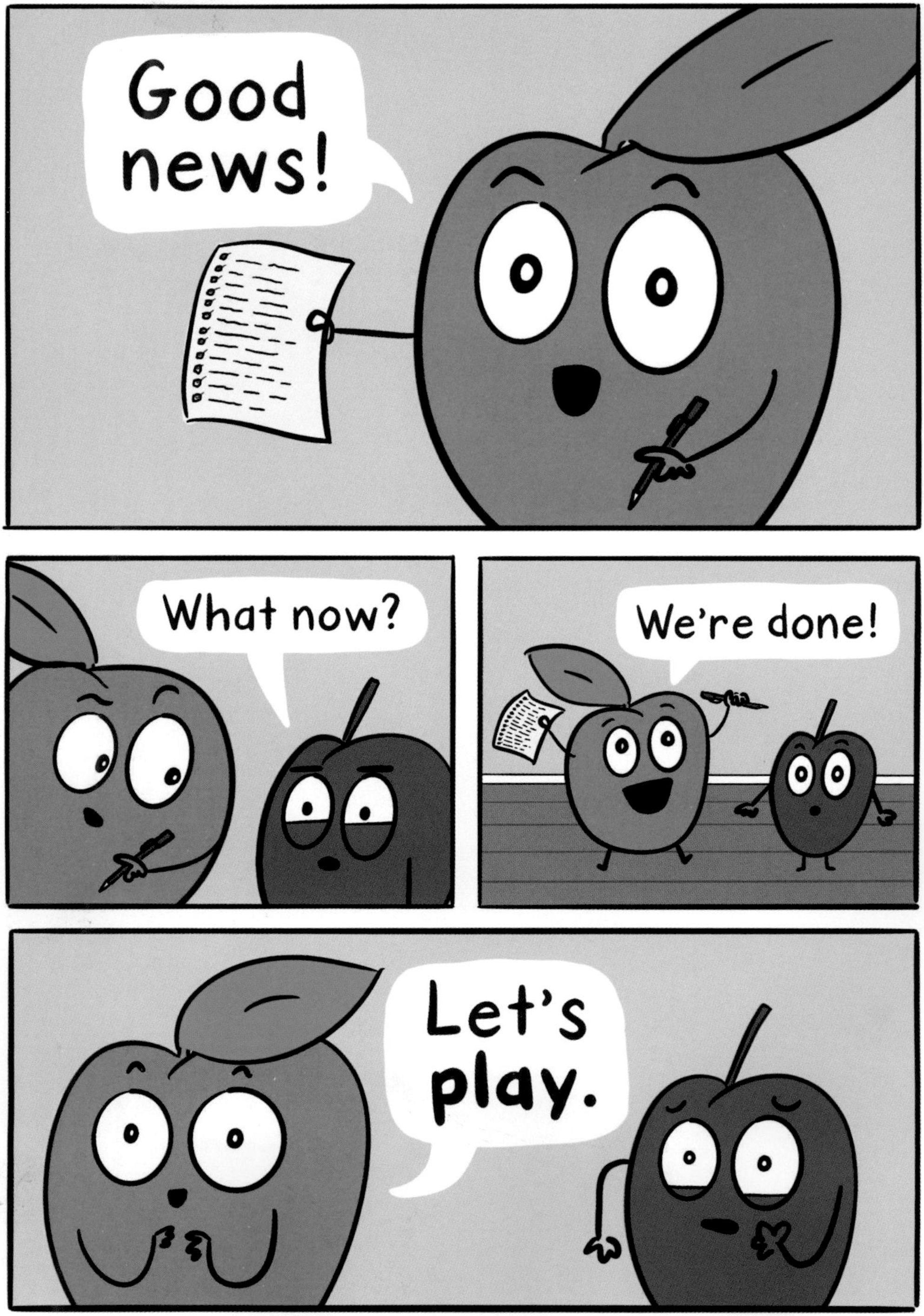

Good news!
What now?
We're done!
Let's play.

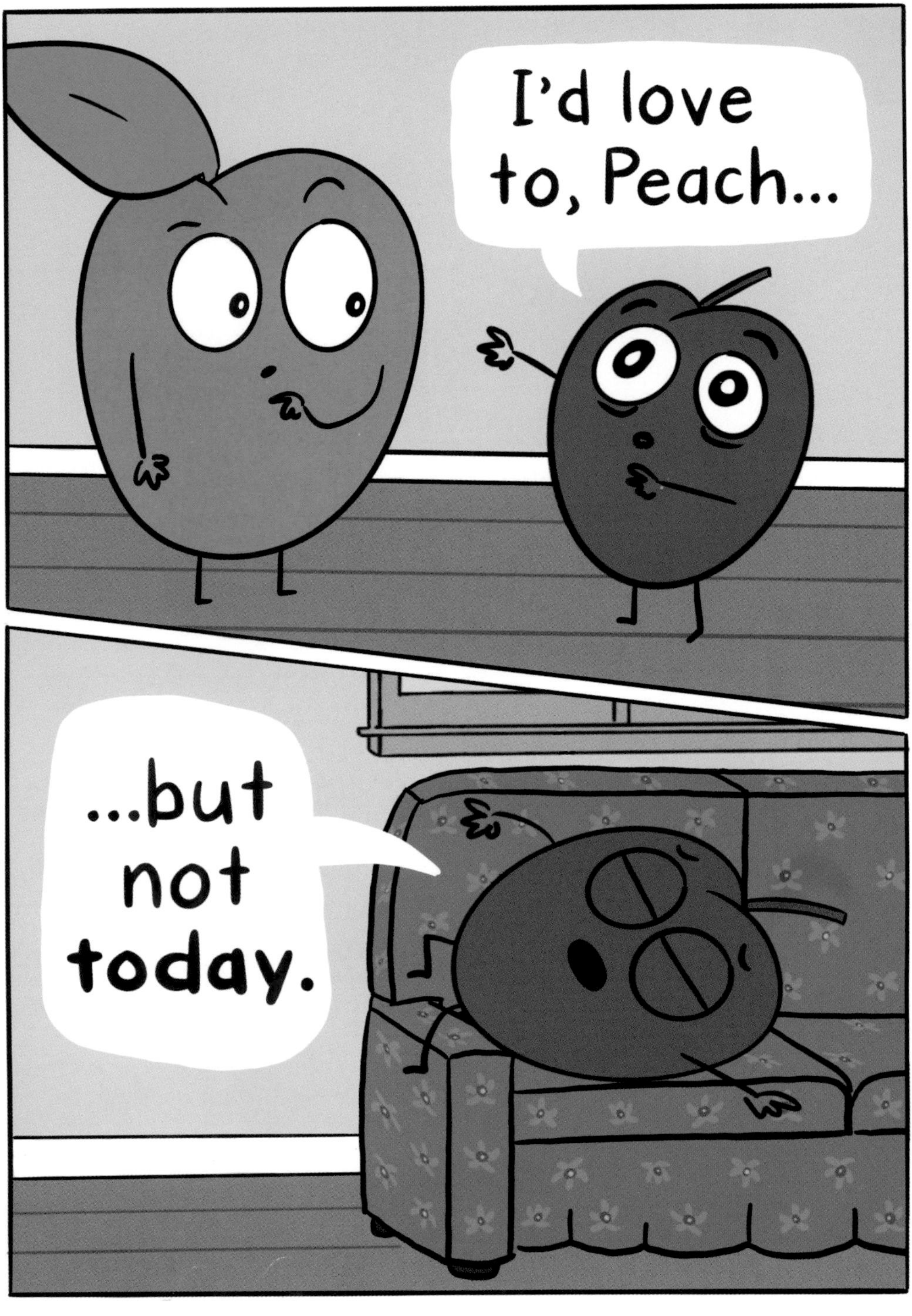
I'd love to, Peach...
...but not today.

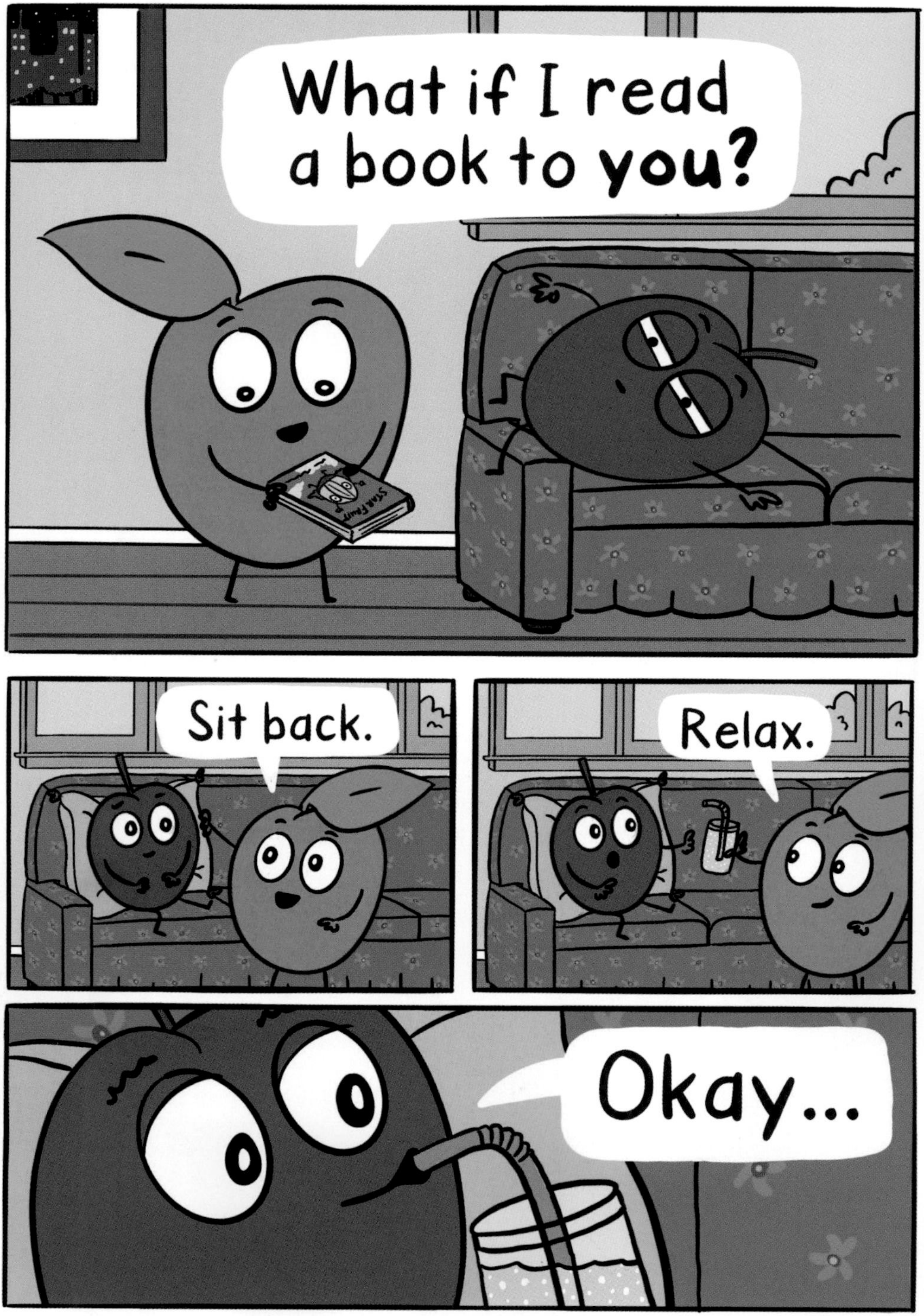
What if I read a book to you?
STARFRUIT
Sit back.
Relax.
Okay...

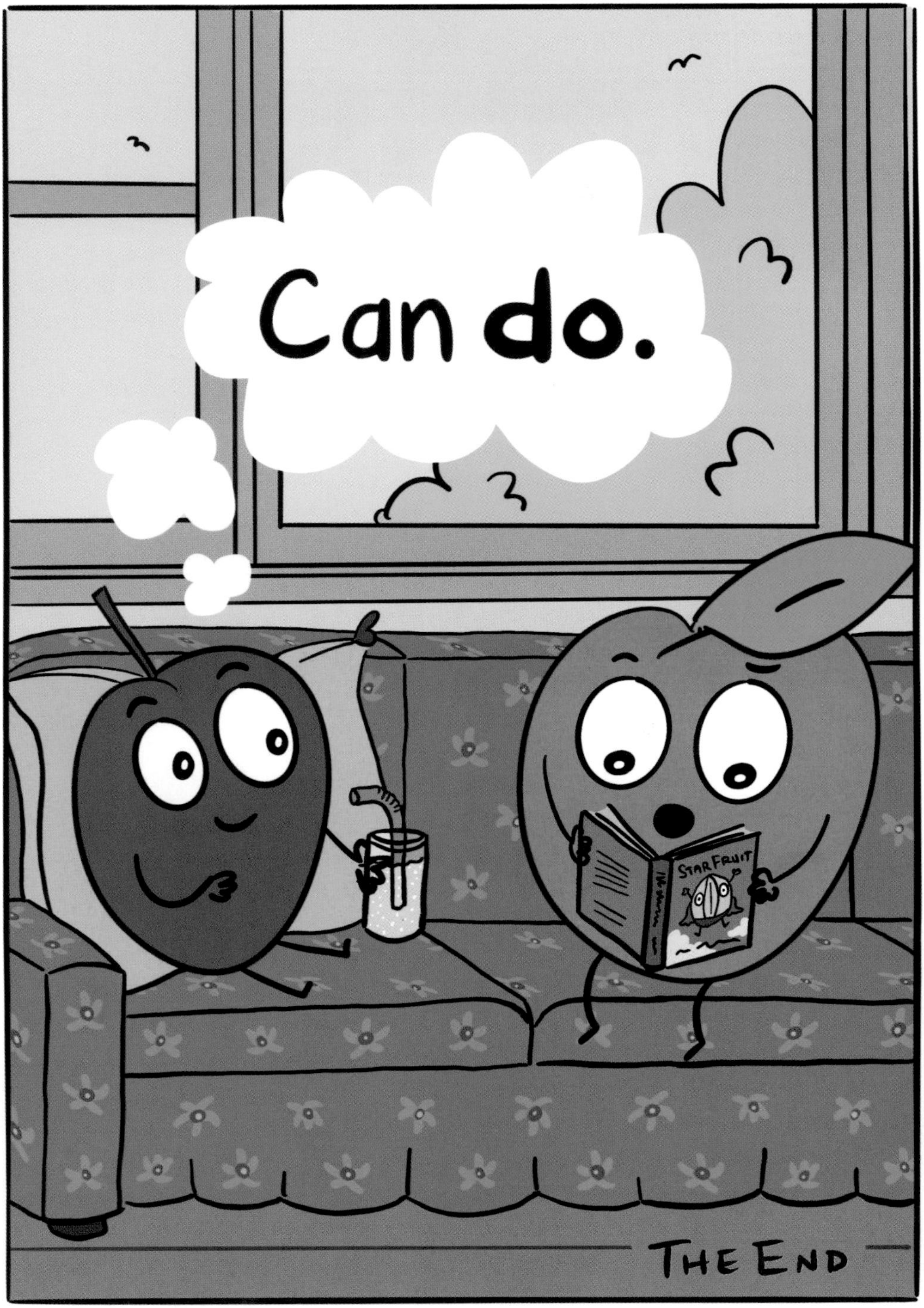
Can do.
STAR FRUIT
THE END

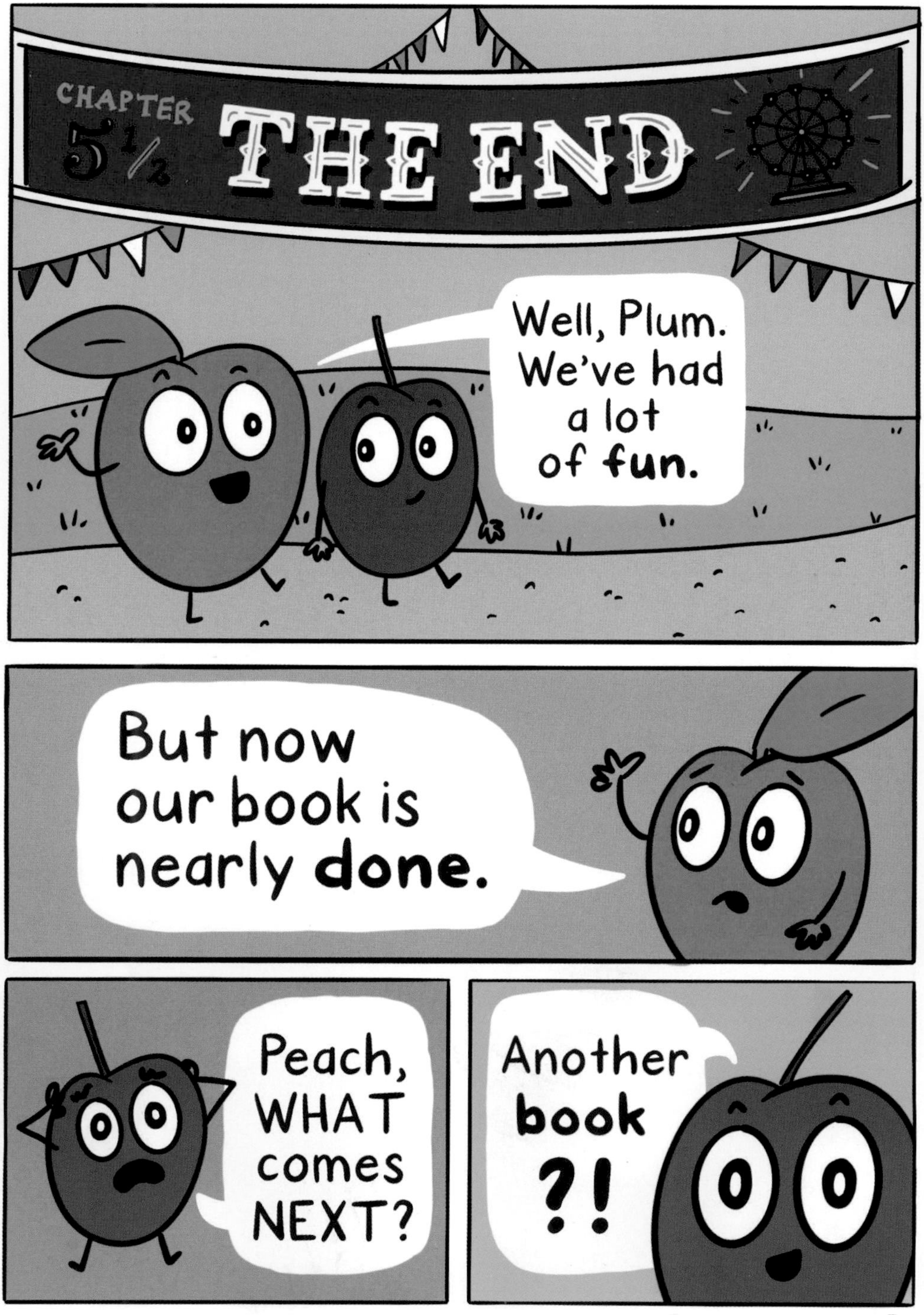
CHAPTER 5 1/2 THE END
Well, Plum. We've had a lot of **fun.**
But now our book is nearly **done.**
Peach, WHAT comes NEXT?
Another **book ?!**

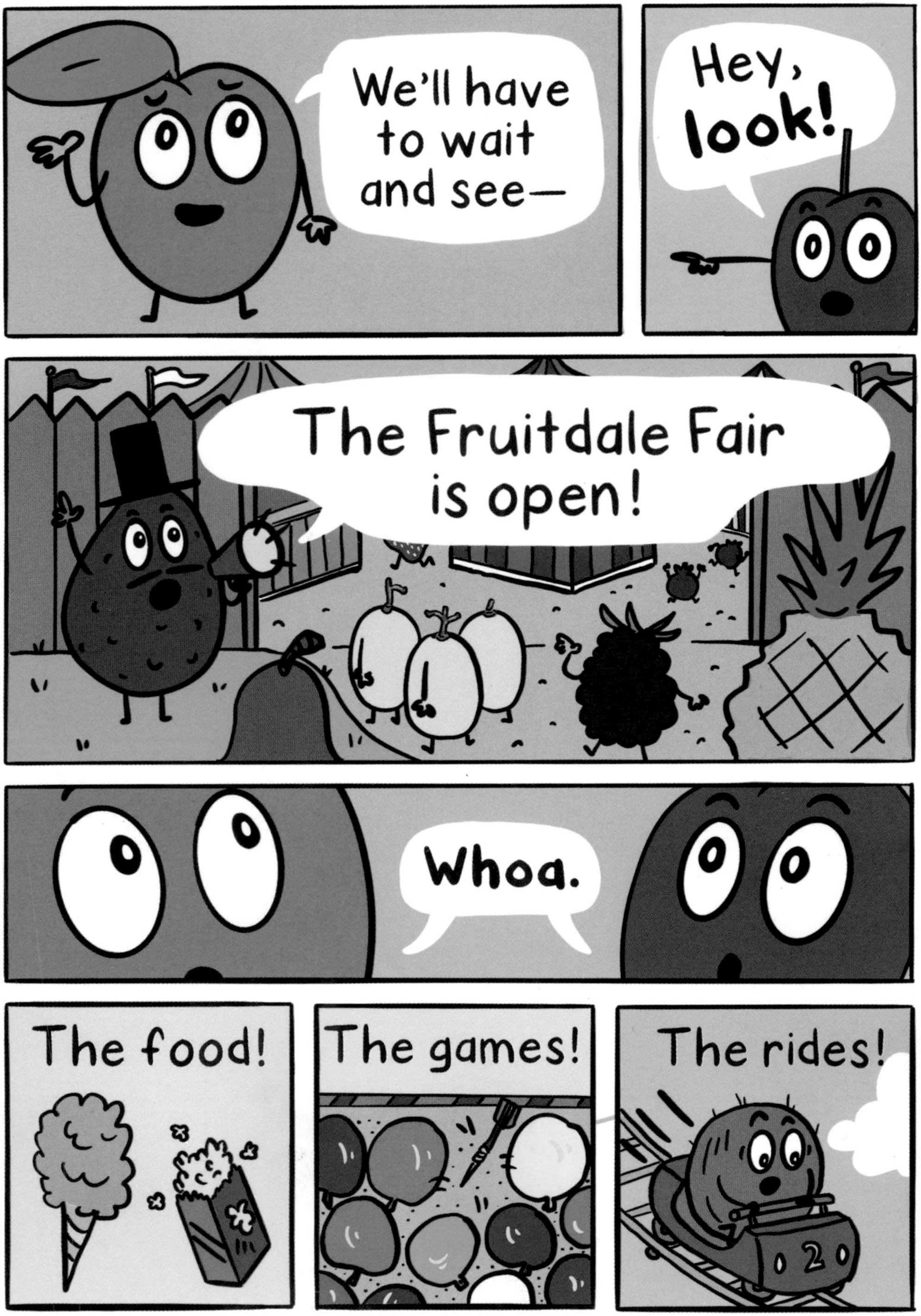
We'll have to wait and see—
Hey, look!
The Fruitdale Fair is open!
Whoa.
The food!
The games!
The rides!
2

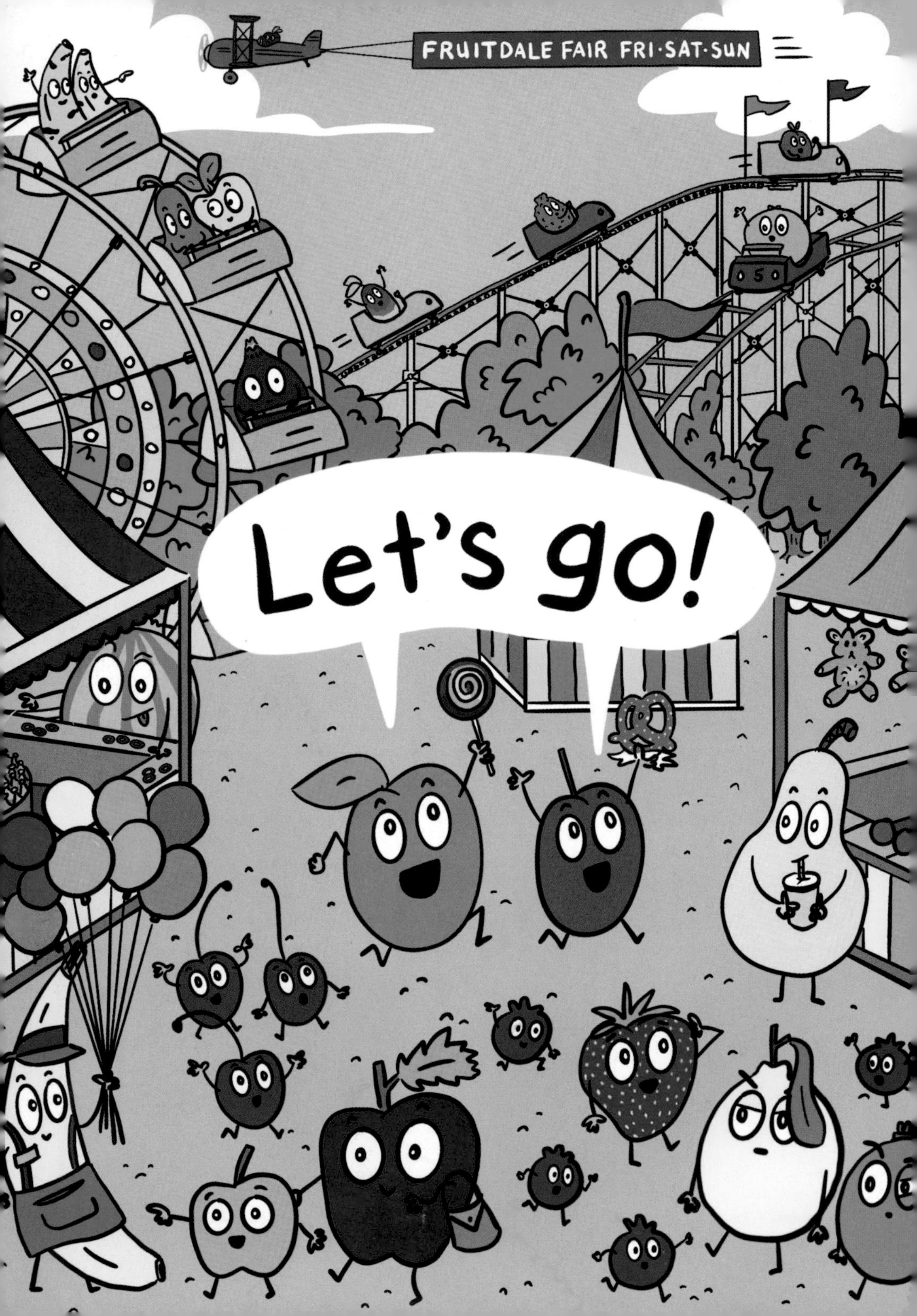
FRUITDALE FAIR FRI·SAT·SUN
Let's go!